THE GOD BOX

Art Wiedebell

THE GOD BOX

Art Wiederhold

iUniverse, Inc.

New York Lincoln Shanghai

The God Box

iUniverse, Inc.

For information address:
iUniverse, Inc.
2021 Pine Lake Road, Suite 100
Lincoln, NE 68512
www.iuniverse.com

ISBN: 0-595-33515-2

INTRODUCTION

▼

After his stunning discovery of a long-lost city in the dense jungles of Guatemala, famed archaeologist Art Wilder set his sights on an even higher project...solving the riddle of the Sphinx.

The ancient guardian sits sixty-six feet high and is almost 240 feet long. Its face, complete with faded pigments of red, yellow and blue, its enigmatic smile and missing nose, is slightly over thirteen feet high. Some archaeologists claim it was built by King Khafre as a sentinel for his pyramid tomb complex 4,500 years ago. Some say it is far older than that, perhaps older than dynastic Egypt itself.

These were just some of the questions that Wilder sought to answer. He had a few questions of his own and—some might say—outlandish theories to prove or disprove.

Such as Egypt's possible ties to the Indus Valley Culture and the legendary Atlantis. When the Ice Age ended, worldwide ocean levels rose over 400 feet, more than enough to cover over 100 miles of coastlines. Any people living in those areas would have had to abandon their cities and head for higher ground to start all over.

This is part of the Great Flood mythology that permeates every known culture on Earth. The Vedas, which are the oldest known books on earth (some experts place them at more than 10,000 years old) tell of the Great Floods and of the continents and cities that were buried by the waters.

Supposedly, the early peoples of India were forced to abandon their vast cities. They fled inland to the Indus Valley and to the Himalayan foothills. There, they built new cities which they mysteriously abandoned nearly 5,000 years ago.

But they did not vanish. These early civilizations mutated into the great Hindu culture of India that still thrives today.

The theories on man's beginning civilizations were turned inside out in 2001 when an ecological team discovered the ruins of two vast cities in the Gulf of Cambay. The ruins showed geometric avenues, wide plazas and high thick walls that looked startlingly like the Indus Valley ruins. Carbon-dated artifacts brought up from the ruins put them at nearly 11,000 years old.

Other offshore ruins, such as the sunken Bimini Wall, the pyramids off the coast of Japan, and lost cities of the Mediterranean coastlines show similar dates.

Wilder knew that Egypt began when the Mound of Creation rose from the primeval sea after the Great Flood ended the Golden Age. Computer analysis of the North African coastline showed that the continent lost over 100 miles of land when the flood waters rose.

Wilder reasoned that if cities lined the coast of India, Egyptian culture which was far older, must also have had coastal cities during the Ice Age. Some of these cities had to have gone back at least 16,000 years, maybe even as much as 20,000.

But Wilder wasn't looking for evidence of fishing villages or tribal pockets. He was looking for stone cities, built by learned men. Cities with all of the trappings of a great, early and advanced culture, such as literature, art, science and medicine.

He was positive that the Sphinx was somehow connected to that Golden Age and that the great Imhotep took the secrets of that age with him to the Afterlife.

That's why he and his associates were also searching for the legendary and never found tomb of Imhotep.

"Find Imhotep and you'll unlock the earliest secrets of mankind's distant beginnings—and learn a lot about yourself in the process," Wilder often commented.

As he and his loyal associate, Dr. Nasi Hawatt of the Egyptian Department of Antiquities probed the mysteries of this most ancient monument, they were unaware of the outside forces that were threatening to stop them at any cost.

CHAPTER 1

▼

Giza Plateau, Egypt, 2005...

It was three a.m.

The middle of the night.

A time when most people are fast asleep.

Unless you happen to be an archaeologist working at the Giza Plateau in Egypt.

Here the afternoon temperatures routinely soar above 100 degrees, making any sort of labor almost impossible. That's why archaeologists like Art Wilder work at night, under the glare of small spotlights.

Cold, neon lights that give off little or no heat.

Wilder and his team were wide awake and hard at work conducting a careful, almost painstaking study of every inch of the world's most enigmatic structure.

The Sphinx.

The ancient Greeks gave it that name.

To the ancient Egyptians, it was Horem Aket—Horus in the Horizon or a depiction of their ancient sun god.

One theory has it being built in the time known as Zeptepi or the Golden Age which flourished long before the rise of Egyptian civilization. It silently guards the Great Pyramid complex on the Giza Plateau.

It probably had another name back then.

It is both a mute sentinel and a monument to ancient man's ingenuity and determination.

Wilder called it the most remarkable thing ever chiseled by man or gods in the entire history of the world. He wanted to prove that it was much older than anyone ever imagined. He also wanted to find that legendary hidden chamber that was supposed to be buried beneath the Sphinx's massive paws.

There were other legends attached to the monument, too. Wilder also theorized that the long-sought tomb of the famous Imhotep was near the Sphinx or might even be part of the hidden chamber.

Of course, most "real" Egyptologists believed those theories were just plain bunk. After all, everyone knew that the Sphinx was built about 4,500 years ago as an afterthought part of the Great Pyramid complex. It was chiseled out of a large rock that just happened to be on site.

Wilder strongly questioned that theory. For one, the Sphinx was actually composed of two distinctly different types of rock. The body was made of hard granite while the enigmatic face was made of much softer limestone. This could only mean one thing: the head was added at a much later date, probably to replace the original one.

This dig was a dream come true for him. For twenty years he had sought permission from the Department of Antiquities to conduct an exploration of the ground beneath the paws of the Sphinx. Each time he was refused on the grounds that such a dig might harm the foundations of the monument.

Despite his youthful appearance and athletic build, at 55 Wilder knew that time was fast running out. He just *had* to conduct a dig at the Sphinx.

Dr. Nasi Hawatt was the one who had denied Wilder permission to dig. In those days, they were bitter rivals and Hawatt viewed Wilder as an upstart who might upset his own stubborn opinions of ancient Egypt.

The "accepted" views.

But when Wilder discovered that lost city in Guatemala that had direct and indisputable links to ancient Egypt, Hawatt knew his position as the Chief of the Department of Egyptian Antiquities was shaky at best.

That's when he attempted to discredit Wilder, but by then it was too late. The media had gotten hold of his discovery and ran with it. It was quite a sensation in that it proved Wilder's theories on how civilizations that were similar to Egypt got started in the Americas.

It also proved that the ancient Egyptians not only knew about America but they had also colonized it. Then they passed their knowledge down to the native tribes in the region, who then added their own bizarre and often gruesome touches.

That's when Wilder received written permission from the president of Egypt to conduct a dig at the Sphinx. The dig was also backed by the World Heritage Foundation of the U.N.

With so many heavy hitters backing Wilder, Hawatt had no choice but to sign off on his request. It was then that Hawatt figured his career was over and prepared to resign from his post.

He was now 72 years old, balding and slightly overweight. He considered retirement.

But oddly enough, Wilder came to his rescue. He asked Hawatt to be his associate on the dig and to share in any discoveries. Surprised and humbled, Hawatt gratefully accepted Wilder's offer.

Instead of being put out to pasture, Hawatt was given a unique chance to jumpstart his stagnant career in archaeology. He felt reborn now and threw himself into his work with a gusto he hadn't felt in years. The activity made him feel young again, like the way he'd felt on his first dig.

It took months to plan and get funding for the dig. Hawatt pulled every string he could as he worked with Wilder to put together the best team of scientists and "archs" they could find. They didn't have too much trouble finding people who wanted to be part of one of the most historic digs of all time. In fact, they had to turn several people down.

Over that time, the two men became fast friends and Hawatt proved to be invaluable to the project.

He had over 45 years experience as an Egyptologist and could easily read hieroglyphs and heiretic symbols. He also spoke fluent English, French, German and Arabic.

Wilder equally impressed Hawatt. Unlike other archaeologists, he never removed a body from its tomb unless it was of significant historical importance.

Even then he usually shipped them to a major hospital for x-rays and CAT scans with the stipulation that it be re-interred in its original resting place once the studies were completed.

He also had a vast knowledge of ancient history and a passion for Egypt that startled his older, native counterpart.

"I'm an archaeologist, not a grave robber," Wilder often said. "I have a deep respect for the ancient customs of these people and believe that their dead should be left where they are found—provided of course that no looters are around."

Looters were a plague to Wilder.

So many times he had entered tombs and cities only to find they had been stripped of anything that had salable value. And looters weren't careful. They left destruction in their wake that wiped out millennia of history.

And when it was gone, it was gone forever.

But many times he'd gotten lucky and discovered unlooted tombs and cities. With artifacts, it was different. He left the more common ones behind in the graves after photographing, drawing and cataloging them. The most beautiful and valuable ones he crated up and shipped to museums—but only the museums of the country he made the find in.

Of course, that's only when there were artifacts to be found.

Or tombs.

Or graves.

Not all ancient civilizations left such things behind. While Rome, Egypt and Greece were loaded with artifacts left behind by their ancestors, some places were strangely devoid of them.

Like the Indus Valley Culture in south central Asia.

About 7,000 years ago, the people of the Indus Valley built several large, well-ordered cities. Then they vanished without a trace.

They left few tombs and graves, no artifacts save a few indecipherable stone tablets. No one knew who they were, where they had come from or where they went.

It was one the world's great mysteries. Unless you had read the Vedas, you had very little idea about this ancient culture. Even then, most scholars thought that the Vedas were only an ancient mythology with no basis in fact.

Wilder, of course, had read the Vedas and he was one of a growing number of archaeologists who believed that the ancient texts were an actual written history of a pre-Ice Age civilization that may have been linked to Egypt during its Golden Age.

Hawatt was aware of Wilder's theories. And he *respected* them. Guatemala proved that Wilder should never be taken lightly. Even the real skeptics in their field paid close attention to everything he did or said now.

"The Indus Valley is my next dig," Wilder said to Hawatt one evening at dinner. "I want to find out what happened to those people. I want to know what made them leave and where they went.

I love a good mystery. Don't you?"

"Of course I do. Maybe I'll go with you—if you don't mind," Hawatt said.

"You are more than welcome, Nasi. Between the two of us, we have a real good chance of finding something there," Wilder replied.

That was several weeks ago. That was the first time the Wilders had dinner at Nasi's home. His wife, Fatima and their daughter Hathor, had spent hours preparing a veritable Egyptian feast. Hathor was a pretty young girl of 14 who showed a keen interest in Egyptology. Art's wife, Maria, also thought the teenager showed a very keen interest in Art as well.

But that was a few weeks ago.

Right now, they were concentrating their efforts on what was happening between the paws of the Sphinx.

"History is exciting to me, Nasi. The more things I discover about our ancestors, the more I realize how very little about them we really know," Wilder said.

"That is so true, my friend," Hawatt agreed. "For instance, until we found Dynasty Zero and the tablet of the Scorpion King, we always believed that the wheel, mathematics, writing and agriculture originated in Sumer. But Dynasty Zero predates Sumer by more than 500 years and they had all of those things even then."

"That just proved one of my pet theories about civilization actually beginning in Egypt on the plains of Abydos—not Mesopotamia like everyone else insisted," Wilder said as they approached the Sphinx.

"You talk about Egypt with a lot of pride, Art," Hawatt said. "It is as if you were born here. Maybe you were an Egyptian in a past life."

"Could be. All I know is that I was hooked on Egyptian history from the moment I first read a book about Cleopatra," Wilder said.

"And history is dynamic. It is forever changing, being rewritten as new facts and civilizations are unearthed. That's why I love this job so much. Anyone who says history is boring is stupid in my book," he added.

"In mine, too," Hawatt agreed.

The distant call of a jackal interrupted their talk. The sound echoed through the plateau and momentarily sent Wilder's thoughts back to ancient times.

As they reached the large space between the Sphinx's paws, they saw Dr. Rudolph Heider and his assistant Albrecht Kuyder checking the connections to a device that was about the size of a washing machine.

From the back of the machine snaked several cables. These led to what appeared to be backyard lights atop four foot poles.

Heider looked up and greeted them as they drew near. He was tall, lean, blond and middle-aged. He had flashing blue eyes and a ready smile for those he liked. He liked Art and Nasi.

"Guten morgen," Heider said as he shook their hands warmly.

"How's it going?" asked Wilder as he nodded toward the poles.

"We have just finished planting the sonar probes. Al is checking the connections now and the batteries are powering up. Once they are fully charged, we can begin," Heider explained.

"What is this device?" asked Hawatt.

"It is called a below ground sonarscope. It's similar to the sonar devices used by various navies to detect submarines and avoid underwater obstacles. Only this has been modified to detect hollow places beneath the earth," Heider explained with more than a hint of pride.

"How does it work?" Hawatt asked, his curiosity now piqued.

"The towers are actually individual sonarscopes. They send sound waves into the earth at intervals of ten feet. When the waves enter a hollow spot, such a cavern or underground tomb, they send echoes back to the towers. The echoes are then sent to the control panel here and the built-in architectural software programs convert them to images," Heider continued.

"In other words, the computer uses the echoes to draw a fairly detailed map of the open space," Kuyder interjected as he looked up from his chore.

"How detailed?" asked Wilder.

"The images will be similar to those done by architects. It will also provide us with important measurements, like length, depth, width and even show very large features of the hollow," Heider said.

"So if there is something down there, we'll be able to find it?" Wilder asked.

Heider nodded.

"In the last century, archaeologists tried to use ground imaging radar devices to locate tombs and buried cities. But the details were so poor that we needed to find another way of doing this. This is the first time that this device is being used on an actual dig," Wilder said.

"That's what makes it so exciting. Eh, doctor?" said Kuyder, who was shorter than Heider but just as blond.

"The red light is on. The batteries are fully charged now," he added.

"Good. Let us begin," said Heider as he flipped a few switches.

The scientists watched as a bank of eight green bulbs flickered on one-by-one.

"Each light represents a sonar tower. The poles are ten feet long, six feet of which is buried in the ground," Heider said.

"When will get the first reading?" asked Wilder.

"Right now," Heider said as he pointed to the large screen atop the device. "This is at ten feet and it shows nothing. See? The line in the center of the grid is still flat."

"Go to twenty feet," Wilder said.

A few seconds later, the line was still unchanged.

"Try thirty feet," said Hawatt. He was truly fascinated with the device now.

"The line's quivering," said Wilder. "Does that mean we've found something?"

"Ja. And from the way it's jumping around, I'd say it is a fairly large space," Heider replied excitedly.

Wilder and Hawatt watched as the grid reformed into a rough rectangular shape.

"It looks like a chamber of some sort," Heider said.

"Can you get a printout?" Wilder asked.

"Sure. It will take about ten minutes for all of the data to be collected," Heider replied.

"That's okay. Any coffee left?" Wilder asked.

Heider pointed to a wooden folding table about fifty feet from the left paw of the Sphinx.

"There's some in that Thermos, but it's probably cold by now," he said.

"That's okay. It's 92 degrees out here, so hot coffee isn't all that necessary," Wilder said as he and Hawatt headed for the table.

They found the Thermos half full. Wilder took two paper cups from the stack on the table and filled them. He then handed one to Hawatt and turned to look up at the face of the Sphinx.

"How accurate is that device?" Hawatt asked.

"I'm not sure. Like I said, this is the first time it's ever been used on a dig. If it works, it will save us years of hit and miss digging," Wilder said.

"Amazing how science advances in so short a time. I wish that there was such a thing back when I first entered the field. It would have saved me years of backbreaking labor. Maybe I wouldn't look so old today," Hawatt said with a chuckle.

"This field can add years to a man but it's all worth it," Wilder said.

He looked back up at the Sphinx.

"I wonder what secrets you're guarding?" he said aloud.

"Perhaps many. Perhaps none. But in any case, we will soon find out," Hawatt said.

He took a swallow of the coffee as he watched Heider work.

"Where is your lovely wife? I have not seen her for the past two hours," he asked.

"Maria's probably wandering around with her camera shooting every square foot of the Sphinx," Wilder said. "She's really thrown herself into this project."

Maria Wilder stood five-feet-three-inches, had a slim, sexy body, long brown hair, hazel eyes and a tan complexion. Although she was from Puerto Rico, many of the locals mistook her for an Egyptian.

"She is a remarkable woman. Where did you meet her?" Hawatt asked.

"That's an interesting story," replied Wilder as he launched his narrative.

Maria and her then-husband Miguel had accompanied Art on his Guatemala dig. They first met each other in St. Louis when Art helped them house hunt. They spent several days at his house while they roamed the city. That's when Art and Maria developed a strong attraction for each other.

A year later, Maria and Miguel accompanied Art on his Guatemalan dig. One thing led to another and, before they realized it, they'd fallen in love. The following year she divorced Miguel and married Art. Miguel was a sport about it. He even agreed to be Art's best man at their wedding.

The trip to Egypt was sort of a working honeymoon. It took several weeks to set the dig site up and hire the right people to work it. During that time, the Wilders took several boat trips up and down the Nile while Art explained the history of Egypt and the significance of the monuments.

When they were working, Maria was Art's official photographer, cataloguer and artist. She also assisted the men in laying out the grid patterns for dig sites.

Despite the often oppressive heat, Maria remained upbeat and enthusiastic about all things Egyptian. She soaked up every bit of knowledge like a sponge. She even began to learn how to read heiretic, the simplified form of ancient Egyptian writing.

Her abilities to adapt and learn impressed the other members of the team. Even Nasi Hawatt took a liking to her and had started teaching her to read hieroglyphs.

"What does the word hieroglyphics mean?" she once asked.

"It's Greek. It means 'holy or sacred writing'," Wilder explained. "They called it this because when they traveled to Egypt, they saw the priests carving them onto temple walls and assumed that it was only used by the holy men.

Hieroglyphics can be read top to bottom, left to right or right to left. How they are read depends on how many of the symbols are facing in a particular direction. Proper names are surrounded by a carved 'rope' which the French call a cartouche.

In the beginning, the pictures were actual representations of what they were meant to portray. They later evolved to represent specific sounds or letter combinations, while some remained as pictures."

"The priestly scribes and more learned of the common Egyptians used the simplified heiretic symbols," Hawatt added. "They were easier to draw and much easier to read. But like the hieroglyphs they are derived from, they have no vowel sounds and that makes them more difficult to interpret."

"There's a third form of Egyptian writing," said Wilder. "It was developed around 700 BC and it's called demotic, which is Greek for popular. You could call it Egyptian shorthand. But it, too, contains no vowels."

"Because of this, we are not exactly certain how words or names are pronounced. Our assumptions are based solely on the translations from the Rosetta Stone and from what is most comfortable for us to say," said Hawatt. "We are guessing a lot."

"Years are also difficult to pinpoint. The Egyptians had several different methods of marking time, some of which were used concurrently," said Wilder. "A year could be named after a ruler or an important event, such as a census or counting of cattle or even a battle or natural disaster."

"Confusing!" Maria said.

"But that's what makes it so very interesting!" said Hawatt.

"Didn't you say that the ancient Egyptians referred to the Sphinx as 'Horus in the Horizon'?" Maria asked.

"That's right. And since Horus was a hawk headed god, I believe that the Sphinx had a hawk's head at that time," Wilder said.

"What happened to it?" asked Maria as she looked up at the face.

"Most likely one—or several pharaohs—modified the head into likenesses of themselves as a symbol of their power both here and in the Afterlife. That's why the face doesn't resemble any one particular pharaoh," Wilder explained.

"Interesting. So the first head was a hawk's?" Maria asked.

"Probably not. Several archaeologists, me included, believe that its head was originally that of a lion. But when it was carved and by whom remains a mystery," Wilder replied.

"Perhaps we shall find the answer to these questions once we locate the fabled hidden chamber beneath the monument," suggested Hawatt.

"It sounds like you're starting to believe my theories, old friend," teased Wilder. "Better watch out or your colleagues will brand you a heretic!"

"Let them call me what they like—so long as we find the truth," Hawatt said with a broad smile.

Wilder and Hawatt watched as the rest of the team made some preliminary tests of the ground sonar imager while Maria just continued to stare into the face of the Sphinx.

She had to admit to herself that she was awed by the monument. And drawn to it as well. Just like she was awed by and drawn to nearly everything in this most ancient of lands.

Maria really blossomed in Egypt. She fell in love with its history, its monuments and its modern culture as well. She loved shopping in the bazaars, dining in the sidewalk cafes (where they were usually mobbed by a dozen or more cats which roam freely throughout Cairo and other major cities) and mingling with its peoples.

The cats fascinated her. When she asked about them, Hawatt smiled and explained that in ancient times, cats were sacred animals.

"We even have a cat goddess. She is called Bast or Bastet. Cats are very graceful and mysterious, two qualities the ancients held in high regard and which were associated with gods," he said.

"Cats were also very useful. In ancient times, much like today, they kept down the rodent populations that threatened our granaries."

"Are cats sacred today?" Maria asked as she tossed a piece of fish to a waiting, mewing feline.

"In a way. They are still highly regarded. Anyone who harms a cat on purpose faces a stiff fine and some prison time at hard labor. Many people still practice the ancient funerary ritual of shaving off their eyebrows when a pet cat dies. This shows they are in mourning," Hawatt explained.

"I believe that the cats know this, too. See how they roam about the streets? They go wherever they please with the knowledge that they will be treated kindly by all they choose to associate with," he concluded.

"In many ways, Egypt hasn't changed for thousands of years," Art added. "They still sail up and down the Nile on reed boats. They still plant and reap their crops the same way their ancestors did. Many dress the same and follow the age-old customs of welcoming strangers, they have strong familial ties and have the same deep, national pride."

But Egypt was also a paradox. Especially its crowded capital city, Cairo. It delighted Maria in many ways and puzzled her in some.

There were older sections of the city that dated back to the time of the Mamaluks who had swarmed down from Turkey during the 11th century to conquer Egypt. It was the Mamaluks who stopped a Mongol invasion a century later, then turned and drove the Crusaders from their strongholds less than twenty years after that. The Mamaluks were Muslims and they left behind minarets, tiled walls, mosques and fountains of great beauty and grace.

Centuries later, the French wrested it from what was left of the Mamaluks. That was in 1798 when Napoleon Bonaparte invaded Egypt and set his army of scientists to work uncovering the Sphinx. It was a French officer who found the

Rosetta Stone that enabled Europeans to finally decipher ancient Egyptian writings.

The British under Wellington then drove the French out. They held it until 1965 when Nasser finally got them to leave for good.

The British modernized Egypt. Nasser continued its modernization as did his successors.

Now Cairo was a bustling city of nearly ten million people. It was the biggest, most modern, most cosmopolitan city in the Middle East.

Although Egypt was still predominantly Muslim, the concept of religious tolerance was deeply engrained in its people. Here one could see Catholic and Protestant churches, synagogues and temples standing alongside of ornate mosques. Here people of all races, religions and standing mingled, intermarried and lived side-by-side with little or no unpleasantness.

What really struck Maria was the fact that unlike in other Muslim nations, Americans were not only tolerated in Egypt—they were welcomed with a warmth and sincerity that simply could not be faked.

The Egyptians made her feel at home. They made her feel as if she belonged here.

And Cairo's nightlife was *kicking*!

Maria loved the discos, cabarets, stage shows, theaters and other trappings that reminded her somewhat of New York or London—but with their own Middle Eastern twists. She discovered that she loved Egyptian food, Egyptian beer, Egyptian music and even the way they dressed.

Wilder and Hawatt were in mid conversation when Maria walked up. She had her camera slung around her neck and a heavy canvas camera bag slung over her left shoulder.

"Hello, my dear," said Hawatt. "We were just talking about you."

"Nothing bad, I hope," Maria said as she put the bag on the table and unslung the camera from her neck.

"We're out of 1000," she said, referring to the high speed film she used for night photography.

"Already? You *have* been busy," Art said.

"As usual. Anyway, what were saying about me?" she said.

"I was just saying to your husband how like an Egyptian you are becoming. You really like Egypt, don't you?" Hawatt asked.

"Yes. I like it very much. I feel comfortable here," Maria answered as she stuffed the camera into the bag.

"Not even the heat bothers her anymore," Art added. "She hardly perspires now. It's as if she's been here her entire life."

"Sometimes, I feel as if I have," Maria said. "I can't explain it, either."

"Egypt has a way of getting into a person's soul. I have been told by many foreigners that after they had seen Egypt, they were forever changed. They no longer thought of themselves in terms of nationality. They became simply people. It is a most remarkable phenomenon," Hawatt said with a smile.

He turned and looked up at the huge stone face behind them.

"What do you think of the Sphinx?" he asked.

"I'm not sure yet," Maria replied. "He appears to be alive somehow. It's as if he's waiting for some predetermined event to occur. I like his expression, his gentle smile. It makes me feel at peace with myself."

"Well, in all of my years, I have never heard the Sphinx described in such manner. It is almost as if you have some psychic connection to it," Hawatt said.

"Does anyone know who built it?" Maria asked.

"No. It is one of our greatest mysteries. We do know that what we see now is not its original face. It most likely had the face of a lion at first and one of the pharaohs—Khafre perhaps—changed it. Like your husband has said, we are not really certain who that pharaoh was," Hawatt said.

"How old do you think it is?" Maria asked Art.

He shrugged.

"It's at least 5,000 years old. I believe its construction or modification began during the life of Imhotep under the direction of Djozer. In fact, I believe it was built to mark *and guard* something the Egyptians considered to be of great importance," he said.

"I remember when some scientists came here in 1986 and used that ground imaging radar. They found an anomaly beneath the right paw of the Sphinx. When they asked for permission to dig, the government denied it. About that time, we found the first of the three 'passages' in the monument. When we explored them, we found they led nowhere and the only artifact we found was a woman's shoe from the 1930s," Hawatt said with a smile.

"Three passages? Where are they?" Maria asked.

"One is directly at the base between the paws. It goes into a small chamber with plain limestone block walls about fifteen feet beneath the sand," Hawatt said. "The second is directly behind the monument's head at the base of the neck. It only goes about twenty feet into the Sphinx. We can tell from the way they were constructed that both were dug long after the Sphinx was built."

"Who dug them? Maria asked.

"Treasure hunters would be my guess," Art answered. "Part of the legends depict the Sphinx as a guardian of Egypt's vast wealth. That would have enticed quite a few would-be robbers."

"I see. What about the third passage?" asked Maria.

"That is near the right hind leg of the monument. It goes down about forty feet or so and is a roughly carved circular passage about five feet wide. That's where the shoe was found. I can tell from the way it was dug that it is very old, perhaps nearly as old as the Pyramids behind us," Hawatt replied.

Just then a very excited looking Dr. Heider came running up. He had several large sheets of paper in his hands which he quickly spread out on the table next to them.

"*You have got to see this!*" he said.

CHAPTER 2

▼

Mahomet Ali Anazhur was a lean, goateed man with a jagged scar running from the lobe of his left ear to his jugular vein. The scar was a "gift" from his father who slashed Mahomet with a knife when he was just nine years old. The scar ran deeper than it appeared.

Much deeper.

He killed his father by driving an axe through his skull six months later. His mother turned him over to the police and he ended up in a home for the criminally insane.

He was beaten daily and even raped by the callous guards. They wanted to break his spirit.

They only succeeded in pissing him off. When he escaped from that hell two years later, he became a typical Cairo street thug. He spent the next twenty years in and out of prison.

At thirty, he was recruited into a group called The Vengeance of Allah. It was the turning point in Mahomet's life.

He now had a purpose, albeit a twisted one. He and his band of fanatics had sworn a blood oath to Allah to drive out all Western and other foreign influences in Egypt and turn it into a hard-line Islamic Republic.

They bombed the U.S. and British Embassies, then had the nerve to proclaim it on a televised feed that was easily traced. The Egyptian police raided their headquarters and killed nearly a dozen of the "martyrs" in a ferocious gun battle that lasted six hours.

The group fled into Libya where, fearing western reprisals, Qadaffi had them arrested. After spending six miserable years in prison, the Libyans kicked them out of the country.

That's when the Vengeance of Allah got real busy. They assassinated the French ambassador in Algiers, car-bombed a Legion outpost and tried to hijack several passenger jets. The hijackings ended with the deaths of the would-be hijackers who were gunned down by sky marshals and armed pilots and the Algerian army hunted down most of the other members and killed them on the spot.

Anazhur spent eight years in an Algerian prison before he escaped and wormed his way back into Egypt. He laid low for a while, then began recruiting new members for his band. He was very successful at first. Then he decided to launch an attack against a group of German tourists near Luxor.

The attack left nine tourists dead—six of them women—but the local (and very well-armed Egyptian police) managed to kill all five of the terrorists.

The attack at Luxor made all of the news channels and also made Anazhur's movement a household name.

But the movement was petering out. The Egyptian police had either captured of killed more than half of his followers. The others were still with him but demoralized.

They needed something to catch the world's eye again. Something big. Something (or so Anazhur hoped) that would tie his band in with Egypt's ancient legacies. Something that would somehow *legitimize* their agenda and pave the way for his eventual takeover of the nation.

And Wilder's dig might be just what Allah ordered.

That's why he read the newspapers daily. That's why he had his men watching every single thing that went on at Giza.

If the legendary Box of Thoth did exist, Mahomet wanted it. He believed that the box might contain the secrets of the ancient gods of Egypt and provide him with the claim to the power he so craved.

But there was another, more compelling reason he wanted the box. He was aware of the ancient legends surrounding a weapon that was so terrible that the Gods themselves decided to hide it from mankind lest they use it to destroy the world. One of the legends went on to say that the secrets of that weapon were locked away in the Box of Thoth.

Such a weapon, if it did exist, would enable Mahomet to blackmail the Egyptian government into making him a pharaoh.

That would place him in complete control of Egypt's modern armed forces and enable him to launch a Jihad against the non-believers within and outside of the nation. He would destroy the enemies of Islam and make himself a god.

But in order to find out if the legends were true, he had to get his hands on the box—if that, too, existed.

That's why his spies watched every moment of the dig at the Sphinx. Mahomet wanted to know if Wilder and Hawatt found anything and what that anything was the moment they uncovered it.

Mahomet was also quite cracked. Besides his belief that he was a direct descendant of Ramses the Great and heir to the throne of Egypt, he was a paranoid schizophrenic. He trusted no one and hated all who didn't follow his rather twisted interpretation of the Quran.

He especially hated America and its allies and vowed that he and his army would one day wipe them from the face of the Earth.

All of this, combined with animal cunning and an explosively violent nature, made Mahomet dangerously unpredictable.

Even for his followers.

That's why his "army" numbered less than twelve.

But now, Anazhur was preparing to take on someone he both admired and respected—the famous Dr. Arthur Wilder. He'd done his homework on the archaeologist, too.

He knew that Art was the son of Arlin Wilder, who was also an archaeologist. Arlin Wilder was considered to be a crackpot by most of his peers because he had some radical ideas concerning the actual ages of various monuments, especially the Sphinx. He was also positive that Egypt was much older than anyone had guessed.

Because of these theories, Arlin Wilder was dismissed by the scientific establishment and faded into obscurity.

Art Wilder had his father's curiosity and thirst for knowledge. He'd accompanied his father on many digs and long trips and learned how to look for traces of lost civilizations in the jungles of Central and South America. When Arlin died at the age of fifty-six, he left behind all of his voluminous notebooks, maps, artifacts and a large fortune in a Swiss bank account.

By that time, Art Wilder had served in the U.S. Army Special Forces and the Navy SEALS. He'd fought in several battles and traveled to the most remote and dangerous parts of the globe.

Like his father, he also had some "heretical" theories about the dawn of man's civilization. These, too, were dismissed by "serious" scientists and archaeologists.

Then Art found Dynasty Zero in the southwestern desert of Egypt. The find—a series of ancient tombs dating back to 5,500 BCE—proved that Egypt was a mighty nation *before* Sumer appeared in Mesopotamia.

The find turned accepted history on its ear and made Wilder a household name. A few months later, he helped uncover the craftsmen's city near Giza and proved that slaves *did not* build any of the monuments on the plateau.

Then came his incredible Yucatan finds. Three years later, he led an expedition into the unexplored region of the peninsula and uncovered three intact Mayan cities along with dozens of their ancient books.

Two years later, he found the lost city in Guatemala and firmly established a link between the ancient cities of Central America and Egypt.

Today, Art Wilder was the most respected archaeologist in the world. Anazhur hoped to use that fame in his favor.

But he failed to find out *everything* about Wilder. He didn't know about his mercenary background or the network of "friends" he had all over the world. And Wilder was *fearless.*

Unpredictable.

Daring.

"There is no doubt of it, Art," said Heider as they stood around the table staring at the printouts. "There is an open space between the paws of the monument. Judging from its exact measurements and configuration, it has to be a man-made chamber. A large one, too."

"How large?" asked Wilder.

"According to this printout, it measures 14 feet high, 22 feet wide and 34 feet long," Heider said.

"And it's thirty feet down?" Hawatt asked.

"Thirty-six to be exact," replied Heider.

"What shall we do, Dr. Wilder?" asked Kuyder.

"We'll rope off the exact measurements first thing tomorrow afternoon, then try to find some way in that won't disturb what's down there," Wilder said.

"See here? The chamber is a little bit off-center. Part of it is to the left of the Sphinx's left paw and the rest goes under the body at a ten degree angle," Heider pointed out.

"There are probably more rooms beneath it," Hawatt said. "The ancient Egyptians always built vast complexes in which to bury their kings or to safeguard treasures. They did this to thwart would-be looters."

"Unfortunately it didn't work most of the time," Wilder added. "Let's hope we got lucky."

"Yes indeed!" agreed Hawatt.

Wilder studied the printout carefully.

"This could be just the tip of the iceberg," he said. "We need to know more before we go for the gold."

He looked at Heider.

"Can you probe deeper? Will the sonarscope be able to detect chambers that might lie beneath this one?" he asked.

"I think so. Want me to try?" Heider asked.

"Yes. Get me a reading at forty, fifty and sixty feet. Then get me printouts of the readings," Wilder said.

"Okay. This will take some time," Heider said.

"What's a few more hours when you've been waiting over 4,000 years?" Kuyder chimed in.

Wilder turned to Maria and Hawatt.

"If there are more chambers down there, we need to know where and how large they are," he said. "I don't want to go into this blindly."

"I agree," said Hawatt. "With any luck, the new printouts may even show us a way into the place."

Wilder laughed.

"A couple of years ago, you were willing to do anything short of murder to keep anyone from finding out what was down there. Now, you can't wait to go in," he said.

"Let us say that my eyes have been opened. My attitude is similar to your own, Art. The ancient secrets are waiting to be unlocked and it is up to people like us to find and share them with all Mankind," Hawatt said with more than a little conviction.

"I'm certain that the great Imhotep would have agreed with us," Wilder said.

"Imhotep?" asked Maria.

"Imhotep was the chief architect, scientist and physician of King Djoser, the second ruler of the Third Dynasty about 2686 BCE. He was also a sage, an astrologer and grand vizier.

He has been credited by many historians with initiating the Old Kingdom. He designed and oversaw the building of the first stone temple at Edfu and the famous step pyramid at Saqqara in Memphis. That is the oldest stone structure on Earth and it is over 200 feet high.

Imhotep was a physician of considerable skill and is still worshipped as the God of Medicine. He has been credited with mapping the stars, refining the process of mummification and even inventing beer and wine," explained Hawatt.

"He was the reigning genius of his time. He may have been the single most brilliant man who ever walked this Earth. His influence is still felt today," added Wilder.

"Without Imhotep, there might not have been an Egypt. Hell, there might not have been a real human civilization," he concluded.

"Where is he buried?" Maria asked.

"That's just it, my dear," said Hawatt. "No one knows. Imhotep's tomb has never been located. Ancient sources tell us that his entire library was buried with him so that he could use it in the Afterlife. If so, think of what a find that would be!"

"Maybe it's right under our feet," suggested Wilder.

Hawatt nodded as he sipped his coffee. Wilder's off-hand remark may hold more truth than anyone suspects. What more fitting a resting place for Egypt's greatest mind than beneath the Sphinx?

Wilder continued.

"Archs have been going over Saqqara with a fine tooth comb for over 200 years now. So far, all they've come up with are Greco-Roman cemeteries, a few older graves, a handful of shrines and a few other artifacts. They spent 200 years looking for Imhotep's tomb and came up empty. That tells me that he was never buried there. If he was, then someone moved his tomb to protect it from robbers."

"That is a good point," said Hawatt.

Wilder nodded.

"So I asked myself just where would a *god* be buried?"

He paused and smiled up at the Sphinx. Hawatt smiled, too.

"I used to think you were mad. That you were just another foreign crackpot. I still think you are mad—but I am also convinced that you are right. I believe now that Imhotep's tomb is either near or beneath the Sphinx," he said.

Wilder laughed.

"I guess that makes *you* as nutty as I am, eh, Nasi?" he joked.

"Then we are both mad together, my friend," said Hawatt as he pounded Wilder's back.

"You once said that Imhotep was the pillar upon which Egyptian civilization was based," Maria said.

Hawatt nodded.

"Without him, there would be no pyramids, no stone buildings, no mummies, no modern medical or surgical procedures. In fact, without Imhotep, human history in general would now be quite different," he explained.

"No wonder they made him a god," Maria mused. "You said he perfected mummification? Did he invent it?" she asked.

"No. The very first mummies, as far as we can tell, were made by the ancient Peruvians. Their dry, hot climate was ideal for such things and they began doing it about 7,000 years ago—at least 600 years prior to the Egyptians," Wilder said.

"Imhotep *perfected* the process. He made mummification into a true art form and also created the religious ceremonies that went with it," added Hawatt.

"I see. Did the Peruvians treat their mummies differently from the Egyptians?" Maria asked.

"Oh Hell yes!" said Wilder. "For one, they didn't bury them—they kept them in their homes and treated them as if they were still alive. The dead could own property, make important decisions, predict the future and even attend feasts with other mummies. Dead generals and emperors were carried into battles at the heads of armies. The whole Cult of the Dead was quite bizarre because they had no afterlife. Death was merely a transition into a more permanent, more stable form."

"Dinnertime in the average household must have been pretty weird," Maria remarked.

Both men laughed.

"Before the Incas, who took the Mummy Cult to almost obscene lengths which actually led to their downfall, a group called the Pekiyacta started the mummy thing.

A warlike people called the Juari invaded the region. To keep the Pekiyacta in line, they gathered up their ancestral mummies and took them to their fortress city high in the mountains. There, they placed the "hostages" in niches they had built into the walls. They allowed the Pekiyacta to visit and place offerings with their ancestors, but they were never allowed to take them back home.

The idea was simple. To control the living, one first had to control the dead. The Juari and Pekiyacta both believed that they owned the land through their ancestors. If you destroyed their ancestors, you took away their right to the land. In ancient Peru, if you didn't own land, you'd starve to death.

So when another tribe invaded the region, they conquered the Juari fortress and destroyed all of their ancestral mummies, thus breaking any claims they had on the land.

The Incas eventually replaced these peoples but the Mummy Cult survived and thrived until the Conquistadores and the Catholic Church put an end to it during the 1700's," explained Wilder.

"Mummies have been found all over the world but nowhere else but Egypt has the process been carried to such a level of perfection," added Hawatt with more than a hint of pride.

"The sun is rising," Maria pointed out.

They watched as a rose-colored sky chased away the darkness in the east.

"The Great God Amun Re is returning from the Underworld and bringing the Atun with him to shine its life-giving rays upon the world," Wilder said.

Hawatt smiled. Wilder's reverence for the culture of his ancestors never ceased to amaze him. Maybe he, too, was Egyptian in a past life?

Soon the plateau would be awash in bright rose and gold and the temperature would rise as much as 30 degrees. Then it would be far too hot to continue working.

"Let's get back to Cairo," Wilder suggested. "We'll get cleaned up, take a short nap and meet you at your office in the museum."

He then turned to Heider and Kuyder.

"I'd like you both to be there as well," he said.

"What time?" Kuyder asked.

"Whatever's good for you. I'm flexible," Wilder replied.

"How about two o'clock?" Hawatt suggested.

"Two it is then," Wilder agreed as the others nodded their approval. "Pack up the sonarscope as soon as you've taken those other readings then bring the printouts to the museum with you."

"What about lunch?" asked Maria.

"Let that be on me this time," said Hawatt. "I'll have the museum chef prepare something special."

"As long as there's plenty of that good Egyptian beer to go along with it", Wilder said with a grin.

They all laughed.

"We Egyptians brew the best beer in the world. After all, we've been brewing it for nearly 6,000 years," Hawatt said. "That was more than enough time to perfect it, don't you think?"

"It *is* just about the most perfect beer I've ever had," Wilder agreed. "What do you say, Dr. Kuyder?"

"It's not as good as Dutch beer but it will do," he said wryly.

Then he and Heider headed back to their sonarscope while Wilder, Hawatt and Maria climbed aboard the Land Rover for the drive back to Cairo.

Hawatt went home and showered the sand from his aching body. He was tired, so he headed up to bed for a nap.

But he couldn't sleep.

After several minutes of tossing, turning and adjusting his pillow, he gave up the battle. He rose, dressed and went down to his study to go over the photos and notes from the day's dig.

The sonic scans fascinated him. Wilder had been right all along. There *was* something down there.

Something big.

Was it a royal tomb?

A hidden vault?

Perhaps both?

Hawatt sighed. He went into the kitchen and brewed himself a pot of coffee. It was eight a.m. and Cairo was alive with the sounds of traffic and people going to work.

It was rush hour.

Hawatt smiled at the phrase.

It was coined in America but it fit so well everywhere. Even the Chinese called it rush hour. It was the perfect description for the morning madness.

His thoughts turned to Maria Wilder. He'd known her only since her arrival in Egypt several months ago. She knew hardly anything about Egypt then and everything seemed like such a mystery to her. She couldn't even identify a single hieroglyph nor pronounce any Egyptian words.

Now she was able to read the ancient writings as easily as her own language and had little or no problems with pronunciation. It was as if she had been speaking the language her entire life.

"Maria is a fast learner," Wilder had said.

But she learned almost too fast. It was unnatural. Almost supernatural.

She also adapted to daily life in Egypt much faster than her husband. She seemed to have an inborn knowledge of Egyptian customs and rituals, even the more obscure ones that had fallen out of common use.

Even Hawatt's colleagues remarked on how easily Maria Wilder had made the transition.

"Are you sure she is not one of us?" one man had asked. "She looks and acts more Egyptian than many people who have lived here all their lives."

"It is as if she had been born in Egypt over 3,000 years ago," Hawatt had pointed out to Wilder. "It is uncanny."

Yes. The changes in Maria Wilder had occurred so fast that they scared Hawatt. But he kept his fears to himself.

"Maybe she is just experiencing something from a previous life?" he thought. "Maybe she was Egyptian in that life and she has finally found her way back home?"

In his younger days, he would have written off such thoughts as superstitious nonsense. Now, especially after watching what was happening to Maria, he wasn't so sure.

CHAPTER 3

▼

Mahomet Ali Anazhur sat and listened as his spies told what they'd seen at the dig. When they were finished, he simply nodded and dismissed them with his usual "imperial" air.

He turned to his second in command, a short, scar faced man named Hasmir who stood nearby filing his nails.

"What do you think?" he asked.

Hasmir shrugged.

"So they found something. At least it appears they have. So what?" he replied. "This information is no good to us now and won't be until they uncover what we hope they will."

"True," agreed Anazhur.

"Even then, the problem then becomes just how do we get them to turn it over to us? Wilder has a reputation for being a man that is best not trifled with. He's left a trail of broken corpses all over the world to prove this," Hasmir pointed out.

"Also true," agreed Anazhur. "But even *he* has a weakness—and it is one we may be able to exploit."

"His wife?" Hasmir asked with a raised eyebrow. He didn't like where this was going. He was all for doing the "terrorist thing" but even he thought his leader was mad. And he didn't believe even for a minute that Anazhur was descended from Ramses the Great.

"Exactly," said Anazhur with a serpentine smile.

"Terrorism is one thing—but screwing with a man like Wilder—that's *another* matter entirely," Hasmir said.

"Don't worry. I have a plan…" said Anazhur.

It was then that Hasmir began to do just that.

Back in their hotel suite, the Wilders had just finished showering together. Art had breakfast sent up and they sat on the balcony while they ate. Maria was still wound up from the evening's dig. In fact, she seemed far more excited about the discovery of the hidden chambers than he was—and it didn't escape his notice.

"Do you think we'll find Imhotep's tomb down there?" she asked.

"Perhaps. If not, it's still a very important find. It may be proof that Egypt's legendary Zeptepi actually existed," Wilder replied.

"The Golden Age," Maria sighed. "What a find *that* would be!"

"It sure would. According to several ancient legends, Egypt's Golden Age began around 10,500 B.C.E. That was roughly the time that Atlantis supposedly sank. The Greeks believed that the survivors of Atlantis fled to various parts of the world, bringing their culture with them. If this is true, then the ancient Egyptians were their descendants," Wilder theorized.

"How long did Zeptepi last?" Maria asked.

"About six thousand years or so—until the rise of Egypt around 4,000 B.C.E.," Wilder said.

"What made it end?" Maria asked.

Wilder shook his head.

"The ancient Egyptian texts don't make mention of that. They simply left the region and took most of their recorded knowledge with them," he replied.

"I believe that Imhotep discovered some of their lost records and used them to jump start Egyptian—and human—civilization overall," he added. "But that's just a guess on my part. I also believe that the people of the Golden Age carved the Sphinx and left it behind to remind the Egyptians of their glorious beginnings."

"That means Egyptian civilization dates back to the Ice Age?" Maria asked.

"At least," Wilder said as he finished his coffee.

He stood up and stretched.

"We'd better get some sleep. We have to meet with Nasi in three hours," he said.

"I don't feel like sleeping. I have something else in mind," Maria said.

"What?" Art asked with a wicked grin.

"Your hard dick and lots of cum!" she replied as she opened her thighs and pulled him into her.

As usual, their lovemaking was passionate.

It was erotic.

It was perfect.

Art plunged into her as deep as he could, then moved his hips counter clockwise so that his penis massaged nearly every part of Maria's happy vagina. At the same time, she used her inner muscles to squeeze and engulf his penis and met his every down thrust with a hard upward thrust of her hips.

Art adored making love with Maria. She was enthusiastic, playful and incredibly sensuous. And she always seemed to be horny. He had never known anyone like her before.

To Maria, they were a perfect couple. She was always horny when she was near him and Art's own horniness was usually quite obvious.

He made her wet.

She made him hard.

"What," she thought, "could be more perfect than that?"

More importantly was the fact that their orgasms were strong, long lasting and usually triggered at the exact same time. Tonight was no exception.

As Maria felt herself spiral to another good climax, she wrapped her arms and legs around Art's shuddering body and held on tight as he emptied every last drop of come he had into her more than willing vagina.

After a short rest, they went into the bathroom and showered again.

Together.

As they soaped each other's bodies, they naturally paid special attention to their erogenous zones. Before long, they were both very horny. Maria wrapped her fingers around Art's penis and jerked him off until he was real hard again. Then she turned her back to him, leaned over and gripped the taps in the shower. Her gorgeous behind was slightly up and her feet were wide apart.

Art got behind her and eased his cock into her from behind. Maria sighed and enjoyed the ride. It was a nice, easy ride and she really enjoyed the position she was in. A few good thrusts later, Art came again and pumped everything he had left into her hungry pussy.

When he saw that she hadn't orgasmed yet, he turned her around and licked her slit until she did. Then they dressed and went down to the lobby. Once there, Art called the limo and had the driver take them to the museum.

The Wilders arrived at the museum an hour early. While they waited for Hawatt, they wandered through the exhibits in the main gallery. Each time she passed the mummified remains of an ancient king, Maria stopped to marvel at his state of preservation.

"Much of what we know about the ancient Egyptians was gleaned from tombs and the Book of the Dead. We still know comparatively little about the everyday lives of the average people," Wilder explained.

"It seems like they were preoccupied with death," Maria remarked as they stopped to examine the remains of Seti I.

"That's a very wrong-headed assumption based upon incomplete historical data," Wilder said. "To really know the Egyptians, you have to look beyond the mummies and tombs. You have to read between the lines so to speak.

They loved life so much, they extended it into the idea of an afterlife. One didn't "die" in the sense that we know it today. One simply left this world and went into the next which they believed was a continuation of Egypt. In the After-life, one didn't feel pain, get sick or grow old. One lived forever—provided that your physical form also survived.

They believed that you'd need your physical body to make the transition to the Afterlife. That's why they went through such great pains to preserve it and to bury people with the things they would need once they got there, like their favor-ite possessions, food and body organs."

"Once you got to the Afterlife, you would live forever," said Hawatt as he walked up behind them. "The Afterlife was a paradise, a mirror image of Egypt. After all, what could possibly be better than Egypt?"

"Hi Nasi," Maria said as she hugged him. "The Afterlife sounds like a wonder-ful place."

"I'm sure it is—but I am in no hurry to get there," Hawatt joked.

"Of course there was a slight drawback to their Afterlife," Wilder pointed out. "Once you got there, you continued the same life you had before. So if you were a laborer or farmer or priest in Egypt, that's what you remained in the Afterlife. But you would never age or go hungry."

"Of course you must realize that life for the average person in ancient Egypt was very good, even by today's standards. So even if you went into the Afterlife as a laborer, you still had it pretty good," Hawatt added as they walked back to his office.

"Provided, of course, that you passed the test to enter the Afterlife," Wilder said.

"I know about that! Your soul went before the god Anubis and he weighed your heart against a feather. If they weighed the same, you could pass through to the Afterlife. If your heart was heavy with sin, your soul was fed to Sobek, the crocodile-headed god," Maria beamed.

"If one possessed the right spells, the test was easy. Of course, the priests always made sure that one had the right spells. So just about everyone entered the Afterlife," Hawatt said. "I have never found any archaeological evidence to the contrary."

Wilder seated Maria on one side of a large mahogany table. Then he grabbed a chair and slid next to her. Maria watched as Hawatt's chef set the table.

"It must be very crowded in the Afterlife," she said as she helped herself to the food before them.

"Yes—but very pleasant. I believe the early Christians derived the concept of Heaven from the Egyptian Afterlife," Wilder said as he opened a bottle of beer.

"Finding that space under the Sphinx was exciting, don't you think so, Nasi?" Maria asked.

Nasi smiled and nodded.

"Yes it was. We should have more exact images this evening. Once Al gives us the pictures, we can decide where and how to enter that chamber," he said.

"I can hardly wait. This is what I've been looking for my entire career. I hope it's what we're after," Wilder said as he drank from the dark brown bottle.

"Even if it isn't, it's still an incredible find. Think of the secrets that might be hidden there! Of course we must do it on live television. I want the whole world to be there when we go inside," Hawatt said with a broad grin.

"I agree. This belongs to everybody. It could be the single most important find in history. At the least, I expect it to change a lot of what we thought we knew about the Egyptians," Wilder said.

"By the way, where are Al and Rudy? It's past two," Art asked.

"They said they needed to recheck their data. They will meet us back at the dig," Hawatt said.

"That's what I like—dedication. Now, hand me another beer," Wilder joked.

Maria sat quietly and listened while they talked. Wilder looked at her and smiled.

"I hope you have plenty of 1000 speed film. I want lots of photos of the chamber," he said.

"You mean I'm going in with you?" she asked.

"Of course you are! You're my right-hand girl," he replied. "I wouldn't have it any other way."

"That's great! I'd better go out and buy some more film today. We're down to two rolls," she said.

"Get a hundred rolls. That chamber looks pretty large," Hawatt suggested. "I don't want to miss a thing."

That afternoon, Maria left to purchase film while Art and Nasi drove back to the Sphinx to consult with Kuyder and Heider.

The day was very warm so Maria walked along the more shaded side streets in search of a good place to buy film and other camera attachments. She soon came to a very small shop on the corner of a narrow street. It had no windows. Only a weather-beaten sign proclaimed its presence. Maria peered up the sign. It was so worn out she couldn't read it.

She shrugged and opened the wooden door. Inside was a low glass counter. Behind it sat a rather beautiful woman of indeterminate age. She smiled at Maria.

"Can I help you?" she asked in Arabic.

"Do you have any film?" asked Maria in English as she held up a spent roll.

"Film? No we do not sell film here," the Woman replied.

Maria looked around at the empty shelves and crinkled her nose.

"What do you sell?" she asked.

"Come. I will show you," the Woman replied as she motioned Maria to come to the back room.

Inside, Maria saw several long shelves lined with all sorts of dildoes, beads, pumps, books, vibrators and lots of other sexual devices. Maria smiled. The Woman smiled back.

"I sell sex things," she said proudly. "Even though Islam has taken over our country, we Egyptians love erotic pleasures."

Maria walked around the room and examined some of the vibrators and the various attachments. The Woman watched as she picked up a realistic-looking dildo and fondled it appreciatively.

"That is our most popular one," the Woman said. "It is very lifelike."

"It feels like real flesh," said Maria as she put it back on the shelf. "Do you use any of these things yourself?"

"I have tried all of them," the Woman assured her. "The one you just fondled is my favorite."

"I love sex, too. Lots of sex. I feel horny most of the time," Maria said.

"Me too," said the Woman. "You like men or women?"

"Men—mostly," Maria said with a smile. "I haven't had a woman in a long time."

"You can visit me after closing hours if you like," the Woman suggested. "I can show you how some of these toys work."

"I like that. I'll come back tomorrow or the next day. Right now, I need to buy film," Maria said as they walked to the front of the shop.

"There is a camera store two streets down on the left. You can purchase film there cheap," the Woman said.

She escorted Maria to the door. Maria turned to say good-bye. Before she got a word out, the Woman kissed her on the lips. Surprised, Maria kissed her back. Before she realized it, their tongue had merged. As their kiss grew more passionate, the Woman undid Maria's shorts and eased her hand down into her panties. Maria opened her stance and sucked the Woman's tongue as she allowed her to liberally fondle her hot, moist cunt.

They stayed like that for several minutes, then Maria grew bold enough to slide her hand down the front of the Woman's skirt.

"Take me. I am yours!" the Woman said. "Take me now!"

Maria locked the door of the shop. The Woman took her hand and led her into the back of the shop, then upstairs to a very clean, well-decorated bedroom.

Naked, they fell into each other's arms and kissed passionately as they virtually melted into the bed. Hesitant at first, Maria cast away all doubts and threw herself into the affair with wild abandon.

It soon became a wonderful, wild ride. Lips met lips, then graced necks, chests, nipples and navels. As their tongues played across their bodies, excited fingers explored their moist, warm folds and danced deliciously within eager slits.

This being new for Maria, she let The Woman do as she pleased with her at first, then followed her lead until both women were burning with lust.

Maria's cunt fascinated The Woman. Her labia were like tender flower petals. Soft and pliant, they quivered noticeably when The Woman caressed them. Her slit was long, moist and deep pink in color. It glimmered in the sunlight and her wonderfully swollen clit peeked at her invitingly from beneath its fleshy cover. This marvelous cunt was covered with a rich, brown carpet of silken pubic hair.

"You're so beautiful," The Woman said.

Maria shivered, still amazed that her new friend was feeling her pussy. She was about to have sex with a beautiful woman. She wondered just how far The Woman wanted to go. Would she go beyond touching? If so, was Maria ready for that?

Despite her inner conflict, Maria gave herself willingly to The Woman. Maybe she was really bisexual. It was a part of her she never had the chance to explore until now. If she was, who better than The Woman to bring that side out into the open?

The Woman inserted two fingers into Maria's cunt and moved them in and out. Maria groaned with passion as The Woman kissed her navel and licked her way slowly downward.

"Do it! Eat me!" Maria whispered.

When The Woman's soft, warm tongue touched her swollen clit, Maria nearly jumped off the bed. She grabbed The Woman's head and opened her legs wide as that wonderful, knowing tongue played and danced between her thighs.

"Aiee! Aiee—yes!" Maria yelled.

She humped The Woman's face wildly now as orgasm after orgasm surged through her body. At the same time, The Woman slid two fingers deep inside Maria's cunt and massaged her g-spot. This increased the intensity of Maria's orgasm and she shook all over as the stars exploded in front of her eyes.

She let go of The Woman's hair and fell, arms akimbo, back onto the bed. The Woman moved upward so her cunt was merely inches from Maria's lips. The delightful aroma of The Woman's open pussy enticed Maria. She reached up, gripped The Woman's behind and pulled her down onto her tongue.

Then Maria ate her.

The Woman tasted sweet.

Inviting.

Intoxicating.

Maria felt wicked. She was eating her best friend's pussy—her first and only pussy—and she loved it. She loved the smell, the feel and especially the flavor. She explored The Woman from cunt to asshole several times, then settled down and concentrated on her pretty little clit and barely noticed that The Woman was still eating her.

The Woman came.

She actually made The Woman come.

Maria felt her bittersweet juices jet into her mouth and hungrily lapped them up. The taste was sensationally erotic. It blew Maria's mind so much, she came again and they both held on to ride the waves that surged through them.

"Th-that was unbelievable!" Maria gasped. "My head is spinning like crazy!"

"Mine, too. You are a good lover, Maria. You eat me very good," The Woman replied as she came down from the clouds.

Maria smiled at her lovely sex partner, then reached out and ran her fingers over her soft, black pubic hair. It felt so natural to be with The Woman like this. Maria told her this, too.

The Woman smiled.

"If you want me, Maria, you can have me anytime you like," she said. "I am all yours."

She was feeling Maria's pussy now. As she inserted two fingers into it, Maria moaned and glanced at the clock. It was only 11:00. The day had just begun…

While Maria looked over the many wonderful things at the local bazaar, Wilder, Hawatt, Heider and Kuyder were hard at work back at the dig. The four men were standing in the tent looking over the ground sonar images that Kuyder had made of the complex beneath the Sphinx.

"I can tell you one thing for certain, Art," said Kuyder. "The place is big. Much bigger than any of us expected."

"Besides that large entry chamber, the map shows several more chambers," said Hawatt as he peered at the printout.

"Twenty-seven to be exact. There are twenty small ones that measure about 15' x 15' and seven larger ones. The other five are odd-shaped rooms. There are two circular ones. Two rectangular and one octagonal room," said Heider.

"They appear to be laid out on four other levels with the octagonal one on the lowest," added Kuyder.

Wilder studied the map carefully. He then picked up a pencil and pointed as he spoke.

"My guess is that the six smaller rooms on the first level are offering chapels. There are three on the left and three on the right of this long passageway. I don't see a way down into the complex," he said.

"The sonarscope couldn't find one," said Kuyder. "The first level may have been above the ground at one time."

"That would make sense. Offering chapels were put there to accommodate members of his cult. They would have needed easy access to them," said Hawatt. "If they were placed below ground level, they could not have been more than ten feet deep."

"How deep is this first level?" asked Wilder.

"Fourteen and a half feet. The second level is twenty-two feet below that and the third is twenty feet beneath the second," Kuyder said.

"What's this?" Wilder asked as he pointed to a narrow corridor running northeast from the octagonal chamber.

"I'm not sure. Most of it is beyond the range of the scope," explained Heider. "It's a passageway I guess."

"But where does it go?" asked Wilder.

He stepped outside and looked to the north. His eyes saw only the Great Pyramid of Khufu. He removed his hat and scratched his head as he went back inside.

"That's odd," he said. "If your map is right, that passageway leads straight to the Great Pyramid—which wasn't even there when Imhotep lived."

"Maybe it was," suggested Kuyder.

"I see what you're getting at, Al," said Wilder. "You're saying that the pyramid was built by Imhotep."

"Or it was *already* there before he was born," Kuyder said. "You once told me that nobody knows exactly how old the Sphinx is. Yet most Egyptologists say it was built the same time the Great Pyramid was built. If this is true, then both must pre-date the First Dynasty."

"But it is common knowledge that Khufu built the pyramid about 4,500 years ago," said Hawatt.

"Think about it, Nasi. That knowledge is based on the assumptions of Egyptologists from nearly 100 years ago. Yet we have never found one scrap of papyrus nor any other hard evidence that proved Khufu actually had them built. Like many ancient kings, he may have simply modified monuments that already existed to proclaim his own greatness," said Wilder.

"Exactly my point," said Kuyder. "If no one knows exactly how old the Sphinx is, how can anyone know how old the Great Pyramid is?"

"Just thinking about that makes my head hurt," said Hawatt as he plopped down in a chair. "Does your map show a logical way into the complex?"

"Not really—wait. The surface scan we did earlier seems to show an anomaly right at the edge of the right paw," Heider said as he scrolled through the data.

"Yes! Here it is," he said as he dragged the mouse over the screen. "It's a slight one, though."

"Hmm. I've seen something like that before. Haven't you, Nasi?" asked Wilder.

The older man squinted at the screen and nodded.

"Yes. That appears to be the door to the complex. We'd better have the laborers dig there to see if I'm right," he said.

Wilder walked out of the tent and signaled for the diggers. Seven ragged-looking men scrambled over to him. He showed the foreman the map and instructed him to start digging. The foreman nodded then turned and barked orders to his crew. Moments later, they were hard at work with picks and shovels.

Wilder watched them for a little while, then went back inside.

"That should take a few hours," he said. "Let's break for now and return after dark. It's too damned hot to work right now."

"What about the diggers?" asked Kuyder.

"I'll stay and watch over them," said Hawatt. "If anything happens, I'll call you at the hotel."

"Okay. I'll bring Maria back with me after dinner. Make sure the diggers get plenty of cold water and rest. I don't want anybody falling out," Wilder said as he headed for the Jeep.

Maria was surprised how easily she had given herself to The Woman. She never had any real lesbian inclinations before, even though she often fantasized trying it just once to see what it was like.

As she lay naked on the bed, she looked down at the pretty Egyptian lovingly licking her cunt and smiled. It seemed and felt so natural now.

And so very, very good.

She closed her eyes and enjoyed the ride. Soon, she would sink her tongue into The Woman's delicious cunt. She sighed as The Woman nibbled her clit.

God, she was good at this.

"The best," Maria thought.

A sudden surge of pleasure roared through her. She arched her back to take The Woman's tongue deeper into her cunt, then came seconds later. As she did, she humped The Woman's tongue and cried out in Spanish.

Sex with The Woman was intense.

Very intense.

Maria groaned and fell back to the mattress. The Woman stopped licking and sat back to watch Maria's petal-like labia throb visibly as her orgasm subsided.

"You're very beautiful, Maria," she said.

"You are, too. I wish we could fuck," Maria replied.

Wordlessly, The Woman got on top of her and began rubbing her cunt against Maria's nice and easy. Maria's eyes went wide. The Woman was actually fucking her! It was the most incredible thing she ever felt. She moaned softly and dug her fingers into the bed as her body took control and fucked back.

"Yes!" The Woman gasped. "Yes! YES!!!"

Maria didn't hear her cry out. She was completely lost in the sex they were having. All she cared about was the way her cunt felt as it ground into The Woman's and the fact that she was coming...and coming...and coming...

She couldn't recall ever coming so much, so many times. Sweat covered her—and The Woman—from head to foot as they continued to make love all through the warm afternoon. The bedroom was filled with their sexual aromas now. The scent only served to heighten their lovemaking.

They soon switched positions. Now, Maria was on top and the two women fucked away in the scissors position until their bodies literally ached. They were tired, sweaty and almost unconscious by the time they'd each come for the last time that afternoon.

When Art arrived at the hotel, Maria was already in their suite. She was seated at the coffee table. Two dozen rolls of 1,000 speed film were laid out in front of her. She smiled when Art walked in.

Back at the Sphinx, Hawatt leaned against the left paw of the monument and watched as the workers loaded sand into baskets and lugged it away. Every ten minutes, the men stopped to drink water and get out of the boiling sun. Despite the heat and hard work, they seemed to be in good spirits as if pleased to be a part of what might be a great historic event.

A hundred yards away, two men watched the site through binoculars, ready to report anything unusual, no matter how slight, to Anazhur.

Things at the hotel were going in an entirely different direction at the moment.

Art lay on his back with his hands behind his head, watching as Maria straddled his thighs. She grabbed his penis, gave it several easy pulls, then moved her hips so that the head of his cock pointed directly at her labia. Satisfied that he was hard enough, she guided his penis up into her slit. When she felt her pubic hairs mingle with his, she began to rock back and forth.

Art reached up and played with her erect nipples, sending delicious tingles all through Maria's taut, sweaty body. She gasped then began moving up and down on his penis as slow and a deep as she could. She kept at this until she realized Art was about to come. She stopped and waited a few seconds.

When she felt she was back in control, she continued. Four times, Art nearly came. Four times, Maria stopped until it passed, then loved him again. This was the longest fuck Art could remember. It was the longest time he'd ever been erect and it was the most his balls had ever ached.

By the time he was ready to blow again, he begged Maria to let him come. But she was already in the beginning throes of her own orgasm and didn't hear a word.

The room was spinning wildly for her now as her orgasm entered the explosive stage. She began shaking out of control as she raised her hips one last time then slammed herself down onto Art's cock as hard as she could.

They both came within seconds of each other. Art grabbed her behind and thrust his cock hard up into her vagina. Maria toppled backward onto her elbows, taking Art with her. He rolled so that he was on top and his penis was still inside her wonderful, quivering vagina.

He humped for a few more seconds as he continued to spew his cum deep inside her eager body. Maria clawed his back and used her pussy to milk him of every last drop.

"Love me, Art! Oh love me!" she cried as everything went white.

CHAPTER 4

▼

After ten hours of intense digging, the workers finally removed the sand and struck solid stone. The foreman called to Art and Nasi. They came running over with Maria and the others a few steps behind.

Art looked down at the large stone slab and whistled. Nasi shook his head with awe.

There before them was a large, square block around ten feet wide and long. It was scratched and worn from exposure to sand and wind but the raised images upon it were still very visible.

The image was of a man seated crosslegged. There was a writing board on his lap. He held a reed pen in his right hand and seemed to be gazing intently at something in front of him.

Behind him was the sun disk or Atun, radiating down on his shoulders. There were no other markings.

"He appears to be scribe," Art guessed.

"If so, he was a very important one because the rays of the Atun are shining down on him," Nasi said.

"Let's call the members of the press. I want them to be here when we open this," Art said.

Nasi nodded.

At ten pm that night, four camera crews from the National Geographic, The History Channel and two major news networks, along with an army of reporters, gathered between the paws of the Sphinx.

"We believe this slab is the entrance to a series of chambers located beneath the Sphinx. Our workers have spent the entire day clearing the sand away and digging slightly around the edges so we can attach a block and tackle to the slab," Hawatt explained to the reporters.

"We're ready to lift it, Nasi," said Art.

Hawatt and the reporters gathered around the slab to watch the "grand opening" as Art called it.

"We are taking great care with the slab. This is a priceless relic from our distant past. We do not want to damage it more than we have to," Hawatt explained.

The cameras rolled as the workers attached the ropers of the block and tackle to the corners of the heavy slab. This done, they looked at Wilder. He nodded to the foreman, who then barked out orders in Egyptian. At first, the ropes went taut as the block stubbornly refused to budge. After three attempts to lift it, several workers attacked it with pry bars while two others operated the winch. After several frustrating minutes, the block lifted a few inches.

Once it was clear of the opening, the workers swung the block to the side and laid it down carefully so as not to damage it. Then everyone gathered around as Wilder took a brush and carefully removed the sand from a second slab that was hidden beneath it.

Then he sat back and whistled.

The slab depicted a standing Thoth holding a staff and an ankh. Behind him were the pyramids and a partially eroded cartouche that bore two hieroglyphs. There were still traces of red, blue, yellow, brown and green paint on the carvings.

Hawatt leaned over and translated.

"Im—"he read. "I would be willing to bet that the missing portion of the cartouche once contained the symbols for O-T-E-P."

"Me too," agreed Wilder.

Again everyone waited as the workers attached the block and tackle to the second slab and gently pulled it from the frame.

"Let's have a look in that hole now," said Wilder.

He and Hawatt picked up their flashlights and aimed them into the hole. They saw the lights reflecting off a hard-packed stone floor some thirty feet below. Wilder sat back on his haunches and looked at Hawatt.

"That's some drop," he said. "We'll have to rig a rope ladder to the winch and place it alongside the hole. Then we can safely descend into the chamber."

Hawatt nodded, then turned and explained what they needed to the foreman. One cameraman hurried off to film the workers setting up the rig. The rest of the TV crew followed Hawatt and Wilder back into the tent. Inside, they found

Heider and Kuyder, pouring over a computerized map of the underground complex. Kuyder handed it to Wilder who quickly perused it.

"How accurate is this?" he asked.

"It shows everything down to a depth of severty-two feet. Beyond that, you're on your own," Kuyder replied.

"That's fine. Most likely, the tomb—if this is indeed a tomb—is here in this hexagonal shaped chamber on the lowest level," he said as he pointed it out to the reporters.

"What are the chances of there being lower levels than that?" asked one reporter.

"Quite good actually," said Hawatt. "Many important tombs go much deeper than 72 feet. The burial crypt itself may not be lower, but usually there are several more rooms beneath the crypt."

"And there can be any number of rooms. The tomb of Ramses the Great at last count contained 144 chambers. Since that's an ongoing project, there's no telling how many more there are down there," added Wilder. "If this is indeed Imhotep's tomb, there could be over 100 chambers down there."

"Dr. Wilder—how can you be sure this is Imhotep's tomb?" asked the NG reporter.

"We can't. We won't know whose tomb this is until we find a cartouche bearing the deceased's name. Our best guess is that this is probably Imhotep's tomb because of the way it was sealed. I imagine that he'd be the only one to have the God of Knowledge inscribed on the seal," Wilder replied.

"What if this isn't his tomb?" asked the other reporter.

"Right now, that doesn't matter. This is a spectacular find because no one ever thought this was here," said Hawatt. "If it is not Imhotep's tomb, then we will catalog and document our findings, then continue our search."

"We're going to locate Imhotep's tomb or die trying," said Wilder. "Now, let's stand back and allow our expert workers some room to do their thing."

An hour later, Wilder turned on the electric lantern and descended into the opening. A few seconds later, his feet touched bottom. He turned the lantern up to high and looked around the chamber.

"What do you see?" shouted Hawatt.

"I'm in a large chamber with a high ceiling supported by eight columns. The walls and columns are covered with some of the most exquisite paintings I have ever seen. Get down here, Nasi! You must see this!" Wilder called back.

A few minutes later, the reporter from NG came down. He was quickly followed by Hawatt with his lantern. Then came Maria and her camera. Then finally the cameraman.

Hawatt took off his hat and wiped the sweat from his brow as he looked around.

"Incredible," he said.

They found themselves standing in a large rectangular room. On either side stood what appeared to be doors with the image of the deceased etched into them. Five images were seated. The sixth was standing with arms outstretched before him. The images were all brightly painted.

The walls were painted with scenes of daily Egyptian life—farmers planting and reaping grain, women making bread and preparing meat, children playing games. There were some images of a man looking down at another lying on a large table. In his hands were delicate instruments. Behind the standing figure were another man and a woman bearing a tray with more instruments.

Hawatt smiled.

"This painting shows someone performing surgery. He is dressed in a pleated white kilt that shows he is a man of high station. He is definitely a physician," he explained.

"Imhotep was a physician," said Wilder. "This could be a painting of him in action."

He looked around. Then he scowled.

"There are no hieroglyphs in this room. Nothing at all to tell us whose tomb this is," he pointed out. "This can mean that anyone who saw the paintings instantly knew who is interred within. Most Egyptians could not read or write, so it was important that paintings could tell the story."

"What about those doors? Where do they lead?" asked a reporter.

"Five doors lead nowhere. They're false doors. Only the spirit or life force of the deceased could enter and leave by this door," answered Hawatt. "The second door should lead into the tomb."

"False door?" asked Maria.

"Yes. All the tombs have at least one such door. They served a dual purpose. The first, as I've mentioned, was to allow the life force of the deceased to leave and re-enter the tomb. The second purpose is to fool would-be tomb raiders. Usually, they led into blind passages or into a deep pit. You have to be real careful with false doors," Art explained.

"It was also a place where the deceased relatives or worshippers could place offerings of food and drink," added Hawatt. "See how there are several bowls and clay pots in front of this one? The priests would periodically remove the offerings. Sometimes, they would consume them for the deceased. Sort of nourishment by proxy."

According to the map, the entrance is directly behind this standing statue," said Art. "Look around for some sort of catch or hidden door."

Maria photographed Art and Nasi as they looked on either side of the statue, then above it then finally at the sand-covered base. Art knelt down and brushed some of the sand away with his hand. When he'd cleared it from the base, he sat back and read the glyphs etched into it.

"It says something about seeing through the eyes of the great Imhotep, Master of all Earthly Things," he translated.

"What does that mean?" asked a reporter.

Art stood up and studied the statue. He especially studied its serene face. After a while, he leaned forward and stared directly into its eyes. Several seconds later, he smiled.

"I think I've got it," he said as he reached up and pressed his thumbs against the statue's eyes.

He felt them give a little. He pressed harder. They gave a little more, then stopped. He let go and stood back. There was a loud grinding sound, like rock against rock, as the statue slowly slid to the left to reveal a rectangular pit with a set of steep stone stairs leading down into it.

Wilder smiled.

"How did you know?" asked Hawatt.

"I don't know, Nasi. I just *did*," he replied. "Shall we take a look?"

"That's what we are here for, my friend," Nasi answered as he lit his lantern.

They climbed down slowly with the cameraman directly behind them so he could shoot over their shoulders. The walls of the lower chamber were adorned with vivid scenes of Egyptian life and very lifelike paintings of plants and animals.

In the middle of the floor was yet another stone slab. This bore the raised, painted image of Thoth and a series of hieroglyphs.

"It says that herein lies the enlightened one, a true man of wisdom and seeker of the divine truth," Nasi translated. "There is no name here, though."

Again they managed to pry the slab loose and push it aside. Nasi shone his lantern into the opening to reveal yet more steps.

This time, they found themselves inside a six-sided chamber. Each wall contained a sealed door with a raised image of who was inside.

"These are the burial chambers for his closest relatives. This one here is described as Jenhetsut, the Eldest Daughter and Priestess of Thoth," Wilder read as he held his lantern to the door.

He walked over to the next one and shook his head sadly.

"Herein lies Imhotep, First Son, gone to the Afterlife in the sixth summer of his youth," Wilder translated.

Hawatt looked over the others and told the reporters that one contained a very young woman, probably his daughter, another his mother and the last his wife, Nankhsunamun.

"But here, half of her image has fallen away so we cannot know what she might have looked like," he said.

"Over here, Nasi!" shouted Wilder. "I found another door."

This one was very plain and surrounded by an ornate arch. The arch was well-painted but the door itself was simply left bare.

"Well?" Wilder asked.

"Let's do it," said Nasi.

CHAPTER 5

▼

They pushed aside the door and entered a long, dark passageway. Wilder and Hawatt illuminated the way with their lanterns while the cameramen shot footage of their every step. The passageway was also painted with scenes of the deceased's life. They depicted him writing, working with tools, looking up at the stars and conferring with the pharaoh and other high officials.

The next thing they came to was a large room about fifteen feet square. The walls were painted with beautiful figures. Art stood back and allowed the cameramen to film while he explained where they were.

"This is the mortuary chapel. As you can see, the wall directly ahead of us contains a niche about six feet high and four feet wide. There is a statue of what appears to be an important man seated on an ornate chair. There is no crown on his head, so it's safe to assume he's not a pharaoh.

This image represents the person who is inside the tomb in the prime of his life. On either side of the room, there are figures of people bearing gifts to this man.

These images are not just art. They have purpose. The deceased lives through them. After his death, his ka, or life force, is able to return to this world through the images.

The ka was sustained by people bringing offerings of fresh food and drinks. But if they couldn't make it for some reason, or had forgotten, he had the walls of the chapel painted with images that could sustain his ka."

Wilder stepped forward and examined the figures.

"That's odd," he said.

"What is?" asked Hawatt as he moved closer.

"Normally, the painted figures would be carrying gifts of food and drinks. But these appear to be bringing other things," Wilder pointed out.

"See? This one is bringing a large scroll. This one is carrying what appears to be surgical instruments. This one is carrying a large round object that looks like a globe," he said.

"You are absolutely right. They aren't bringing food or drinks. They are bringing books and other things. Whoever is inside this tomb is sustained by knowledge. That is his ka," said Hawatt.

"Look at the figure closest to him—she's bearing a long, black box. You don't suppose that's the legendary Box of Thoth, the Box of Knowledge?" asked Wilder as the excitement built inside him.

"The Box of Thoth. Maybe it is *not* a myth. Maybe there is truth to the ancient tales," Hawatt offered.

"If the Box existed, does that mean the god Thoth also existed? That he was *real*?" asked Maria as she photographed the paintings.

"I'll go you one better, Maria. If Thoth existed, what about all the *other* Egyptian gods? Were they also real? If so, what happened to them? Where'd they go?" asked Wilder.

"If this is the mortuary chapel, where's the actual tomb?" asked a reporter.

"Patience. Imhotep has waited 4,500 years for us to find him. Surely we can wait a little longer? This tomb is very large. There are many rooms and chambers to explore. Who knows where the actual tomb is?" cautioned Hawatt with a twinkle in his eyes.

Wilder held up the map that Kuyder had made and looked it over. He took out a pen and put an "X" through the first room.

"This is where we are now," he said. "According to this, there are more rooms beyond the chapel."

Hawatt looked around.

"How do we get there? I don't see another way in or out of here," he said.

"Most likely, the actual door was hidden to deter grave robbers. Check around the walls. It has to be here somewhere. But be careful. A man as clever as Imhotep would have set traps," warned Wilder as he shone his flashlight on the statue.

But there were none. Instead, they discovered that the large statue of Imhotep slid easily to the right to reveal yet another opening with steps leading into the darkness.

The steps led down some twenty feet and stopped at a sealed granite wall covered with a raised image of a seated man holding an ancient writing desk on his lap. Above him in a cartouche where three hieroglyphs.

Hawatt smiled as he ran his fingers over them an translated.

"Imhotep," he announced. "We did it, Art! We found it! This is Imhotep's tomb!"

The two men grabbed each other's arms and jumped up and down while their workers clapped. Maria stood at the top oif the steps snapping pictures of their spontaneous celebration.

"Now we must open it—but carefully," Art said.

He looked back up the steps into the lights of the cameras.

"We don't want to damage the magnificent artwork on the door. Our best bet would be to carefully chisel out the seal around the edges then somehow pull it free with a block and tackle," he explained.

One of the reporters pointed to a series of small doors on the right side. There were five such doors. He asked where they led to.

Wilder looked at his map.

"Judging from the sizes of the rooms, I'd guess they're small chapels. They probably contain images of the gods of the Underworld or of Imhotep's relatives that are entombed here with him," he said.

While the men worked to open the door, Maria and Art wandered through the other rooms to get a better idea of the size of the complex.

Alone in the side chamber, Maria stopped before an ornate double-doored wooden box. As she stared at it, Wilder came up behind her.

"What is it?" she asked.

"It's a shrine. It should contain the image of the god Amun-Re. It was placed here so that the spirit of whoever occupies this tomb could rise up each morning and perform the appropriate ritual to assure that the sun will rise and the balance of the universe or Maat will be maintained," Wilder explained.

"What ritual?" Maria asked.

"The ritual of renewal," he said. "Normally, this shrine would be inside the innermost sanctum of a temple. Each morning, just before sunrise, the king would go into the sanctum and announce his presence to the god. Then he would open the shrine, say the appropriate spell and make his offering."

"What was the offering?" Maria asked.

"The king would jack off into a bowl and fill it with his sperm. Sperm creates life, so in effect, the king was offering his life force to the god," Wilder explained.

Then it happened.

The dark room shimmered and faded. Instead of a small room in a tomb, they found themselves standing in the inner sanctum of a vast temple complex. The sanctum was well-lit by torches. On either side of the sanctum stood ten bald-headed priests dressed in white kilts, their heads bowed in respect.

Maria looked at her husband. Gone were his dusty fatigues and pith helmet. In their place was the white linen kilt and head dress of a pharaoh. He had rings of solid gold around his neck and wrists. She looked down at herself and discovered that she, too, was dressed like Egyptian royalty.

Wilder walked up to the shrine and reached for the handles.

"It is I, the king," he announced.

He pulled open the doors to reveal a solid gold statue of Amun-Re. Before it stood an onyx bowl.

Wilder hesitated as he tried to understand what was happening.

Maria didn't. She undid his kilt, reached inside and pulled out his already-half hard member. Then she knelt before him and began jerking him off.

She did it faster and faster. Wilder shivered as waves of pleasure raced through his body. Maria stared at the swollen knob and licked her lips as pre-cum oozed from the slit.

She did him faster now. When she sensed that he was about to come, she stood and aimed the head of his prick at the offering bowl. Then she did him even faster.

Wilder grunted and spewed his cum into the bowl. Maria kept at it until he was completely spent. She stopped and looked up at her husband.

That's when the scene shifted back to the present. There she was, standing before a wooden shrine in Imhotep's tomb with Art's limp prick in her hand. She gave him a few more pulls, then slid it back into his pants.

"My God. Did you see *that*?" she asked.

"Yes. Weird, wasn't it? We were back in ancient times. In Karnak," Wilder said as his head cleared.

"That was too weird. What happened?" Maria asked as she leaned against a wall.

"I don't know," Wilder said as he looked at the bowl of cum. "But I think we satisfied Maat—and me at the same time."

"Let's move on," she said as she took a deep breath.

They walked through three other rooms and found them filled with statues, boxes and jars. They then went down the hall to the last—and smallest chamber. This one contained some sort of adobe-like bench and little else.

Maria removed her helmet, then placed it and her camera bag on the floor against the wall. She turned and looked around.

"Looks like it's just you and me," Maria said with a smile.

She unbuttoned her shorts and let them fall to the floor. Art watched them slide down her pretty legs, then fixed his gaze on the prize between them. He was already rock hard as he slid to the floor and pressed his lips against her fleecy cunt. As his tongue entered, Maria sighed deeply. Usually, Art licked her pussy just long enough to get her ready for his cock. This time, he tongued her labia and clit until she came.

Maria groaned, then convulsed as her nectar gushed into Art's open mouth. He lapped up every drop, then stood up. Now, Maria knelt. She pulled down his jeans and stared as his throbbing cock. She gave it a few strokes with her hand then twirled her tongue around and over the knob. Art moaned.

Maria was good.

So very good.

She licked him to the balls then back several times before slipping the swollen head into her mouth. Moments later, Art grunted and Maria drank his first load of cum as it jetted down her throat.

"No one does that better than you, Maria. You're the best," Art said.

She smiled, then grabbed hold of his prick and led him to the bench. Within moments they were completely nude and locked in a hot embrace. Maria kept hold of his prick and pumped it until he was hard again. She spread her thighs, laid back and guided him into her open cunt.

He slid into her nice and slow. Her cunt felt tight, hot and comfortable as they began to fuck in their usual style. Both liked it slow, deep and easy.

Maria wrapped her arms and legs around his body and pressed her lips to his. As their tongues merged, the tempo of their union increased. Art used deeper thrusts now. Penetrating strokes that made Maria sigh with pleasure each time he moved inward.

She let her body take control and began driving her hips upward to meet him each and every time, taking his cock deeper and deeper into her hungry cunt. It was a hunger only Art could feed now.

Art moved his arms so Maria's legs draped over them. He leaned forward then, almost pressing her thighs to her chest, and driving his cock into her as hard as he could. Maria gasped and dug her nails into Art's shoulders. This was something new for her. Something exciting.

Art ground his cock into her and she shivered as magical sensations emanated from deep within her cunt and tentacled through her entire body. She was soon speeding uncontrollably toward orgasm.

Art shivered, too. Maria's cunt felt warm, tight and incredibly delicious as it clutched his prick. They fucked good and hard now, sweat beading up on their naked bodies.

Maria came first. It was deep, hard come that rocked her to her very soul. She drove her hips up and down on Art's prick and cried out in Spanish as her pussy took complete control of her. She fucked Art like she'd never fucked before and begged him to come inside her. At the same time, she tightened her cunt muscles to increase the friction—as well as Art's pleasure—as much as she could.

That did it.

Art exploded—no erupted—and kept filling her cunt with what seemed like gallons of thick, hot cum.

Maria rolled him over and straddled his cock. He was still hard. She was still horny. And the day was young.

As she bounced up and down on his prick, Art played with her dark nipples. He was still coming, too, and his cum oozed out of Maria's cunt and covered his balls. Maria kept fucking and fucking. She seemed insatiable now. She lived only for the feel of Art's prick inside her cunt.

Art caught his second wind. He gripped her thighs and drove his prick upward into her cunt. This was, by far, the longest, most sensational fuck he ever had—that either of them ever had. They were as one now. Two halves of a whole who lived only to please each other. They fucked until both ached from the strain. Just when Art thought he was about to collapse, Maria came.

She threw her head back, screamed with delight, shook violently on his prick, then fell on top of him. She lay in his arms, her eyes closed, emitting soft cooing sounds as she basked in the afterglow of their lovemaking.

"We'd better find Nasi. They should be ready to open that door by now," Art said as the dressed.

"I can hardly wait to see what's inside," Maria said as she followed him out of the side chamber and down the corridor.

CHAPTER 6

▼

As soon as the door was pulled away enough to allow them to enter, Hawatt grabbed his lantern and walked through the opening. Wilder and a cameraman followed him.

The chamber was fairly large—about twenty feet square. Four ornately-decorated pillars, one at each corner, supported the high ceiling. Around the room was a four-foot high stone shelf that was built up from the floor and etched with depictions of the various gods of Egypt, all skillfully painted and like the rest of the tomb, perfectly preserved. Standing on the shelves were twenty-seven tall ceramic jars or various colors. Each was sealed with a wax-covered ceramic lid. Four of the jars were topped with decorative heads of men and beasts and painted with hieroglyphs.

Hawatt aimed the beam of his lantern at them and explained what they were.

"These are canopic jars. They are vehicles that were used to preserve the major organs of the body, such as the liver and the heart. The organs were then interred with the deceased so they could be used again in the Afterlife," he said.

"What about the brain?" asked the reporter.

"The brain was removed through the nose one piece at a time and discarded. The ancients believed that it served no real purpose," Hawatt said.

"Considering some of the people I've met over the years, they might have been right," quipped Wilder.

Their attention then fell on the life-sized statue of Imhotep in the center of the chamber. The image was startlingly realistic. So much so, that Maria remarked she could almost see him breathing.

Wilder studied the image. The eyes seemed to look straight at him, almost *through* him, as if Imhotep were seeing him from a distant world that only the dead could know. He felt a cold shiver go down his back and shook it off.

That's when he spotted another door. This one was painted with the Eye of Horus symbol. He stopped before it then checked the map.

"It's behind this door," he said. "The burial chamber is behind this door."

Again they called for the workmen and instructed them to open the door without damaging the paintings.

"How long will this take, Dr. Hawatt?" asked the reporter.

"At least one hour, perhaps more, depending on how well it was sealed," he said.

The reporter checked his watch and told the crew to break for lunch. Then most of them headed back out to get some air. Art and Maria decided to wander through the other rooms while Nasi stayed to watch the workers open the door.

As they passed the jars, Art stopped to examine some of the symbols that were painted on them.

"We'll have the men remove these jars and take them back to the museum for study," he decided. "What's inside could be what we're looking for. They could very well contain the legendary books of Imhotep."

"We have an hour until the door is opened. How about a quickie?" asked Maria as she dragged him into a small side-chamber and set her camera down on an ornate wooden box. This room, too, was filled with jars. Smaller ones and most were open.

"Offerings to Imhotep. The jars probably contained food and prayers," Art explained as he picked one up and examined it.

He turned and looked at Maria. Her shorts were already off and piled on the box next to her camera. He smiled and removed his jeans.

Maria looked it over and smiled. Then she leapt onto the wall and sat down with her thighs wide open and facing Art.

The smooth adobe wall felt cold to her bare bottom and she fidgeted as she sat there. Now, Art got an even better look at her vagina and the sight was breathtaking to say the least.

Her labia were thick and flowery like and her clit was swollen and shiny. A rich carpet of soft brown pubic hair delightfully highlighted this.

The sight of Maria's vagina and the erotic atmosphere of that moment caused Art's penis to stir. Maria watched with apparent glee as it returned to its full glory. She reached over and stroked it a few times.

Art sighed. He leaned closer. Maria threw her arms around his neck and wrapped her legs around his waist so that her vagina touched his cock. Art gripped her pretty behind and lifted her onto the stone shelf.

As he released his hold on her, she grabbed his penis once again and gave it several long, easy jerks. Art moaned, then pulled away to undress.

Maria quickly took the rest of her clothes off. Art stared at her nice firm breasts with the taut hard nipples that seemed to beg him to suck them. She cupped her hands under them and teased her nipples until they stood straight out.

"You like them?" she asked coyly.

Art responded by sucking first the left, then the right nipple while he massaged her already wet vagina and she kept jerking him off. After a little more sex play, Art pushed the willing teenager down on the bed and kissed her from her lips all the way down to her pretty vagina. As he stopped to suck her hard clit, Maria gasped and pushed her hips upward. Art responded by easing two fingers into her vagina and moving them around. He soon located her g-spot and massaged it. The sensations nearly made Maria come on the spot.

Her buttocks clenched as his touch made her feel like she was either going to piss or come. This turned into a delicious tingling sensation that quickly brought her to one of the most ferocious climaxes she'd ever had.

Maria groaned and shook all over. Art kept fingering her g-spot gently, then withdrew his fingers and replaced them with his tongue. This again sent Maria over the top and she almost tore his hair out as she humped his tongue. She thrashed wildly as Art continued to lick and suck her quivering vagina.

She wanted to scream but found that she had no voice. All she could see was white. All she could feel were the waves of intense pleasure washing over her as she came again and again.

Before she could gather her senses, Art moved between her thighs and rammed his hard penis into her still trembling vagina. His sudden move delighted the girl and she moaned with pleasure as he did her nice and slow.

When Art began to moved his penis in that counter-clockwise manner inside her pussy, she thought her legs were about to fall off.

She had never felt anything even remotely like this before. His penis rotated wonderfully inside her tight hold, massaged every delicate fold and crevice. Even her g-spot got a good going over. She was so overwhelmed by his expertise, she could only lay still and enjoy the ride for a few minutes.

And what a ride that was!

After a little while, Maria decided to show Art a few things that she had learned. She started out by matching him thrust for thrust, then used her well-trained vaginal muscles to squeeze and massage every inch of his penis as it moved in and out of her vagina.

Now it was Art's turn t be impressed. He couldn't believe what Maria was doing with his penis. She had the expertise and control of the best Philippine bar girls and he momentarily envisioned her picking up a stack of coins with her vagina.

"My God! Where'd you learn that?" he gasped.

"I teach myself. You like it?" she said as she fucked him harder.

"I love it!" Art sighed.

They kept going like this for several minutes more. Each time either felt they were about to come, they stopped and waited for the orgasm to subside. Then they did it even harder. They did this four times. Then it happened.

Unable to hold back any longer, Art plunged into Maria's pussy as hard as he could, then let himself come. Maria felt his cum spurting inside her vagina and fucked him with everything she had left.

"Fuck me, baby! Fuck me good! Yes!" she cried as her body shook violently and she, too, erupted like a volcano.

She held Art close.

"Don't pull out, Art. Please don't," she begged as he lay on top of her with his penis still buried in her vagina.

She rested a while, and then started working his penis with her inner muscles once again. Art moaned. He'd never felt anything like that before. It was like she was jerking him off with her vagina. In no time at all, he had another good erection. It was the fastest recovery of his life.

This time, they tried a few other positions. They began with the scissors position, then Maria got on top and rode him as she faced away from him. She bounced up and down his penis until she almost came. Just before she orgasmed, she slid off and moved her body back until her vagina was right on Art's mouth.

He grabbed her behind and started licking. Maria shook, moaned and then engulfed his penis with her mouth and started sucking away on it.

It felt so good that Art blew his wad right away. It went straight down Maria's throat and the sex-wizened nymph hungrily lapped up nearly every drop before Art's tongue brought her to another thundering climax.

After a few minutes rest to catch their breath, Art and Maria dressed. He handed her a bottle of water and watched as she took a deep swallow. The water was fairly warm by then, but still wet and quenched her thirst. She put the cap back on and smiled coyly at him.

"That was one of the best we ever had," she said.

"You seem especially amorous since we entered this tomb," Art said.

"There is something about this place, something I don't understand yet, that makes me feel very horny all the time," Maria said. "It's a nice feeling, but weird. All I want to do is fuck."

"Me, too. Maybe it's the excitement of finding it. Maybe there's something very magical here," Art guessed.

"Yes. Magical," she said.

As he watched, Maria opened her shorts then slid her hand into them. Art could tell that she was masturbating by the way her fingers were moving beneath the khaki. The sight transfixed him to the spot.

Maria smiled at him, and then winked mischievously as she worked her middle finger down into her pussy. When she knew that she had Art's undivided attention, she decided to make her big play.

She kicked off her shoes, then slid her shorts down. She did this slowly in order to make sure that Art could see every inch of her sexy, shapely legs. When the shorts reached her ankles, she kicked them off and left them on the floor. Then she sat down and opened her legs as far as she could.

Art's penis began to expand in his shorts as he watched Maria use her fingers to pull open her thick labia. She saw the bulge in his pants and nodded her approval, and then she inserted her fingers into her vagina and put on one of the most erotic shows that Art had ever witnessed.

"Show me yours," she said.

Art unzipped and pulled out his erection. Maria eyed it carefully and ran her tongue over her lips as she continued to twiddle her clit.

By then, Art was so far gone that he began jerking off. Maria smiled as he did this and urged him to do it faster. She did the same. Minutes later, Art began sending streams of cum onto Maria's legs. A moment later, Maria screamed. She raised her hips off the shelf, frantically fingered her slit for a few seconds, then sighed and sat down.

Art could see that her labia were still twitching as she beamed at him in a most suggestive manner. Maria stood and walked over to him and leaned over. She made no attempt to cover up. Neither did Art.

His half-limp member still dangled from his zipper. Maria looked it over and smiled. Then she leapt onto the shelf and sat down with her thighs wide open and facing Art.

The sight of Maria's vagina and the erotic atmosphere of that moment caused Art's penis to stir. Maria watched with apparent glee as it returned to its full glory. She reached over and stroked it a few times.

Art sighed. He leaned closer. Maria threw her arms around his neck and wrapped her legs around his waist so that her vagina touched his cock. Art gripped her pretty behind slid into her once more as she thrust her hips forward to take him all the way in. As they kissed, Art fucked her nice and easy and Maria matched him stroke for stroke. Soon, Maria's body trembled. Art realized she was about to come. He leaned forward and pressed her knees to her breasts as he fucked her faster and faster. Maria groaned, then exploded.

Art kept at it until he felt his balls jerk. Just before he came, he pulled out of her pussy. Maria was still in the throes of her orgasm so he didn't notice when Art put the head of his cock against her anus and pushed it halfway into her. Since it was still coated with Maria's juices, it slid it rather easily. Art stopped about three inches in, then began to move in and out gently as he emptied a huge amount of sticky white cum into her tight, sexy ass.

Maria wrinkled her nose at him when he pulled out. She looked down and saw a river of cum oozing from her puckered rear door.

"You fucked me in my ass?" she asked.

"Almost. I didn't go all the way in. I'd love to though. Maybe one day," Art replied.

"Maybe I'll let you—one day," she said as she slid off the ledge and picked up her clothes.

They were nearly dressed when they heard Nasi calling to them. They finished up and hurried to the vault, arriving just in time to watch the workers pull the heavy door from the wall and slide it to the side.

Hawatt smiled at Art.

"After you," he said.

Art lit his lantern and walked through. After a few seconds, he called out for the others to join him. What they saw held them transfixed in stunned silence for several minutes.

The crypt was quite large and eight-sided. It had a vaulted ceiling that was painted to depict the Egyptian sky at night, complete with wispy clouds and several bright stars that sparkled like precious gems. The walls were decorated with exquisitely detailed paintings and reliefs of Imhotep overseeing a huge construction project or performing surgery. Each wall also had a large, recessed niche about four feet up from the floor. In each niche was a large, ornately-painted wooden chest.

"We'll send the boxes to the museum with the jars," Nasi said. "They must contain something very important to have been interred so close to Imhotep."

The most incredible thing in the crypt was the sarcophagus itself. It stood eight feet long and five feet high and the base was made of highly-polished granite. It was etched with spells from the Book of the Dead to help ease Imhotep's passage into the Afterlife. The sarcophagus rested atop a base of highly polished black stone.

The lid was even more impressive. It was sculpted from a single slab of pure white alabaster into a life-sized image of Imhotep. The image was realistically painted with lifelike colors and skillfully decorated with gold and turquoise.

"It's beautiful!" exclaimed Maria as she snapped photo after photo. "Beautiful!"

"This lid is made from fine alabaster. Normally, such things are reserved for kings or queens. This proves that Imhotep was very highly respected by the royal court and the Egyptian people," Nasi explained for the cameras.

"Let's open it, Nasi," suggested Art. "Right now!"

"Of course. This is why we are here, is it not?" Nasi agreed.

They stepped back and allowed the workers to slowly chip away the wax seal around the lid. When they were finished, the foreman waved his men away to allow Nasi and Art access to the sarcophagus.

"Let's do it," said Art.

With the cameras rolling, Wilder and Hawatt carefully pushed the heavy stone lid off the sarcophagus. As workmen lowered the lid to the floor, the two archaeologists and Maria looked down in awe at the ornate coffin.

"This is incredible! I have never seen anything like this in all my years' experience," exclaimed Hawatt as the cameraman zoomed in to get a close-up of the ornately handsome figure on the lid of the coffin.

"Unbelievable. Instead of the usual wood, this appears to be made entirely of some metal alloy. It's not pure gold, but I can see that there is a lot of gold in it," Wilder said.

"It might be electrum," suggested Hawatt. "But the ancient Egyptians never made such an alloy—at least I never saw anything made from it before now."

Wilder leaned down and motioned for the cameraman to zoon closer as he pointed to a series of hieroglyphs on the lid.

"You see these glyphs? They translate to "Imhotep". There's no doubt about it, Nasi. We've found our man. This is indeed Imhotep's tomb!" he announced.

Maria leaned forward and snapped several photos as Wilder and Hawatt looked into the cameras and explained again who Imhotep was and why finding his tomb was so important. Then they returned to the sarcophagus and talked over various ways to open it to get a good look at the mummy inside.

Then the two men stepped back and watched as their workers moved forward. An hour later, and with the help of a block and tackle, they slowly lifted the heavy lid from the coffin. Once it was above the stone sepulcher, the workers moved it out of the way so the archaeologists could study the mummy.

What they saw amazed them.

Inside was a tall, thin mummy in what Hawatt described as the most perfect state of preservation he'd ever seen. On his face was a solid gold funerary mask. A wide gold collar bearing several ancient symbols was around his neck and his crossed arms held a large leather-wrapped bundle.

"The mummy appears to be in excellent condition," explained Hawatt. "Before the embalmers finished wrapping a mummy, they usually placed several golden charms, ushabtis and prayers inside the bandages. These charms would allow the deceased to pass safely into the Afterlife."

"I wonder what's in that bundle?" Maria asked.

"Let's find out," said Wilder.

As the cameras rolled, he reached down and carefully pulled the bundle from the mummy's grasp. That's when something happened that caused a sensation throughout the modern world.

As soon as Wilder freed the bundle, the mummy sat up and turned its face toward the stunned archaeologists. Then its mouth opened wide.

"Nai!" it said.

Its voice was like a distant echo from beyond the grave.

Then the mummy slowly fell back into the coffin.

Maria stood and stared like she was in shock. Wilder's mouth opened and his lips moved, but he said nothing. Hawatt ran his hands over his face.

The reporters and cameramen were also in a state of shock.

"I wonder how Imhotep managed to do *that*?" asked Wilder after several minutes of silence.

"I have opened many sarcophagi and have seen many mummies during my career. Yet this is the first time any of them ever sat up and spoke," Hawatt said.

"That was amazing. I almost had a stroke when he did that," said the National Geographic reporter.

"Me, too," said Maria. "I am still shaking. Just what happened here, Art? What's going on? What does 'nai' mean?"

"It means 'no'," Hawatt said. "But what did he mean by it? Did he say no because you took the bundle from his arms? Or did he say no because he didn't want anyone to disturb his tomb?"

"I feel like I'm in a sequel to 'The Mummy'," said Wilder. "This is too fucking weird!"

"Imhotep was supposed to possess great magic powers. This could have been his last great spell to scare would-be robbers away," suggested Hawatt.

"This bundle must really be important if it was buried with him," said Wilder as he examined the package. "It's even tied with golden wires."

"Are you going to open it now, Dr. Wilder?" asked one of the reporters.

"No. We'll take it back to the museum first—along with those large earthen jars in the antechambers. Don't worry, boys. We'll make sure that you're all present to film us opening each jar. Along with us, you'll be the first people in nearly 4,500 years to know what's inside," Wilder promised.

"Right now, I'd like to take a closer look at the mummy to try and find out why it did what it did," he added.

"I, too, am curious," said Hawatt. "But I don't want to move him. Not yet. It may destroy the mummy."

"How about a portable CAT scan device? That would enable us to take pictures of Imhotep's insides without moving him," Wilder offered.

"That's a great idea. Any idea where we can got one?" asked Hawatt.

"I have some friends in Boston. They shoot a series for the National Geographic Channel called "The Mummy Roadshow". I'll call them tomorrow and ask them to fly out here," Wilder said.

That decided, they left the tomb and told the foreman to post six guards at the entrance.

"Make sure they are armed," Nasi cautioned. "Tell them to shoot anyone who tries to get inside without express permission from either myself or Dr. Wilder."

The foreman selected six rather rough-looking men and passed out sidearms to them. He then led the rest of the crew back into the tomb and, under Wilder's supervision, they carried out the earthen jars and loaded them into the back of a truck.

Once all of the jars were aboard, Wilder tucked Imhotep's bundle under his arm and climbed into the Land Rover. Maria got in next to him while Nasi got into the back seat.

Wilder dropped Nasi off at the museum where he could oversee the unloading of the precious jars. Just before Nasi got out, Wilder handed him the bundle.

"Take care of this, Nasi. I'll be back in a few hours," he said.

Then he drove on to the hotel. There, he and Maria quickly removed their dirty clothes and jumped into the shower where one thing quickly led to another.

As tired as Art was, the sight of her soft brown muff caused his cock to stir. Maria gave him a come hither look and walked into the bedroom with Art right behind her.

There, they kissed passionately as Maria wrapped her fingers around Art's penis and gave it a few easy strokes. Then she sat down on the edge of the bed with her thighs apart. Unable to resist, Art fell to his knees and slowly licked her already juicy slit. Maria sighed as his tongue danced in and out of her vagina and fell back on the bed. Art cupped her cheeks and pulled her to him as he ate her.

"Oh, yes!" she sighed as Art's tongue sent shivers up her back.

She loved the way he ate her. No one else, she decided, could do the things he did with his tongue. She was always happy and eager to feel it dancing between her legs.

As for Art, he adored her bitter-sweet-salty flavor and delightful scent. Maria tasted and smelled so different. So delightfully sexy.

Now, he was as hard as could be. He stood up, pushed Maria's legs as far apart as possible and slid his penis into vagina all the way to his balls. Maria gasped. She wrapped her legs around his hips and closed her eyes as they began that slow, deep-penetrating love they both loved.

It was the most incredible sex they could have. It was exhilarating, wonderful sex. But it was far more than that. What they had now went far beyond the mere physical union of two people. It was an incredible melding of two into one—a perfect union of body and spirit.

Art took his time with Maria. He always went as slow and as deep as possible, not only to give her the utmost pleasure but also to savor the feel of her silky-smooth vagina as he moved in and out of her. The way Art made love to her made Maria feel especially wonderful.

Wanted.

Sexy.

Each time they made love, they added more cement to their blossoming relationship. Each time, the bond between them grew stronger and stronger.

Soon, Maria felt herself coming and began humping Art faster. He caught her signal and tried to hold back as long as possible. He wanted to time their orgasms perfectly. To make this one really special.

He did.

Both he and Maria erupted at the same moment and became suspended in time for a few seconds. They clung to each other like there was no tomorrow and humped until their bodies ached and sweat covered them. At the height of ecstasy, Maria cried out.

"I love you, Art! I love you!"

To her delight, he echoed her words. They rested now. Art was still on top of her, his semi-hard penis still buried inside Maria's pulsing vagina, their lips fused together in a long, hot kiss. When they broke off, Maria looked into Art's eyes and saw the love in them.

Maria used her inner muscles to squeeze Art's penis. The delicious sensations caused him to harden once again. Instead of doing her, Art slid to the floor and used his fingers to pry apart Maria's pussy lips. The center was dark pink now and very moist. He leaned forward, sniffed her heady perfume, and then licked her thighs near her slit.

Maria shivered with anticipation as she waited for his tongue to work its magic. She didn't have to wait long. Art slipped it into the bottom of her vagina then moved it slowly up toward her swollen clit. Maria gasped and emitted a deep "ah!" as his tongue swirled around her love button.

It felt so good.

So very very good.

Art ate her for a long, long time. Each time he sensed her about to come, he eased up, then did it all again. Several times, he brought her to the brink or orgasm and stopped short of making her come. Soon, Maria was begging him to finish her off.

When he did, she blew like a volcano and just about rolled off the bed. Then Art did the unexpected.

While she was in mid-come, he climbed on top of her and rammed his penis into her vagina hard. Maria screamed with joy. She wrapped her arms and legs around him and they gave each other a nice, steady—and somewhat harder—love. The movement of his hard-on inside her convulsing vagina caused Maria to come again and again. Each orgasm was stronger than the last and she soared ever skyward and became lost in the clouds.

"Yes! Yes! Love me, Art! Love me good!" she screamed as her body trembled uncontrollably with each hard thrust f his penis.

She was getting the best love of her entire life now and she didn't want it to end any time soon.

Art humped her harder. Maria clung to him, unable to move, unable to love him back. All she could do now was to take it, to enjoy the glorious ride he was giving her. Then her quivering, quaking body became too much for him. He rammed his penis into her as deep as he could and groaned as streams of white good jetted into her pussy.

He stayed motionless as Maria milked him until her pussy was flooded with his cum. Then he leaned over. They kissed passionately. Maria tasted her vagina on his tongue. The taste excited her again and she began humping his half-hard penis. Art trembled as she humped him. He was nearly exhausted now. He just hovered over her and let Maria do the work. He was so numb, he barely noticed he was still coming like crazy inside her wonderful vagina.

Then Art pulled Maria to him and squeezed her behind. Maria giggled and slipped free. Maria's body was nearly perfect and her legs were gorgeous. He played with her nipples as she jerked him off. When he was ready, she ran her tongue over the knob and along his shaft several times. Art groaned as she eased it into her mouth and sucked it gently. She soon felt his balls spasm. She stopped and smiled up at him.

"Not yet," she said. "I want this to last."

She spread her legs as Art sunk his tongue into her cunt. Now it was his turn to tease her and he kept nibbling and licking at her swollen clit until he senses that she was ready to come.

Maria pushed him onto his back, then straddled him and slowly impaled herself on his erection. She lowered her hips until their pubic hairs merged, then proceeded to bounce up and down slowly. Art grabbed her behind and began humping her back harder and harder. Soon Maria's head fell back and she emitted a deep, satisfied moan as she came. Art kept driving in and out of her until he came, too. Then he pulled her down on top of his cock and emptied his cum into her pussy until it ran out of her and coated his balls and stained the sheets.

Still not finished, Art rolled Maria onto her side and kept hammering away at her. Maria screamed and moaned with each hard, deep thrust of his cock. Then she felt him spasm again as he added yet another good load of cream to his earlier deposit. They rested for a few minutes, then Art began to get hard again. Maria eyed his growing cock and smiled.

She laid on her back.

"Want to try something different?" asked Art.

"Okay. What?" she asked.

"You'll see," he said. "It's a little strange but I think you'll like it."

He then sat on her chest and placed his erection between her breasts. Maria stared at the swollen glans which was just an inch or two from her chin as Art used his hands to push the sides of her breasts against his cock. When it felt nice

and snug, he began moving his hips back and forth. Maria was totally surprised—and somewhat mesmerized—with the sight of his cock moving in and
out between her breasts. She'd seen this in porno movies before but never once
thought of doing it.

As Art humped her, he played with her swollen—and sensitive—nipples. That
sent delicious tingles racing all through Maria's body and she began to writhe in
pleasure. Art was also enchanted. He'd always wanted to try this with her. She
had the greatest breasts her ever saw. Now that he was doing it, he realized how
good this was. Laying her breasts was nearly as good as laying her pussy and it was
an incredible turn-on.

Maria felt Art's balls jerk suddenly. She saw his knob expand and watched as
the first of several long streams of cum rocketed from his cock. This one splattered the underside of her chin and neck. The second landed from her chin to her
hairline and the third across her lips and nose. As Art kept humping, Maria
opened her mouth. She caught most of the next few spurts on her tongue, then
bent her head and allowed his cock to move in and out of her open mouth. As it
did, she licked the knob several times, which caused Art to ejaculate even harder.

She gripped his behind and pulled him forward until he was laying her mouth.
Art groaned and heaved one last load straight down her throat. Maria swallowed
every last bit of it, too. Then Art rolled off. Still horny, Maria straddled his face.
Art gripped her behind and licked away until she came several times. Then both
lay still to catch their breath.

"That was incredible! Awesome," Art said after several minutes.

"Yes," Maria agreed.

CHAPTER 7

▼

When the flight from New York landed in Cairo two days later, the Mummy Road Show crew disembarked and walked down the ramp. Art, Nasi and Maria greeted them.

The Road Show team consisted of radiologist Arlin Coombs, Art Holder the expert cameraman and archaeologist Jennifer Wong from the Brooklyn Museum.

As soon as Jennifer Wong laid eyes on Art, she ran up to him and threw her arms around his neck. Then she proceeded to stick her tongue into his mouth for a good, long and somewhat steamy kiss.

Taken by surprise, Art simply stood there. Maria frowned as she looked the woman over.

Jennifer was about five feet four inches tall, slender and had long, shiny black hair. She also had nice round breasts and a firm, sexy behind. Now that she was having sex with women, Maria decided that she liked Jennifer. Maybe even enough to sleep with her.

Art broke off the kiss and introduced Jennifer to Maria and the others.

"How long have you known my husband?" Maria asked, making certain to put a lot of emphasis on the word *husband*.

"Ever since we became lovers about ten years ago," Jennifer replied.

"We were examining a mummy in Mexico at the time. One thing led to another and the next thing you know." Art began

"You were fucking like rabbits," Maria finished with a coy smile.

"But that's all behind us now," said Jennifer.

"And a lovely behind it is," said Maria.

Jennifer looked at her. That's when Maria winked and ran her tongue over her lips as if to signal that she's like to try her, too.

When Maria passed by on the way to the car, Jennifer took Art aside.

"What's up, Jenny?" he asked.

"Did you notice the way your wife looked at me?" she asked.

"Yes. Strange, wasn't it?" he replied.

"Very. Is she bisexual?" Jennifer asked.

"Maybe. I know she had sex with a female arch when we were in Guatemala. I thought that was a one-time experiment though," Art replied.

"Maybe she wants to experiment again," Jennifer said.

"I can't blame her. You're still one hot, sexy woman," Art said.

"So is Maria. She has a great looking ass," Jennifer said.

"It sounds like you want to give her a tumble, Jenny," Art joked.

"Maybe. But what I'd really like is to fuck you until you can't see straight," Jennifer said.

They watched as Holder supervised the off-loading of the team's special x-ray and CAT scan equipment. Another man with curly brown hair and thick glasses walked over and introduced himself as Todd Jackson.

"I'm the MRS director," he explained. "The other six people you see are our roadies. They schlep the equipment around and set it up at each site."

"I'm happy to meet you, Todd," said Art. He then introduced him to the rest of his crew.

"The first thing we need to do is go to the museum and check out the maps you made of the tomb so we can figure out exactly what we need at the site," said Jackson. "After that, we'll go to the site and make sure everything fits together."

"That makes sense. The maps are in my office," Nasi said as they all headed for the cars.

While the others worked on their plans for the upcoming broadcast, Maria flirted openly with Jennifer. At first, Jennifer pretended not to notice. After a while, she began flirting back.

Art watched them and laughed. He assumed that things were about to get real interesting once they returned to the hotel suite.

He walked over to the table and leaned down to study the map. As he did, Jackson asked him questions about the ceiling heights, inside humidity and best way to get in our out of the main chamber. At that point, Jennifer also walked over and asked Art about a specific detail at the top of the map. Art pointed to it and explained that it was a directional symbol placed there by the sonarscope.

Maria walked past Jennifer while she was leaning over the table and gently ran her hand over her behind. When Jennifer turned, Maria simply smiled and headed for the ladies' room.

Jennifer followed. She found Maria waiting by the door, which she locked as soon as the stunning Asian entered.

Before Jennifer could say a word, Maria pressed her lips to hers. Shocked, Jennifer simply gave herself to Maria.

Sensing Jennifer's compliancy, Maria undid her jeans and slid her hand into her panties. Jennifer sighed as Maria massaged her clit.

"That feels nice," Jennifer whispered.

"Ever have sex with a woman?" asked Maria.

"Not for a long time—but I'd love to do it with you—Art, too," Jennifer answered as she felt the heat rising in her cunt.

"You want to do it with the both of us at the same time?" asked Maria.

"That sounds wonderful! You think Art will go for it?" Jennifer said.

"Probably. When would you like to try it?" Maria asked as she massaged Jennifer's clit faster and faster.

Jennifer suddenly stiffened, then sighed deeply and relaxed as she came. Maria withdrew her fingers and licked them. She smiled at Jennifer.

"How about as soon as we're finished with Imhotep?" Jennifer suggested.

"Okay. We won't tell Art. We'll just go out for dinner that night, then spring it on him when we return to the hotel," Maria replied.

When they got back to Nasi's office, they found the others packing up their gear.

"We're heading out to the tomb," said Holder. "The equipment's still in the van. Are you ready?"

"I'm always ready," Jennifer said as she grabbed her shoulder bag.

CHAPTER 8

▼

Holder and Coombs looked the tomb over carefully while they made notes about where and what equipment to set up. Holder then called for the lighting crew. When the three men arrived, he walked around with the crew chief and explained how much light they would need.

The crew chief got on his cell phone and barked some orders. Ten minutes later, two more men arrived bearing a small generator.

"We use the generator to power the lights. It is gasoline powered but the main system is in the back of our truck topside. They will connect this smaller unit with cables. In this way, no gas fumes will enter the tomb," Holder explained as the crew went to work.

"What about the heat from the lights themselves?" asked Hawatt.

"These are special bulbs. They do not produce any heat at all when lit," said Coombs. "Once the lights are up, we'll have the techs set up the x-ray machine, which will be suspended from a u-frame that will straddle the sarcophagus."

"What powers that?" asked Wilder.

"Batteries. They can hold a six-hour charge. The same system powers the CAT scan," Holder replied.

"How will you manage the CAT scan without risking damage to the mummy?" asked Hawatt.

"That's where it gets a little tricky," said Holder. "We'll try to slip plastic hammocks under the mummy then use a pulley system to lift him out of the sarcophagus. Once he is high enough, we'll slide the bottom half of the CAT scan under him. Then we'll gently lower him to it and slide the top half the machine over him," said Jennifer.

"We'll take pictures of him from every angle, do cross sections of his entire body, including whatever organs that may still be inside. By this time tomorrow, we will know a great deal about Imhotep," added Coombs.

"It will take us at least four hours to set everything up. You might as well get some rest before we begin shooting," said Holder.

Once outside the main vault, a reporter stopped Wilder and Hawatt to ask some questions.

"Dr. Wilder—what do you hope to learn from these scans?" he asked.

"The scans will give us a lot of information, like how old he was when he died, if he had any diseases or ailments, the condition of his teeth and if he died from anything other than natural causes," Wilder answered.

"These tests are very valuable because they enable us to get a good look at the mummy without having to actually unwrap him or move him. That means there is little or no risk of damaging or destroying the mummy," said Hawatt.

"Do you do this with all the mummies you find?" asked the reporter.

"We do it only when conditions allow it, like here in Egypt or on the dry plains of South America. In places like Guatemala or other rainforests, this would be nearly impossible," said Coombs who had come out for a smoke.

"And why is that?" asked the reporter.

"The humidity and heat there wreaks havoc on the equipment. The machines don't work when they get hot and damp," Coombs said as he lit his cigarette.

"But it gets hot here in Egypt," said the reporter.

"True. But it's not so humid here. The sand gets on everything, which can make for a real pain in the ass, but usually we can blow it off with air hoses," Coombs explained.

Just then, several other members of the MRS crew arrived with several pieces of the metal u-frame that was to go over the sarcophagus. Coombs put out his cigarette and led them back into crypt.

Art looked at Maria. She smiled and walked down the corridor toward one of the smaller side chambers. Art smiled and followed her.

When he caught up to her, she hugged his neck and kissed him.

"I'm horny," she said. "Fuck me."

She turned and placed her hand on the now-visible bulge in Art's jeans. Art pulled her to him and stuck his tongue into her mouth. He moaned as she sucked it eagerly and slowly pulled down his trunks.

Before he realized it, Maria had his erection halfway down her throat and was sucking away hungrily on it. Maria stopped just as he started coming into her mouth. She wrapped her fingers around his penis and smiled at the gobs of white cum jetting from it as she jerked him off. Most of the cum landed on her chest and face.

Art noticed that the more his cum covered her, the hornier Maria was getting.

To her delight—and Art's surprise—his penis remained rock-hard. She led him to a raised altar, then pushed him down onto it and almost tore his jeans off. Within a minute, both were completely naked and Maria was happily bouncing up and down on Art's penis.

He reached up and grabbed her smooth, firm ass as he drove his penis hard and fast up into her vagina. been missing. Maria was an incredible lover. She had a slender, sexy body and she really knew how to use it to its greatest potential to give Art the best ride of his life.

Art groaned as his body stiffened for a moment. Then he emptied his balls up inside Maria's lovely vagina for the first—but not the last—time that night.

Maria hadn't come yet. Still craving release, she slid her cum-filled pussy up onto Art's mouth and begged him to finish her off. The flavor of his own cum excited Art, and as he licked Maria's quivering slit, he began getting hard all over again. By the time she came and fell across his face, Art was fully erect.

He turned Maria onto her belly, and then pulled her up to her knees as she slid his penis into her from behind. Maria screamed with delight as he rode her hard and fast. It was an intense, almost numbing screw that ended with both of them climaxing at the exact same moment.

They rested for a while, and then dressed and went up the stairs to join the others who were now seated on the paw of the Sphinx, drinking cold beer and eating sandwiches.

Al Kuyder handed Art a beer as he climbed up and sat next to him. Kuyder pointed toward a high dune near the river.

"Have you noticed those men over there? They are watching our every move with binoculars," he said.

"I spotted them two weeks ago. They're not real good at concealing themselves are they?" Art replied as he opened the beer and took a deep swallow.

"I wonder who they are? Maybe police?" Kuyder said.

"No. I'd know if they were police. Whoever they are, they seem real interested in what we're doing here. *Too interested*," Art said.

"We'd better keep our eyes on them. I have a feeling they are after something," Kuyder cautioned.

"Me, too. Although I can't imagine what they could possibly want from here," Wilder agreed.

At that moment, Coombs popped his head out of the entrance. He looked up at Wilder.

"We're ready!" he announced.

CHAPTER 9

▼

When they raised Imhotep out of his sarcophagus, Wilder and Hawatt looked inside. The two men stared at each other in wonder, for there on the bottom of the sarcophagus lay three wooden tubes.

Wilder reached down and retrieved them, then showed them to Hawatt and the TV cameras.

"Scrolls! I wonder why these were interred with Imhotep instead of being placed in the jars with the other scrolls?" Hawatt said as he turned one of the tubes over in his hands.

"There are no markings on the tubes. There's no telling what's inside. They must be of tremendous importance to be buried with Imhotep," Wilder said as he examined them.

"Whatever is inside can wait for now. We'll take them back to the museum and go over the contents when we open the Box," Hawatt said as he passed the scrolls to Heider.

Then everyone stood and watched as the mummy of Imhotep underwent a CAT scan.

"I wonder what he'd think of this machine?" Hawatt mused.

"Imhotep was the greatest physician of his age. I think he would have been able to see the medical importance of it. Hell, he might have been able to *improve* on it," Wilder said.

As the cameras rolled, Holder took center stage while the crew worked behind him.

"First, we x-rayed Imhotep to determine the condition of his skeletal structure at the time of his death. We found no signs of broken bones or ones that had been broken and were knitted together again. We also saw that he retained all 32 teeth. They showed the usual wear and tear due to the sand that gets into all of the food here in Egypt.

So we concluded that Imhotep lived a long and healthy life. Judging by the wear and tear on his teeth, I'd say he lived to be at least ninety, perhaps older."

"This is not so unusual among Egyptian upper classes," added Nasi. "Ramses the Great lived to be over ninety years old. Many other pharaohs lived well past eighty. In those days, the food was all natural. The air and water were clean and the average Egyptian ate a healthy diet of grains, green vegetables, beer and a little bit of meat. It is much like the diets prescribed by doctors today."

Holder turned to the crew. One man gave him the thumbs up signal. He nodded.

"Let's do it!" he said.

Imhotep was lowered gently onto the bottom bed of the CAT scan. Once he was secure, they team lowered the concave shell over him and bolted it into place. Holder turned the machine on. As the images were fed into the large screen, he gave his interpretations of the data.

"As expected, all of the internal organs have been removed and placed into canopic jars. The brain was also removed through the septum, judging from the broken bones in the upper nasal cavity," he said.

"No surprises there," said Wilder. "That was always done prior to preserving the body."

"Other than the slit in the side where the organs were removed, I see no other signs of trauma or deterioration caused by disease. No arthritic deterioration either. Imhotep was in excellent health," Holder said.

"Like most important men of his time, he appears to have died of natural causes," added Nasi.

"Does the scan show any sort of implanted device in the mummy that could have helped him pull off that last trick?" Wilder asked.

"Not a thing. There's nothing inside of him that indicates anything artificial. I guess we'll just have to list that one under "unexplained mysteries" and leave it go at that," said Jennifer.

Wilder reached out and touched the mummy's face. To his surprise, the flesh was still soft and pliable. He pushed a finger into Imhotep's cheek and moved back. The flesh almost immediately returned to its normal position.

"Unbelievable! It feels like living tissue," he gasped. "I've seen good examples of embalming before, but never in all my experiences did I see anything to compare with this," he said.

"We will have to take samples for a full spectrum analysis to see if any special materials were used to mummify him. I would also like to take some hair and skin samples for DNA testing," Hawatt said. "We are dealing with something new here. Something that we have never before encountered in all of the history of Egyptology."

"But how did he pull off that sitting up and talking trick?" asked Kuyder. "By magic?"

Hawatt and Wilder looked at each other and smiled. Kuyder rolled his eyes.

"For now, that is as good an explanation as any," said Hawatt. "After all, Imhotep was supposed to possess awesome magical powers. Perhaps he used the last of that power to perform that trick."

"When it comes to the ancient Egyptians, it is always best to keep an open mind," said Jennifer.

"A *very* open mind," added Art.

They went back over a few more details for the film crew, then Jackson signaled for them to wrap it up.

Maria gripped Art's arm as they left the chamber. Jennifer was only one step behind them.

"We've decided to take you back to the suite and fuck the Hell out of you. Think you can handle two women at the same time?" she said.

"I'll sure as Hell give it the old school try," Art replied.

As soon as they returned from the tomb, Jennifer pulled Art to the sofa. Maria watched as they sat down and kissed. It was a long, deep kiss that turned her on. After a few seconds, Jennifer unzipped Art's jeans and pulled out his already half-hard penis. She gave it a few easy pulls as it continued to expand in her fist. Art simply sat back and smiled.

Jennifer leaned over and licked his cock from its dark red knob all the way to his balls a few times, then took most it into her mouth. Art groaned as she sucked him.

Maria moved closer and watched as her new friend worked Art's cock like the seasoned pro she was. Nobody, she decided, could do that better than Jennifer. From the expression of Art's face, Maria could see that he agreed with her.

Jennifer bobbed her head up and down on Art's penis. At the same time, she pumped it with her fist. It was all that Art could stand.

He moaned.

Then he came. He sputtered several long lines of sticky cum straight up into the air. Jennifer sat back and continued jerking him off, enchanted by the sight of his cum jetting out of his cock. She never knew that any man could come so much. She tried to catch it in her open mouth.

While this was happening, Maria had masturbated herself into a nice hard orgasm. Art heard her cry out and watched as she fell back onto the loveseat with her legs apart.

Maria caught her breath and smiled. Her shorts were undone and Art could see her pretty brown pubic patch. Jennifer was still seated next to him, her hand wrapped around his penis. Some of Art's cum had missed her mouth and was now decorating the bridge of her nose and her left cheek. Each time Jennifer jerked Art's penis, his balls spasmed.

Maria eased her shorts off and spread her thighs to display her swollen, wet vagina lips and erect clit. The sight of it kept Art's cock stiff and hard, which delighted Jennifer. She slipped it into her mouth and began sucking away again. Art was thrilled. This drop-dead gorgeous woman really knew how to please a man!

Maria walked over and plopped down on her knees as she watched Jennifer suck Art's penis.

"Save some for me," she said as she pushed her aside.

Now, Jennifer sat back and watched as Maria swallowed Art's penis like a sword and happily sucked away. Art groaned. Maria was good, too. Very good and he had a lot of trouble holding back the flood of cum that was threatening to erupt. Meanwhile, Jennifer pulled Art's jeans all the way to his ankles so she could see his entire penis, then squeezed his balls gently.

That did it. Art emitted a loud "Ahh!" and suddenly filled Maria's hungry mouth with cum. Maria gulped down everything she could while Jennifer continued to play with Art's balls. Soon, he was so limp he begged them to stop.

"But I haven't come yet!" Jennifer complained.

Maria unbuttoned her friend's shorts and pulled them down to her ankles. Art dropped to his knees before her, grabbed her firm ass, then pulled Jennifer forward until her vagina covered his tongue. She tasted sweet and salty and smelled heavenly. Art inhaled her womanly scent, then began licking away. Jennifer cried out with pleasure and moved her hips back and forth as if she were fucking Art's tongue. Seconds later, he tasted her nectar as it gushed forth and covered his tongue.

Jennifer had stepped out of her shorts by then. Art looked at her long, dark sexy legs and shiny raven-haired vagina and wished that he could get it up just once more. Jennifer reeled and fell back onto the sofa with her legs apart. Maria stripped completely and sat next to her. Her legs were wide open, too. Art knew what she wanted and he quickly buried his tongue in her crotch. Maria threw her legs over his back and screamed with delight as Art's knowing tongue sent waves of intense pleasure coursing through her trembling body. Seconds later, she screamed again as her orgasm erupted from within her.

"What now?" Jennifer asked with a wicked smile on her lips.

"We have something to drink, rest a few minutes, then go into the bedroom and fuck like crazy," Maria suggested.

Art smiled. He couldn't think of anything else he'd rather do for the rest of the day.

CHAPTER 10

▼

Anazhur listened as his spies told him what they saw at the Sphinx. Wilder had done it all right. He had located Imhotep's tomb. More importantly, he had found the legendary Box of Thoth.

"Where is the Box now?" he asked.

"They have taken it to the museum. It is probably in the main vault," said one of the men.

"Go to the museum and find out exactly where they have put it. Also, keep times on how often the guards make their rounds."

As the men bowed and left, Hasmir entered and looked at Anazhur. His boss barely acknowledged him.

"Then you mean to go through with this?" Hasmir asked.

"Perhaps. Stealing it from the museum would be easier than trying to steal it from Wilder, don't you think?" Anazhur replied.

"I think this is dangerous in either case," Hasmir answered. "The museum is well guarded and Wilder is as deadly as a cobra."

"Still, I must have that Box. Now go away and let me think," Anazhur said curtly.

Hasmir stepped outside and lit a cigarette. He was starting to think that Anazhur was going mad. Taking on Wilder, along with the entire—and ruthless—Egyptian National Police, was insane. It had *suicide* written all over it.

"Maybe it's time I got into a new line of work," he mused as he looked up at the moon.

Back in the suite, Maria watched as Art's penis slowly moved in and out of Jennifer's eager vagina. Each down thrust he made, caused Jennifer to tremble with pleasure. Each plunge caused her to moan softly and claw at his back.

Outside of porno movies, this s the first time Maria had actually watched anyone make love. She was amazed at Art's staying powers, since less than a half hour earlier; he had made love to her. She watched in awe, fascinated with the way Art's penis moved in and out of Jennifer and with the way she drove her hips upward to take in every deliciously hard inch of him. They were in perfect sync now. It was as if they had been making love all their lives. She was amazed at how well they moved together.

"Fuck me, Art! Please fuck me!" Jennifer virtually sobbed.

Maria watched her back arch suddenly as she shook all over. Jennifer's mouth opened wide and her lips trembled as she fucked Art back erratically. Jennifer was in the throes of what appeared to be a powerful orgasm now as Art continued to hump away.

"Fuck me harder, Art! Harder!" she begged as her body spasmed wildly.

Art felt his own body shaking and began to move faster and faster. Maria realized that he was about to come.

"Pull out, Art!" she cried. "Come on her! I want to see you come on her!"

"Do it, Art!" Jennifer echoed. "Come all over me!"

Art kept pumping away, enjoying the sensations of Jennifer's twitching vagina, until he was just about to spew. At the very last second, he pulled out and hovered above her as he sent long streams of sticky, white cum all over her flat tummy and open pussy. Maria reached over, grabbed Art's penis, and pumped him until he had nothing left to give. By then, Jennifer's body was dripping with cum.

Inspired, Maria laid next to her and massaged the cum into Jennifer's vagina. Each time she touched Jennifer's clit, the woman begged Maria to eat her.

Now, it was Art's turn to watch as Maria shoved a pillow beneath Jennifer's fine ass and buried her tongue in her cum-filled snatch. It was the most erotic thing he'd ever seen. So erotic, that after a few minutes, he once again had a good-sized erection.

Maria was already on her knees as she ate Jennifer. Art gripped her behind, then spread her cheeks so he could get at her vagina. Moments later, he was moving in and out of her pleasure pocket like there was no tomorrow.

A few minutes later, they all just happened to orgasm at the exact same moment. It was a long, numbing and exhausting orgasm that left them piled atop one another for several minutes before they could catch their breath.

"Holy shit!" Art gasped as he extricated himself from the tangle of arms and legs. "That was unbelievable!"

From the looks on the ladies' faces, he could see they felt the same.

"Let's fuck" Jennifer said she forced herself to sit up.

Maria just rolled onto her side and smiled.

Art watched in amazement as Jennifer scissored her legs between Maria's so that their vaginas actually touched. She them moved up and down so that her vagina massaged Maria's nice and easy.

Maria moaned with pleasure. This was only the second time she'd ever felt anything like this and the sensation was heavenly. Jennifer was literally fucking her with her pussy. She was doing the one thing that, until recently, Maria thought women couldn't do.

Jennifer's soft labia moved delightfully against Maria's. On each pass, their clits moved across each other. The feeling it produced was incredible.

So different.

So exciting.

After a few strokes, Maria began fucking Jennifer back. The sight of these two beautiful women having sex made Art's penis hard again. He'd seen this in porno movies but in all of his travels, he'd never witnessed anything like it first hand. He never imagined that his beloved Maria would be involved either.

He watched as they moved faster and faster. Their labia made slurping sounds as they rubbed together and became wetter and wetter. The women were sweating now and breathing harder as they moved faster and faster.

Maria came first. Art watched her body stiffen suddenly, then she cried out and fell onto her back with her arms to either side. Jennifer kept moving like crazy until her orgasm rumbled through her lean, sexy body. Then she, too, fell back and gasped for air.

She looked over at Art, grabbed his erection and beat him off as he untangled herself from Maria.

"Fuck her, Art," she said. "I want to watch you do Maria."

Art grabbed Maria's ankles, bent her knees and pushed her legs back until they touched her nipples. Then he slid his hard penis deep inside her stretched out pussy and humped away. In this position, Art's penis massaged her g-spot on each and every in and out thrust. The sensations were sending Maria through the roof as she gripped his sheets with her fingers and moaned with pleasure. It was the most intense love she'd ever felt.

She came again within seconds.

"Pull out, Art!" Jennifer yelled.

Reluctantly, he eased his penis out of her. Jennifer grabbed it just as Maria dropped her feet to the mattress and began jerking him off. Maria watched in anticipation and smiled.

Jennifer beat him faster and faster. Art groaned and trembled and began firing gob after gob of cum onto Maria's writhing body. Jennifer kept at it until Art was completely spent and his penis shrank from her grasp.

Maria was covered with cum from her tits to her vagina. Jennifer pushed Art aside and spent the next several minutes licking Maria clean. When she was finished, she slid upward and sat on Maria's face.

Maria grabbed Jennifer's ass and licked her pussy until she came. Jennifer screamed with pleasure, then fell to the side. The three lovers exchanged long soft kisses until sleep overcame them.

They woke around seven.

"What shall we do now?" asked Jennifer with her usual wicked smile.

Art laughed.

"We go out to dinner, then come back here and do it all over again," he said.

"Sounds like a winner to me, Art. Let's get dressed. I'm already starving," Jennifer agreed.

After their meal, they decided to stop by the museum to see what else was happening. When they reached Nasi's office, they found him there with the other members of the MRS, Kuyder, Heider and a tall, thin man with curly brown hair and a goatee.

The man stretched out his right hand. Wilder shook it.

"I am Dr. Jean Louis LePage," the man said.

"I've heard of you. Your genetic and DNA studies are quite fascinating. You take DNA samples from mummies to try to determine the origins of specific diseases," Wilder said.

"Oui. I am so glad that you know my work, Dr. Wilder. I am also quite familiar with your exploits," LePage said.

"Dr. LePage has taken several DNA samples from Imhotep. He plans on doing a comparison study on him," Hawatt explained.

"I have been trying to find a direct link between modern day Egyptians and those from the beginnings of the ancient kingdom. At first, I wanted to see if there were any genetic disorders that were particular to the Egyptian people. But in doing so, I came upon a most unusual problem," LePage said.

"I know. I've read your papers. Your DNA studies shows no direct links between the ancient Egyptians and over 87% of modern Egyptians," Wilder said.

"That is correct. What's more, those that do have such links have very faint ones, as if they had been watered down over many centuries. I have so far found no strong bloodlines dating back to the pharaohs," LePage added.

"Even Dr. Hawatt's DNA does not match," he said with a nod to Nasi.

"And it should not. My ancestors arrived in Egypt with the Mamaluks prior to the Crusades. We were Arabs."

"Your study only proves what most historians already knew, Dr. LePage. Most modern-day Egyptians are descended from Greeks, Turks, Persians, Romans and Arabs who overran and settled in Egypt at various times. Most of the ancient bloodlines are extinct now," said Wilder.

"True. But I still keep searching for that one strong, direct link to Egypt's past dynasties. Maybe one day, I will find it," said LePage as he rose and picked up his hat.

As he did, he made direct eye contact with Maria. Instantly, he felt himself transported back in time to the age of pyramids and vast palaces and boats sailing lazily down the Nile. He envisioned Maria before him, dressed in royal raiment and seated upon the golden throne.

He blinked and shook his head.

"Mrs. Wilder, are you Egyptian?" he asked.

"No. I am from Puerto Rico," she replied.

"That's odd. I could swear that you are Egyptian," Le Page said.

"Maria is more Egyptian than most Egyptians are," said Nasi as he rose to escort LePage to the front door of the museum. "She has taken to Egypt as if she has lived here her entire life."

"I see. I would like to do a DNA comparison on you, Mrs. Wilder. I am sure the results would be most enlightening," LePage said with a courteous bow.

As Nasi escorted him to the taxi stand in front of the museum, he asked him what he saw when he looked into Maria's eyes.

"Marvelous things. It was like being transported back into time," LePage said.

"I sometimes get the same feelings when I look into her eyes. I believe that her husband also sees this," Nasi said.

"If there is one person alive today who can be traced directly back to the time of the pharaohs, it is Mrs. Wilder. I would be willing to bet my reputation on it," LePage said as he climbed into the back seat of the taxi.

Hawatt waved as he drove off. He would remember his conversation with LePage for the rest of his life.

Art, Jennifer and Maria headed back to the hotel for more and fun and games while the rest of the team headed back to the dig site.

Along the way, Art told Jennifer that he liked her behind so much, he wanted to screw her there. Jennifer blushed and replied that although she's never tried having sex that way, she'd be willing to try it with him—if Maria had no objections.

Maria decided to play Devil's advocate. She told Jennifer that she and Art "always had anal sex and it felt great." But she lied. Like Jennifer, Maria's rear tunnel had never been used for sex. She wanted to see Art do it to Jennifer first before deciding to try it herself.

Art played along with this. Anything, he thought, to get at Jenny's fine ass.

Once back at the suite, they quickly disrobed and jumped into bed. After several minutes of licking, kneading and fondling, Jennifer announced that she was ready for her big moment.

As Art prepared her behind for penetration, Maria sat down in the chair next to the bed to watch. It proved to be quite a learning experience.

Jennifer winced as Art's penis pushed past her puckered anus and slowly penetrated her rear channel. She made a fist and bit down on the knuckles to avoid screaming in pain as his penis worked its way inside her ass. She felt her inner flesh part painfully as Art went where no one else had gone before.

So far, it was not a pleasant experience. When Jennifer told Art she'd do anything that Maria did, she never expected this to be one of them. She wasn't prepared for the pain she was feeling, but since she promised Art she'd try it, she bore it in silence.

Art was being a gentle as possible. He had first coated his fingers with K-Y and worked them into her asshole to prepare Jennifer for what was to come. Then he liberally coated his penis with the lubricant before he invaded her.

"This hurts like Hell," she moaned when he had gone all the way in.

"You want me to stop?" he asked.

"No. Maria didn't and neither will I. Do what you want to do with me. I'll get used to it," Jennifer assured him.

Art ran his hands over her fine behind, then began moving in and out of her nice and easy. After a few strokes, the pain subsided and Jennifer relaxed. She even started moving her behind back into Art each time he thrust into her.

"That's it, Jennifer! By God that's nice!" Art gasped. "What an ass you have!"

"This is kind of fun," she said after a few more good strokes. "I am starting to enjoy it."

She gripped his penis with her sphincter muscles and held him in place as he spewed his love cream into her bowels. It felt so good, Art moaned the entire time.

Jennifer rolled off his penis and laid down with her thighs wide open. Art kissed and nibbled his way from her lips all the way to her vagina, then he ate her. She erupted seconds later.

Now it was Maria's turn…

Art ate her until she came.

Maria was still in the throes of her orgasm when Art undressed her completely. She had just started to fall back to Earth when she felt his long, hard penis push past her trembling labia and delve into her vagina. She closed her eyes and gripped his arms as he began that slow, deep and delicious fuck she had come to love so well.

Maria was totally enthralled with Art. Even though her sexual experience was rather limited, Art was, by far, the best lover she'd ever had.

"He might be the best lover on Earth," she told herself as his knowing thrusts began to send her toward another explosive come.

After a little while, her hungry body picked up Art's rhythm and she began loving him back. As she did, she tightened her pussy muscles to increase his pleasure.

Now it was Art's turn to marvel at Maria's sexual know-how. This Latin beauty really knew how to use her vagina and it was all he could do to keep from coming too soon.

He stopped thrusting and allowed Maria to do all of the work for a while. She responded by moving her hips up and down slowly as she once more tightened her muscles around his penis.

Art gasped.

Maria's vagina was fantastically tight and it felt so smooth and silky as it wrapped itself around his penis. Right at that moment, Art realized that he was getting the very best sex of his entire life.

Maria humped him slowly so she, too, could savor this incredible sex. Art felt her vagina quiver and realized that she was about to come. He leaned forward and began thrusting in and out again. Only now, he did it much faster than he did earlier.

Maria's eyes widened and she emitted several long, deep sighs as his penis massaged her inner vagina. His sudden change of pace had surprised her and virtually robbed her of her ability to breathe. Somehow, she managed to hold onto his hips as she strove to match his new pace.

Then it happened.

She felt something deep inside of her erupt like a volcano. The room turned white. Maria's head dropped back and she arched her back as Art made one last good, hard thrust into her trembling channel.

Maria felt his warm cum spurt into her vagina and she clawed Art's arms as another orgasm washed over her.

"Si! Si!" she cried. "Dios mio! Si!"

They had come at the same exact moment. It was one huge, simultaneous, mind-numbing blast that left both of them gasping for air and covered with sweat.

When Jennifer woke the next morning to pack for her trip back to the States, she could hardly walk. Maria saw her limping around and laughed.

"You look like you're in a lot of pain," she observed.

"I am. That hurt. Was this the way you felt when he did it with you the first time?" Jennifer asked.

Maria giggled.

"What's so funny?" Jennifer demanded.

"I have never had anal sex," Maria confessed.

"You bitch! You set me up for that!" Jennifer shouted.

"I guess I did," Maria admitted.

"Why?" asked Jennifer.

"Art's been bothering me to try that for a long time now. I thought I'd let him do it to you so I could see how you liked it first," Maria said.

"You're still a bitch," Jennifer said smiling. "Are you going to try it now?"

"Maybe. How'd it feel for you?" Maria asked.

"Kind of nice once I got used to it. I doubt I'll do it again any time soon, though. I've heard that some women actually prefer that type of sex, but I'm not one of them," Jennifer replied.

They both laughed, then hugged and kissed each other.

That afternoon, Art and his crew saw the Mummy Road Show team off at the airport. As the plane taxied down the runway, Art led his group back to the parking lot.

"Now what?" asked Heider. "The MRS team is through and Dr. LaPage's DNA sample has been delivered to the museum."

"Now we invite the press corps to the museum to film the opening of the earthen jars we took from the tomb," Wilder said.

"An excellent idea, Art. The whole world needs to see what is inside those jars. The knowledge may prove to be invaluable to us," Hawatt agreed. "I will make the necessary calls as soon as we get back to my office."

"Good. Meanwhile, we'll continue to photograph, catalog and map the tomb. I also want to make sure that Imhotep's sarcophagus has been properly sealed," said Wilder.

Hawatt smiled. Wilder never removed a body from its proper resting place. It was something that set him above and apart from most archaeologists. It was the thing that Hawatt respected most about him.

CHAPTER 11

▼

It took three days for the press people to set up this huge event. There were crews from the History Channel, the Smithsonian Magazine, National Geographic, the BBC and a dozen other major news agencies in Hawatt's conference room that morning.

Wilder and Hawatt sat at one end of the long table. Before them were an assembly of Xacto Knives, magnifying glasses, small paint brushes and light pencils. Behind them stood two armed guards and a double row of earthen jars.

"Shall we begin?" asked Wilder.

The director nodded and signaled to the camera crew to start filming. Wilder leaned over the first jar with a Xacto and gently cut away the wax seal around the lid. This done, he set the blade on the table and started twisting the lid.

He finally removed the ceramic lid, placed the jar on the table, then stepped aside so the cameraman could get a good shot at the eight wooden tubes inside the jar.

This done, Wilder took out the tubes one at a time and handed them to Hawatt who examined the hieroglyphs painted on them and explained what they said.

On the end of each tube was wooden plug. Hawatt removed the plug on the first one, then carefully took out the papyrus scroll and spread it open on the table. As he and Wilder examined it, Hawatt translated its contents for the press.

"This is a very descriptive recipe for beer," he said. "It tells the proper ingredients to use and the exact methods needed to produce several large jars of beer and even how long to ferment it."

"According to legend, Imhotep invented beer, wine and mead," added Wilder. "No wonder they made him a god."

His remarks evoked laughter from the onlookers. They repeated the process with another tube. This contained a drawing of a long staff with what appeared to be a light bulb on one. A long tube led from the other end into an earthen jar. Alongside each were several descriptions in heiretic.

"Amazing! According to the text, the jar was filled with citrus juices and some sort of acid. Inside the tube was a copper wire that fed the energy from the acid mixture to a globe filled with some sort of gas. In other words, this is an ancient version of the electric light!" exclaimed Hawatt.

"Incredible! They had electricity 4,000 years before anyone else. That explains how they were able to paint the insides of the tombs without using oil lamps," said Wilder.

"How do you know this, Dr. Wilder?" asked the reporter.

"Easy. Oil lamps produce an oily smoke which leaves an obvious residue on walls and ceilings. We've never found such residue in any tombs that were opened. We always assumed they had other light sources. This proves it," Wilder answered.

The next tube held a drawing of an intricate machine that resembled pistons and cylinders and rods attached to a central block. Hawatt studied the text carefully, then looked at Wilder in astonishment.

"This is some sort of engine—an early version of the internal combustion engine. But it doesn't state what fuel was used to run it," he said.

"What do you suppose they used it for? They didn't have cars or trucks back then," asked the reporter.

"True. Maybe the next scroll will shed some light on that," said Hawatt.

But the next scroll was even more astonishing. It depicted the plans for what could only have been a powerful steam jet engine.

"It could be that Imhotep was just toying with these ideas and never actually built them—sort of like DaVinci's helicopter and submarine," suggested Wilder.

"The ancient Egyptians were a very practical and pragmatic people. They were great inventors and innovators. If Imhotep drew up plans for such things, I am certain they must have been built and used. They would not have wasted such ideas," said Hawatt.

The next jar contained several scrolls that dealt in great detail with the processes of mummification, as well as the necessary spells and rituals needed to ensure safe passage to the next world. It even included detailed drawings of the proper attire to be used by the priests who presided over the process.

They unrolled several more "books". One contained the detailed plans for a large, deep-hulled sailing ship that looked nothing like typical Egyptian vessels of the time.

"A ship this size could carry hundreds of tons of cargo. From the looks of it, it was designed for long sea voyages," Wilder explained.

Others contained detailed drawings of animals, birds, fish and insects. There were literally dozens of such scrolls in three large jars.

Then came a startlingly detailed map of the entire world, including Antarctica, Australia and Greenland—which the ancient Egyptians weren't supposed to know about. Wilder commented that it sort of went hand-in-hand with the need for long-distance sailing ships and proved that the early Egyptians were great explorers, traders and colonizers.

At least eight other scrolls contained a very detailed medical manual, replete with instructions on how to identify, treat and do follow-up examinations on hundreds of ailments. This also included surgical procedures, pre-op and post-op exams, and a box filled with delicate surgical instruments.

"Amazing! We are holding the very same instruments that Imhotep himself used to operate on his patients. It gives me goose-bumps!" Hawatt said as if he were awestruck by the find.

Then came a series of highly detailed anatomical charts of both a man and a woman's body. Hawatt and Wilder stared at them in wonder.

"These charts are extremely detailed—and look—each organ is labeled in heiretic. I believe it also explains what each organ's function is. Incredible. It is commonly believed that the Greeks were the first to make such charts. Yet this is at least 1,000 years older than any others known to exist," Hawatt gushed.

"He even included cross-sections of the major organs," Wilder added. He looked at the camera again.

"These charts were drawn by Imhotep nearly 5,000 years ago. This proves that he was the world's first doctor and surgeon to make such detailed studies of the human body and put it all down on papyrus. When you put this together with his medical manuals and instruments, it is easy to see why he is truly the father of modern medicine," he explained.

There were several smaller scrolls. When they unrolled them, they were found to contain larger, more exacting drawings of the major body organs. Wilder whistled as he unrolled one.

"These are even more detailed than many modern charts. I think our present-day doctors could learn a lot from them," he said.

"According to legend, Imhotep never lost a patient and he spent many years training other doctors throughout Egypt and other places," Hawatt added with a broad grin on his face.

There were also scrolls on dentistry, veterinary medicine, plants, flowers, trees, agricultural methods, irrigation methods, pest control and several on architecture and building methods.

By midnight, Hawatt and Wilder had opened a half dozen jars and examined nearly seventy scrolls.

Wilder looked up at the wall clock.

"We've been at it for six hours now. Want to keep going?" he asked.

Everyone in the room nodded. Wilder looked directly into the main camera.

"So far, we've opened six of the twenty-five jars we took from the tomb. As you can see, they scrolls cover a wide range of scientific and medical subjects and even include drawings for some of his inventions.

As we continue to examine the contents of each and every scroll, who knows what else they will tell us about this wonderful civilization? Perhaps they will tell us who actually built the Sphinx. Maybe we'll discover the origins of human civilization.

This is a very exciting time for myself and Dr. Hawatt—and for all mankind. We are about to unlock the earliest secrets of the world's greatest civilization and rewrite human history," he said.

The next jar they opened caused quite a stir among the media people present, especially when Wilder took out the largest tube and removed the plug from one end.

As he unrolled the papyrus, he stared in disbelief. The disbelief soon turned to excitement as he spread it out on the table.

"This is it, Nasi!" he shouted. "It's what every archaeologist of the last hundred years has been searching for—and it was right where I said it would be!"

Hawatt gawked, then motioned for the cameras to zoom in on the scroll.

"Unbelievable. These are the building plans for the Great Pyramid. The details are amazing, too. Now we will know exactly how the pyramids were built. Imhotep even included the number of workers that would be needed, support personnel, amount of food, water, beer—it is all here."

"But didn't Imhotep die before the Great Pyramid was built?" asked the reporter.

"We thought so. But since he drew these plans, the work might have been started during his lifetime," said Hawatt.

"Or the Great Pyramid is a few years older than we thought," added Wilder. "After all, Khufu's architect credited Imhotep for its construction. At the very least, Imhotep passed the plans down to his apprentices before he died."

"It appears as if we have many more questions than answers right now. Let's have a look at the rest of the scrolls," said Hawatt.

The other scrolls were also plans for great stone buildings such as temples, dams, irrigation projects, other pyramids and huge monuments. In all, there were twenty such scrolls and the plans were laid out in exacting details—down to the last inch.

"Imhotep was history's first real architect," Wilder explained as he carefully placed the scrolls back into the jar.

"By that I mean he was the first to draw up exact plans and to oversee construction of the buildings."

"Did you find anything in those plans about the Sphinx?" asked one reporter.

"There was one drawing for modifying the head but that's all," said Hawatt.

"Nothing on who actually built it?" asked another reporter.

"No. But perhaps that is best. Perhaps there are some things that we were never meant to know," Hawatt replied.

"What about the bundle?" asked the reporter. "When will you unwrap it?"

"No time like the present," said Wilder as he brought the bundle forward and gently placed it on the table.

As the cameras continued rolling, he cut the leather cords with a knife and slowly pulled away the layers of the bundle. When he was finished, they found themselves looking down at a long, rectangular box.

The Box measured 26" x 14" and was almost 10" high. It was made of some sort of black metal. Wilder guessed it was probably an alloy of tin, copper and iron, covered by layers of shiny black paint and lacquer.

There was an ornate and intricate locking mechanism on the lid and a cartouche bearing the hieroglyphs of Imhotep's name on the right side. There didn't appear to be any kind of hinges.

The cameras zoomed in for close-ups while Wilder and Hawatt espoused some theories as to what might be inside the Box.

By then it was nearly five a.m. and the entire things was being broadcast live by TV stations all around the world.

Anazhur sat in front of the TV set watching as the jars were opened. He paid little attention to their contents or to what Wilder and Hawatt said. His mind was on one thing only.

The Box.

He was convinced the ancient secrets of the legendary Box would enable him to bring down the Egyptian government and install himself as pharaoh. Then he could gather together a vast army and use it to overrun the entire Middle East like an avenging tide. He would "liberate" his Arab brothers from the infidel yoke.

"He who controls the Box, rules the world," he often said, though just where he got that idea remained a mystery to his right-hand man Hasmir.

"He probably heard it in an old movie," Hasmir once told an underling. "And he was foolish enough to believe it."

When Wilder explained to the Smithsonian reporter that the Box couldn't be opened until they figured out the locking mechanism, a disgusted Anazhur rose from his seat and turned off the set. He scowled at his men as he paced the floor a few times. When he stopped, he'd come to a decision.

"I must have that Box," he said. "I must have it at all costs. What's inside could make me the most powerful man in the Middle East."

"How are we going to get it?" asked one of his men. "The Box is inside a vault in the museum and there are several armed guards in the building."

"I leave the details to you and your men. I don't care how you get it just as long as you get it," Anazhur replied. "And I want it by tomorrow evening."

The men looked at each other, then shrugged. Since their boss wanted the Box fast, they had to plan and execute a burglary on short notice. They knew that it would be very dangerous to try and steal it so soon, but Anazhur's orders were explicit and left them no choice but to try.

Wilder returned to the hotel. He'd been up nearly two days straight with no sleep to speak of and was dead on his feet. He took a quick shower, plopped face-down on the bed and fell into a deep sleep.

But Maria was wide awake. Rather than hang around the hotel watching Art sleep, she dressed and headed into the crowded streets of Cairo. She walked down avenues and along narrow alleys until she came to her destination—the secluded little sex shop she'd found while out hunting for film.

Maria felt horny.

Hornier than usual.

Since Art was in no condition to make her happy right now, she decided to seek relief elsewhere. As she walked up to the plain-looking door, she hoped that her new friend was inside.

Maria the doorbell. She was pleasantly surprised to see The Woman open the door. She followed The Woman into the living room and took a seat on the opposite end of the sofa from her. The Woman was dressed—if you could call it that—in a long white T-shirt and she had left her panties off.

She noticed Maria ogling her legs and smiled. She put one foot up on the sofa and allowed her shirt to slide toward her hips. Maria's gaze was immediately drawn to the fleecy black patch between The Woman's thighs.

The Woman realized then that Maria had fallen for her in a big way. She took a good hard look at her and had to admit she was very beautiful.

Exotic and sexy.

With great legs.

Maria smiled sexily at The Woman and ran her tongue over her lips.

"I bet you have an adorable pussy," The Woman said.

As if to assure The Woman she did, Maria stood up and undid her shorts. The Woman watched hungrily as the pretty Latina slid them down and off her lovely legs to reveal her soft, brown haired cunt. The Woman went to her knees and examined the soft, flower like folds and swollen clit, caressing it gently as she did.

"It's beautiful—just like you are," The Woman whispered.

Maria held out her hand. The Woman took it and stood up. Then they walked to the master bedroom. Before long, they were both naked and locked into a torrid "69". They kept at until they both came, then fell apart to rest. After a few minutes, The Woman rose from the bed and walked to the dresser.

Maria watched as she opened a drawer, reached inside and took out a large, fleshy, double-headed dildo. She turned to Maria and smiled.

"Now we fuck," she said.

The Woman slid one end of the huge dildo up into her cunt, then got between Maria's thighs. Excited beyond imagination, Maria threw her legs open wide and closed her eyes. If the fuck she was about to get was anywhere near as good as what The Woman did to her with her tongue, Maria knew this was going to be something special.

The Woman bent over and licked Maria's cunt to moisten it, then slowly eased the dildo into her until their pubic hairs touched.

"Aiee!" Maria gasped.

The Woman smiled, then began to fuck Maria nice and slow. She used deep, easy strokes that stoked Maria's inner fires until she was white hot. It took a little while for Maria to grow accustomed to this huge, latex prick working her gash, but she soon learned to enjoy it.

Really enjoy it!

She was being fucked by another woman. An older, sexier woman who really knew how to use a "prick". Maria began fucking her back, matching The

Woman thrust for thrust as she dug her fingers into the woman's soft back. Now, Maria's legs were wide open and her knees were bent. She was getting the ride of her life, one of the best fuck ever. And it was from a woman!

"Oh, God! That feels so damned good!"

"You're very beautiful, Maria. You have the most gorgeous cunt I've ever seen. I could do this with you forever," whispered The Woman as she increased the tempo of her thrusts.

Maria took a deep breath, and matched her. She knew she was about to blow and gripped The Woman's ass tightly.

"Fuck me harder, please! Ohh, yes!" Maria cried.

The Woman complied. It was just enough to push Maria over the edge and she erupted into an orgasmic bliss. She trembled all over and cried out in Spanish. The Woman fucked her even faster, sending more waves of pleasure surging through Maria's taut, sweaty body. Then The Woman came, too. She shook all over, then fell next to Maria. Both women were breathing very hard.

When she came back to Earth, Maria hugged The Woman close.

After another long rest, Maria looked at her lover who still had the dildo protruding from her cunt. Maria grabbed it and moved it in and out of her a few times while The Woman gently massaged her pussy. After a few minutes of foreplay, they were ready for another round.

Maria lay on her back, her legs wide open, as The Woman once more used the dildo on her soft, willing cunt. As before, The Woman fucked her slowly, sliding all the way in until their pubic hairs touched on each nice, easy down stroke.

On each deep thrust, Maria drove her hips upward to take in every delicious inch of The Woman's artificial "prick". Each thrust brought her closer to orgasm as her body begged for more and more. Maria was in the clouds, on a sexual high.

But she wasn't there alone.

The Woman, too, was lost in a sexual fog as she enjoyed one of the best fucks of her entire life. The soft, moist flesh of Maria's eager cunt swallowed the dildo like a hungry mouth and The Woman took great delight in the way this beautiful woman offered herself to her.

Each inward thrust now made Maria moan softly as waves of intense pleasure began to ripple through her. She dug her fingers into The Woman's back and began to fuck her even harder. The Woman, caught up in the excitement, matched her thrust-for-thrust. Soon, she, too, felt the beginnings of an intensely good orgasm coursing through her.

Maria smiled.

"I'm coming! Oh, Lord! I'm coming!" she gasped as the room around her began to glow white.

"Me too! Fuck me harder, Maria! Give it to me good!" The Woman replied as her body began to shake all over.

Both women stepped up the pace and really hammered each other. The Woman gasped. Maria thrust her hips upward as hard as she could, driving the dildo into The Woman's cunt all the way. The Woman shuddered and emitted a shout of Maria, then fucked Maria back with all she had.

Maria began sobbing with glee.

"Yes! Yes!" she screamed as she milked The Woman's "prick" like a woman possessed.

She was possessed.

Possessed by lust.

An all powerful, all consuming lust.

For a woman!

Both women exploded into a mutual supernova at the exact same second. They laid there, holding each other close, exchanging soft kisses until their orgasm subsided.

"Perfecto!" Maria whispered.

The Woman couldn't agree with her more.

CHAPTER 12

▼

Anazhur looked at his watch and scowled. He turned to Hasmir.

"Are the men in place yet?" he asked.

Hasmir nodded.

"They will hide in the restrooms until the museum closes then go after the Box. With any luck, they won't trip the alarms," he said.

"They had better not. I will not tolerate yet another failure," Anazhur said.

Hasmir nodded again.

There had been a long string of failures for the group. One botched job after another. They were now a laughing stock among other groups in the region. Not even the PLO took them seriously now.

Terrorism was one thing.

Burglary was quite another. That was far out of their field of expertise. Since most of their men were a cross between the Three Stooges and the Keystone Kops, Hasmir had little hope for a successful theft of the Box.

At ten PM, long after the cleaning crews were gone, the three would-be burglars emerged from the rest rooms and slowly made their way to the vault in the basement.

But not everyone had gone.

Unable to sleep, Wilder and Hawatt decided to stay at the museum and examine the scrolls. It was well past midnight and the only other people in the building were seven armed guards.

At one pint, Hawatt happened to glance up from the scroll he'd been examining. That's when he spotted the flashing red light on the opposite wall. Wilder looked, too.

"That is the silent alarm. It appears we have after-hours visitors," Hawatt said. "The police will be here soon to check it out."

Wilder took a .44 magnum out of his briefcase, checked to be sure it was loaded, then stood up and walked toward the door.

"I'm going to check on our guests," he said over his shoulder. "You wait here for the cops."

As he entered the hall, he spotted three armed guards heading for the stairs. He hurried after.

"From where was the alarm tripped?" he asked.

Mamoud, the head guard pointed at the stairs.

"The basement," he said. "Someone tried to break into the main vault."

"Who's down there now?" Wilder asked as they descended the stairs.

"Ali. He is on rounds now," replied Mamoud. "I tried to call him on the radio but he did not answer."

"Our intruders might have overpowered him. You and your men cover the exits to keep our visitors from escaping. I'll check the vault," Wilder said as he raised his pistol.

When they reached the basement, they split up. Wilder walked across the shiny floor of the main gallery, past several cases containing the mummies of long-dead kings, sarcophagi and ancient stone statues. Just before he reached the vault, he stopped and listened. That's when he heard footsteps.

"Sounds like more than one person," he thought.

He moved to the side gallery and looked around. He soon found Ali seated upright against a wall. The guard was unconscious but breathing.

"They must have caught him by surprise. I wonder where they are now?" Wilder thought as he looked around.

That's when he spotted a shadowy figure running through the side gallery and down the hall. Wilder took off after him. He decided to take a short cut through one of the offices. The short cut put him in the hall several feet ahead of the intruder. He hid behind a column and waited.

Just as the intruder passed by, Wilder kneed him hard in the groin. The surprised man went down to his knees in a heap. Wilder brought him down all the way with a blow to the back of his head.

That's when another man appeared from the shadows. He leveled a pistol at Wilder and fired. Wilder rolled out of harm's way and returned fire. The shot caught the thief in the sternum and knocked him back against a wall in a shower of his own blood.

That's when Mamoud and the guards arrived with guns drawn. Wilder knelt beside the man he'd shot and went though his pockets. He found a wallet with a driver's license, several bills and a sacred amulet of the Eye of Horus. He handed them to Mamoud.

"Ever see him before?" he asked.

"Never in my life," Mamoud said. "Maybe the police will know who he is. They have already arrived."

That's when Hawatt entered the gallery with eight heavily armed Egyptian police officers. The tall man next to Hawatt introduced himself as a captain. Wilder shook his hand and explained what happened.

The other officers handcuffed the unconscious thief and dragged him roughly up the stairs. The captain smiled.

"He will be happy to cooperate with us by the time we are through with him," he said. "Egyptian justice can be quite, er, *harsh*."

Wilder nodded.

Mamoud handed the wallet of the dead man to the captain. The captain opened it, took out the bills and handed them to Wilder. The archaeologist looked at them.

"For your trouble, Dr. Wilder. *He* no longer has need of money," he explained.

Wilder handed the bills to Mamoud and told them to give the money to Ali when he came to.

"Tell him it's for his headache," he said.

Mamoud laughed and followed the captain up the stairs.

"An ambulance will be here in a few minutes to take that carcass away," said the captain as he bade Wilder and Hawatt farewell.

Wilder looked at Hawatt.

"I need a drink," he said.

"Me too. I have a bottle of cognac in my office and some ice cubes," Hawatt replied as they headed upstairs to finish their examination of the scrolls.

Much to Anazhur's chagrin and outrage, the local media played the attempted burglary up real big. When Wilder was interviewed about the incident, he hinted that they may have been agents of some clandestine organization intent on stealing the Box of Thoth.

"Although I can't imagine what value it might have to them. It's far too hot to sell and I doubt there's anything of a military nature inside. The Box is a historical artifact. Beyond that, it has no value," he added.

Anazhur scowled at his surviving burglar, then slapped him on the side of his head. The man flinched but did not try to defend himself as his boss cursed him out mercilessly.

"We could try it again," suggested his aide.

"No. They will be more careful from now on. We must find another way to get it," Anazhur replied.

Then he smiled.

It was a wicked, evil smile.

"I know how to get it. We'll use Wilder's wife, Maria," he said.

"She won't steal it for us," the aide said.

"Idiot! I don't want her to steal it for us. I know she'd never agree to something like that. No. We'll kidnap her. Once we have her, we'll contact her husband and offer to return her to him in exchange for the Box. We'll threaten to kill her if he doesn't agree to the trade. That should force his hand," Anazhur said.

"That sounds good. But Wilder can be dangerous. Very dangerous," the aide pointed out. "Besides, we just can walk right up and grab his wife. There are always a lot of people with her."

"True. I want you and Ahmad to follow her for the next few days. See where she goes. Then, when you are certain she is alone, grab her and bring her here. Do you think you can do that without fucking it up?" Anazhur said.

"I think so," replied the aide.

"Good. Now get on it before something else goes wrong," Anazhur barked.

As the aide scurried off to find Ahmad, Anazhur shook his head.

"It's so hard to find good terrorists these days," he moaned.

Hasmir had listened to the entire exchange. Anazhur looked at him and he simply shook his head.

"You disapprove? Why?" Anazhur asked.

"How much do you actually know about Wilder?" Hasmir asked.

"Enough. He doesn't frighten me if that's what you're getting at," Anazhur said.

"Well, he *should*," Hasmir cautioned.

"Explain yourself," Anazhur ordered.

"I have done extensive research on Wilder. His record is quite amazing. At the age of twenty, he was a Green Beret fighting in Vietnam, Cambodia and Laos. After the war, he joined the Navy and became a SEAL. After the SEALS, he was a paid mercenary who fought in several African and Central American wars. He also worked for the CIA and Interpol. He did all of that before age thirty. That's when he decided to become an archaeologist.

He has been highly decorated by the United States, French, Spanish and English military. His military exploits are the stuff of *legends,*" Hasmir explained.

"You make him sound like Rambo!" Anazhur almost spat.

"He makes Rambo look like *Peter Rabbit!*" Hasmir countered. "And there is more!"

"Oh?" Anazhur asked.

"He has friends—*special friends*—who have skills you have only imagined. These friends are all over the world and will drop everything to come to his aid. Not to mention his high-placed political contacts," Hasmir said.

"So what?" Anazhur asked.

"So this—fucking with Art Wilder is like fucking with a rabid wolverine. I advise you, as your friend and second in command, to *forget about the Box.*" Hasmir urged.

"The die is cast. There is no turning from the path I have started on. Now go away and let me think," Anazhur said.

Hasmir stepped outside to smoke. He looked over at three of his men who were sitting around a stone bench playing cards. He walked over. One of the men looked up.

"I was listening at the door when you talked to the boss," he said. "Is Wilder as bad as you said?"

"No. He's much *worse,*" replied Hasmir.

"What would you do in our place?" asked another man.

"Run—and I would not stop to look back," Hasmir said honestly.

The men looked at each other. Hasmir saw the fear in their eyes and realized that not one of them would be around once it hit the fan. Hell, he doubted that *he* would stick around.

Wilder returned to the hotel right after sunrise. Thinking that Maria was asleep, he jumped into the shower to wash the sand and sweat from his body. When he toweled off and walked into the bedroom, he got a pleasant surprise.

His wife was on the bed but she was far from being asleep. He walked over to her after he draped the towel over the back of a chair.

"I've been waiting for you," she said.

Maria lay on her back, her legs wide open. She reached down and pulled her labia apart, enticing Art with the dark, pink moistness of her cunt.

Art climbed on top of her and slid his hard prick all the way inside. Maria sighed happily and opened her legs wider as he began that slow, soft, delicious fuck she loved so much.

Maria let herself go with the flow, allowing her body's natural rhythms match Art's every thrust. She savored every moment of their lovemaking—for that's what it was to her.

Lovemaking.

It went well beyond just great sex.

Each time Art thrust his cock into her steaming snatch, it felt better. More natural. More excitingly delicious than anything she ever felt before. His prick felt perfect inside her and she hungrily accepted every thrust.

This was the third time this evening they'd made love. Each time, the fit was more perfect. Each time, she wanted more and more.

And she gave him more and more.

Art was in Heaven, too. He didn't care that he was fucking his sister-in-law or that his wife had set this up for them. All he cared about was that sexy brown body writhing beneath him and the incredibly silky-soft cunt that was devouring his prick.

Maria felt herself coming. She arched her back. Art felt it, too and began fucking her faster. Their timing was perfect.

Unable to hold back any longer, Art exploded deep inside Maria's cunt. The force of his last hard thrust caused Maria to come, too. They fucked erratically for a few more moments and Maria groaned with each thrust.

CHAPTER 13

▼

Hawatt was just about to go to bed when he noticed that the light was still on in his daughter's room. He walked over, opened it and looked inside.

Hathor looked up at him and smiled.

"Hathor, my child, why are you still up at this hour?" Nasi asked.

"I was just reading Dr. Wilder's book. You know, the one about his find in Guatemala? I can't seem to put it down," the girl replied. "What time is it?"

"It is past two in the morning. You have school tomorrow," Nasi said in his best fatherly voice.

"I know, Papa. But this book is so fascinating. I think I've decided what I want to do when I graduate from high school," Hathor said.

"And what is that, my dear?" Nasi asked.

"An archaeologist. Is there a special school for that?" Hathor asked.

Nasi beamed. He liked Hathor's choice very much. She would follow in his footsteps after all.

"No. You learn in the field, by *doing*. Archaeology is something you must have a real passion for. You cannot learn this from books. You must *live* it," he replied.

"Like you and Dr. Wilder?" she asked.

"Exactly. Now, it is time for you to sleep. We will talk more of this another time. Okay?" Nasi said.

Hathor smiled and closed the book. Nasi shut the door and walked down the hall to his bedroom. As he did, he looked back and saw that Hathor's light was still on. He simply smiled and went to bed.

Maria lay on her back. Her long, shapely legs were spread as far apart as possible as she enjoyed the sensations caused by Art's tongue adoring her willing cunt.

They were in his suite at the hotel and she was in ecstasy. Art, the man she loved more than anyone else, was making sweet, passionate love to her.

Art's tongue danced magically over her swollen clit and labia. Maria trembled with excitement. It felt so good. So very good. She ran her fingers through his hair and bent her knees to take his tongue deeper inside her quivering gash. More shivers raced through her and she moaned softly.

"Eat me, Art. Please eat me," she begged.

And he did.

Maria started coming. It was a deep, strong orgasm, too. Just before she went over the edge, Art stopped licking her. She felt the bed move as he positioned himself between her legs, then cried out with pleasure as he slid his hard cock into her already pulsating channel.

"Yes! YES!" she shouted as she rocked with him. "Do it, Art! Love me. Use me. I'm yours, darling! I'm yours forever! Use me!"

She exploded like a thousand rockets. She came hard. Harder than she's ever come before. She fucked him back with all her might now. She drove her slender hips up as hard as she could each time to take him deeper and deeper into her eager cunt.

"Yes! Yes! I love you, Art! I love you!" she gasped as another powerful orgasm rocked her sweaty body.

At that instant, Art came, too. He emptied every last drop of jism he had left into Maria's gorgeous, exquisitely tight cunt. They kept going until Art's balls and abs ached and they were too worn out to continue.

"I love you, Maria," Art said.

She knew he meant it, too.

Anazhur looked at Hasmir as he walked in and sat across from him. He poured Hasmir a cup of Turkish coffee and watched as he added six cubes of sugar to it and stirred.

"Are the men in place? Are they watching her yet?" he asked.

"Ali and two others are in front of the hotel even as we speak. They plan to follow Mrs. Wilder when she does her normal shopping and sightseeing during the morning. It may be difficult. She is rarely alone," Hasmir said.

"Tell them to keep at it. She has to be alone sooner or later. Then they can grab her," Anazhur said.

"They already know that," Hasmir replied.

"Then *remind* them again, Hasmir! I want no fuck-ups this time," Anazhur growled.

Hasmir gulped down the coffee, shrugged, and went outside.

"You have already fucked up, Mahomet. *Big time!*" he said as he closed the door behind him.

As Maria roamed the streets, bazaars and shops of Cairo in search of film and other Egyptian treasures, she was completely oblivious to the fact she was being followed by three rather sinister-looking men in a blue sedan.

They tailed her for three days, starting from the moment she left the hotel and ending at the dig site after sunset.

The first day, they followed her from the hotel to one of the main shopping areas. She went from shop to shop. While she purchased rolls of film, perfume and Egyptian treats, they waited patiently for her to come out. They followed her to a small café and watched as she ate lunch and chatted with the waiters. Then she got into a taxi and went back to the hotel. The entire time, Maria was in plain view and surrounded by a lot of people.

This made grabbing her too risky. After all, they didn't want any witnesses.

The second day, she and Art went sightseeing through the oldest section of Cairo then took a ten hour boat trip up the Nile to Luxor and back. From there, they went back to the dig where they worked until dawn before going back to the hotel.

The third day was pretty much a repeat of the first and afforded the would-be abductors no chance at Maria.

On the fourth day, they got a break. This time, Maria left the hotel alone to do some souvenir hunting. For much of the day, they followed her through main shopping areas, galleries, cafes and large stores.

They were about to give up when they saw her head back up the main avenue that led to the hotel a few hours later. Then, only three blocks from it, Maria turned left and walked down a narrow, shaded street.

Intrigued, the men followed at a distance.

"If she stays on this street, we may be able to grab her", said the driver of the sedan.

"I wonder where she is going? There are no souvenir shops on this street," said another man.

They parked the car and watched as Maria walked up to an inconspicuous shop and rang the bell. The door opened and a tall, good-looking woman welcomed her inside.

The driver looked up at the sign above the door and laughed. He pointed. The other two looked at the sign and laughed, too.

"A sex shop?" one asked.

"She probably went inside to purchase a few toys. She won't be there long. When she comes out, we'll take her," the driver said.

But as time passed, they realized they were in for a much longer wait than they expected.

Maria watched as The Woman undid her shirt, one button at a time, then took it off. The Woman's breasts jiggled nicely as she tossed the garment into a corner of the bedroom. She smiled as Maria studied her.

The Woman's breasts were large, perky and firm with large aureoles and pert nipples. Maria watched as The Woman fondled herself until the nipples stood hard and proud from the mounds of her breasts.

The Woman smiled. She reached down and undid her shorts, then let them slide down her legs to the floor. Maria's eyes went immediately to the dark, fluffy triangle between The Woman's thighs and stayed there.

She had seen nude women before. She had seven sisters. But this was different. This was the first time she's seen a nude woman she was going to have sex with.

And she was a beautiful, sexy woman.

Maria's heart raced as The Woman approached her. Since Maria was seated on the bed, The Woman's cunt was at eye level. She could see that it was moist and ready. Maria looked into The Woman's eyes. She smiled at her and nodded.

Maria's right hand moved slowly toward The Woman's cunt, then hesitated a moment before continuing. As soon as Maria's long, sexy fingers touched her, The Woman closed her eyes and sighed deeply.

"Yes, Maria. That's it. Touch my pussy. Feel me all over," The Woman said.

Maria explored her slowly. She had resisted The Woman's advances for days, not wanting any part of girl-on-girl sex. Now, all of her fears melted away as soon as she touched The Woman's cunt.

Her soft, beautiful cunt.

Her sexy cunt.

The Woman let Maria feel her for several minutes and nearly came when she slid two fingers inside her. There was doubt now. Maria wanted her as much as she wanted Maria.

Afraid of coming too soon, The Woman moved away and told Maria to stand. She knelt before her.

"What beautiful legs you have," The Woman said as she caressed them over and over.

Her touches made Maria's heart pound harder. It pounded harder still when The Woman undid Maria's shorts and tugged them—along with her panties—to the floor.

The Woman sat back on her haunches and stared. Maria's cunt was magnificent. It was neatly furred, with large flowery labia and an obviously erect clit.

"Oh yes," Maria gasped as The Woman touched her.

Seconds later, they were on the bed, locked in a hot embrace as they fingered each other to their first juicy come of the afternoon.

The Woman took control after that. She happily initiated Maria into the world of lesbian sex. Maria jumped in willingly. They ate each other. They rubbed each other's cunts together until they came. Then The Woman introduced Maria to her favorite vibrator.

They came again and again.

Maria came more times than she could count. Time and again, she shoved her tongue deep into The Woman's quivering snatch or fucked her with the vibrator. And The Woman did the same to Maria. They kept at it until both women were too tired to move. They fell asleep in each other's arms for a good two hours.

When Maria woke, she looked at the beautiful woman lying next to her and smiled. The Woman smiled back.

"That was great," Maria said. "Where did you learn to do that?"

"Mostly from fooling around with my sisters when we got horny. I'm glad you enjoyed it," The Woman answered.

"I really did. This was wonderful," Maria gushed. "I never knew women could do this."

"Is it wonderful enough to try it again?" The Woman asked.

"What do you think?" Maria replied as she bent over and pressed her lips to The Woman's.

It was time for another round.

The Woman let Maria take control. Maria fondled her breasts then kissed and licked each nipple until it tingled with excitement. As Maria played with her tits, The Woman eased two fingers into her oh-so wet cunt. Maria sighed and fell back onto the bed, pulling The Woman with her. As their lips touched, Maria's fingers found their way into The Woman's moist slit and the two lovers fingered each other to another good come.

Maria lay on her back gasping, trying to catch her breath. Maria didn't miss a beat. She straddled The Woman's face then leaned over and began tonguing her

.cunt. The Woman cried out, then grabbed Maria's gorgeous ass and pulled her pussy down on her eager tongue until they came a second and third time.

"I got a new toy," The Woman said.

She walked to the dresser, opened a drawer and produced a large double-headed latex cock. It was at least two feet long with a double set of "balls" in the center.

Maria watched with anticipation as The Woman slid one end up into her hot juicy cunt and climbed onto the bed. Maria spread her long, sexy legs, then grabbed a pillow and stuck it under her behind to elevate her pelvis.

"This lets me take it deeper," she explained.

Maria closed her eyes and moaned as The Woman slid the dildo into her cunt. It was a nice, easy fuck. A long, slow, deep fuck that had Maria begging for more and more. The Woman had fucked her twice so far. Until then, she never knew women actually fucked other women. It seemed weird then. Now, it seemed like the most natural thing on Earth.

The Woman savored every stroke. Each inward thrust also drove her into her cunt deeper so that it was really a mutual fuck. She'd fucked The Woman before. She'd been fucked by The Woman many times, too. As much as she loved doing it with The Woman, she wanted this with Maria more. She was, at last, living out one of her fantasies and she wanted to make it a memorable time for both her and Maria.

Maria suddenly spasmed and stretched her legs out to the sides. She dug her nails into The Woman hips and began fucking her back as hard as she could. By some miracle of timing, they both orgasmed at the exact same moment.

And it was a long, powerful and wonderful orgasm. They lay next to each other for a long time, kissing, groping and talking.

An hour later, Maria left the shop. The kidnappers followed her for one block. As soon as they saw the street was empty, they opened the doors and rushed at Maria.

Maria didn't run as they expected. Instead, she hauled off and punched the first man square in the nose. He screamed and fell to his knees.

"She broke my nose!" he wailed as he clutched his bleeding nostrils.

The second man fared little better as Maria's boot found his groin. She was about to slug the third man when he pulled a pistol out of his pocket and aimed it at her.

Maria threw up her hands.

"You must come with us, Mrs. Wilder," the gunman said. "Our car awaits."

Maria smiled as the man with the broken nose helped the man with the shattered testicles to his feet.

"We must go now," the gunman said as he pointed to the car.

Maria shrugged and walked toward it. The gunman was puzzled by her calm demeanor as he opened the back door. Maria slid in and her kidnapper sat next to her.

The man with the broken nose got behind the wheel while the other man slowly slid in next to him. Maria laughed.

"I must say that you're taking this quite calmly, Mrs. Wilder. You don't seem very worried," the gunman said.

"Oh, I'm worried all right—*for you*," Maria said. She sat quietly for the rest of the trip.

CHAPTER 14

▼

Maria found herself seated before a rather nasty-looking man. On either side of him stood two armed men. Behind him stood the faithful Hasmir.

"I am Mahomet Anazhur, Mrs. Wilder. I bid you welcome to my humble abode," Anazhur said with an evil smile.

"What do you want with me?" she asked calmly.

"You will be my guest for the next few days until I can arrange a trade with your husband," Anazhur replied.

"Oh. I get it. You want the Box. You kidnapped me in order to trade me for it," Maria said. Her calm demeanor did not go unnoticed by her "hosts".

"Exactly," Anazhur said.

"You don't know my husband. He'll never go for it," Maria said.

"If he does not, then things will go badly for you, Mrs. Wilder. Very badly," Anazhur promised.

Maria simply smiled.

"You find that amusing?" he asked.

"Not half as amusing as what will happen to you and your men if anything happens to me," Maria replied.

"That sounds like a threat," Anazhur said testily.

"No threat. A *fact*. You'll be dead within an hour if anything happens to me. *All of you*," she said as she made eye contact with him.

That's when Anazhur felt it. A sudden, almost violent spinning sensation as if he were free falling through some sort of spiral. When it stopped, he found himself standing in front of the great temple of Amun Ra at Karnak, surrounded by bald-headed priests in white kilts.

Startled, he shook his head to clear the vision from his mind.

"Show Mrs. Wilder to our guest room—and watch her," he said to the guards. When they left, Anazhur massaged his temples.

"You have a headache?" asked Hasmir.

"Yes. A big one. It came on suddenly," Anazhur replied. "What do you think, Hasmir?"

"This was a very bad mistake, Mahomet. This will go very badly for us. You should never have kidnapped her," Hasmir said.

"The deed is done. Now we will wait ten hours then call Dr. Wilder at the hotel," Anazhur said.

Hasmir nodded and went outside to smoke. The street was crowded with cars, pushcarts and pedestrians. It was rush hour. People were returning home from work.

Right now, Wilder was arriving at the dig site. He wouldn't be back at the hotel until six the next morning. He wondered what Wilder would say when he got Anazhur's call. He wondered more about the actions he'd take to get his wife back.

Hasmir had a bad feeling about it all. The vengeance of Allah, he thought, would pale in comparison with the vengeance of Art Wilder.

"This is the end for us," he thought.

When Art got back to the hotel that morning, he was surprised to see that Maria was still gone. He figured she was out shopping again, so he went down to the bar to have a few beers. When he returned to the room two hours later, Maria still hadn't returned.

He showered then sat down to watch the morning news reports on TV. An hour later, the phone rang. He reached over and picked it up.

"Dr. Wilder?" said a rough voice on the other end.

"Yes. Who's this?" Art replied.

"My name is Mahomet Ali Anazhur. My associates and I have something that is very valuable to you," came the reply.

"And just what might that be?" asked Art.

"I believe her name is Maria Wilder. She is your wife, no?" said Anazhur.

"She is my wife yes. Am I to assume that you have kidnapped her for some reason?" Wilder asked.

Anazhur noted the dead calm in Wilder's voice. It made him feel uneasy somehow.

"Kidnapped is an ugly word. Let's just say that she is my *guest*," he said.

"And just why is she your guest?" asked Wilder as a plan began to take form in his mind.

"You have something I want—the Box of Thoth," said Anazhur.

"What in Hell do you want with *that*? I mean, it's not like you'll be able to fence it or anything," asked Wilder.

"That is my business. What happens to you wife is *your* affair," Anazhur answered rather curtly.

"I'm listening," Art said.

"I propose and exchange—your wife for the Box," Anazhur suggested.

"I dunno about that. I can always get another wife but that Box is one of a kind. What if I don't feel like trading?" Art asked.

"Then we will kill her," Anazhur answered.

"If you do that, I'll track you down and make you wish that you were dead before I'm finished with you. If you know anything at all about me, then you know this is no idle threat," Wilder threatened.

"You are in no position to threaten me, Dr. Wilder. Don't you know who you are talking to?" Anazhur almost shouted.

Wilder laughed. He'd made him lose his cool. And it was childishly easy.

"No. And I don't give a rat's ass who you are either. Now stop acting like you're somebody important and talk to me," Wilder pushed.

Anazhur emitted a string of curses. Wilder laughed.

"Temper, temper," he chided.

"Look, Dr. Wilder. I have your wife. You have the Box. I want the Box. You want your wife. So let's trade. Okay?" Anazhur said in frustration.

"How can I be sure that you really have her? You don't sound like you're bright enough to kidnap a goldfish much less a live adult woman," Wilder said.

"I will let you speak with her—but only for a moment," Anazhur said as he handed the phone to Maria who was seated next to him.

"Hi, honey," she said calmly.

"Hi, Maria. You alright?" Art asked.

"I'm fine. They are treating me okay so far," Maria said. "I left some rolls of film in the dresser drawer just in case you need them at the dig."

"Don't worry. They'll be there when you get back. See you soon, kid," said Art.

Maria handed the phone back to Anazhur and smiled at him. He seemed stunned by serenity. He wondered if anything could rattle the Wilders. His henchmen noticed her demeanor as well and began to wonder just what on earth their boss had gotten them into.

"Satisfied?" Anazhur asked.

"Yes. That's her, alright. Now, let's talk turkey," Art replied. "Where and when do we make the swap?"

"Do you have an e-mail address?" Anazhur asked.

Wilder gave him the address for the museum's computer and told him he could contact him there. Anazhur promised to contact him in three days with further instructions, then hung up.

Wilder smiled.

He took an address book out of his pocket, looked up a few phone numbers, then started dialing. After he made his initial calls, he dialed the private number of the Egyptian Secret Police. A voice on the other end told him that he would forward his request to the president of Egypt immediately, then hung up.

Ten minutes later, the Chief of Internal Security called him back.

"The President wishes me to inform you that you have carte blanche in this matter. I will contact the local police authorities and tell them to extend their fullest cooperation to you and your associates. They are not to interfere," he said.

Wilder thanked him, then left the hotel and headed for the dig. Once there, he explained everything to Hawatt and the others.

Anazhur looked at Maria with wonder. She saw the puzzled look on his face and smiled. For Anazhur, it was an unsettling kind of smile, as if she knew something he didn't. Something that might bite him in the ass.

"You and your husband are strange people, Mrs. Wilder. Neither of you appear to be upset over your predicament. It's as if you've been through something like this before," Anazhur said.

"We have. That's why I'm not very concerned about this," she replied smugly.

"I see. What happened to your other kidnappers?" Anazhur asked.

Maria simply smiled. Anazhur's aide who was standing behind him, swallowed hard. Anazhur frowned.

"Take Mrs. Wilder into our guest room and see that she is made comfortable," he said.

As two of his henchmen led Maria away, he turned to aide.

"Strange people these Americans," he remarked.

Anazhur was completely unaware of Maria's experiences in Guatemala and her daring rescue by Art. Her behavior bothered him. Most women would be terrified in her situation. Yet Maria Wilder seemed unusually calm and collected, like she knew what was going to happen.

Her husband was even more of a puzzle. When Anazhur told him he had Maria, Art seemed strangely unrattled. He even joked about it.

Anazhur looked at his aide.

"Watch her carefully," he ordered.

At sunrise, Art and Nasi climbed into the Land Rover. Instead of taking the road into Cairo, Wilder steered the vehicle toward the International Airport.

"The airport? Why are we going there?" asked Nasi.

"We have a few flights to meet," Wilder answered with a wry smile.

"Flights? As in more than one?" Nasi asked.

"Yes. I have friends coming in from several countries. They should all arrive before ten a.m.," Wilder said.

"Does this have anything to do with the kidnappers?" Nasi asked.

"This has *everything* to do with the kidnappers," Wilder said. "I'm going to teach those bastards a lesson they'll never forget!"

Anazhur's men watched as Wilder picked up the new arrivals and drove them to the museum. When they reported this to their boss, he simply assured them the new arrivals were just more archaeologists who have come to assist Wilder with the dig. He even told his men to ignore the new arrivals.

But the new arrivals were a rough-looking bunch. They weren't archaeologists. Their expertise lied in *other* areas. These were men who operated just outside the scope of international law, yet were immune from prosecution due to their unusually high connections.

These same men were now in Nasi's office at the museum going over with Art the reason he had summoned them to Egypt.

Wilder sat back in his chair and looked at the faces of his team. They were a strange bunch and they hailed from all over the world.

Hawatt studied them, too. The men looked seasoned. Even dangerous. He decided that these were men that shouldn't be crossed—especially if one wanted to stay alive. He wondered just where and when Wilder had met them and why they dropped whatever they were doing to hurry to Cairo the moment he called.

Wilder had introduced them as his "A Team" and by nationalities rather than their names. Hawatt thought that was a bit strange but decided it would be best not to get too nosy.

The Swede was a tall, lean blond haired man about forty years old. Wilder said that he was a genius when it came to explosives.

The German was shorter and more muscular. His hair was white and he looked to be about sixty or so. He was the team's electronics wizard.

The Frenchman was thin and mustachioed. He wore a beret and smoked ciga-
rettes. Wilder said he could copy anything so precisely that not even experts
could tell his from the originals. A master forger.

The Jap was a trained ninja and master tracker. He could get in and out of
anything without being seen. To Hawatt, the Jap looked to be the most dangerous.

The Jew was a computer whiz. He could track any e-mail back to its source in
minutes, even after the computer on the other end was shut down.

The Spaniard was a veteran of the infamous Tercio, the Spanish Legion. He
did the "dirty work" as needed.

"That's what I'm faced with, gentlemen," said Wilder as he concluded his
explanation. "Those bastards have my wife and they want the Box in exchange
for her."

"Such childishness," said the German. "What would they do with the Box? It
is not a weapon."

"I'm pretty sure that he can't read the hieroglyphs either," said Wilder.

"How many people are in his group?" asked the Spaniard.

"According to my source at Interpol, probably no more that a dozen. He's real
small time," Wilder replied.

"When we get through with them, they will have zero members," said the
Frenchman.

"I take it that you want us to give them the usual treatment?" asked the Swede.

"Exactly. Just like Morocco. I plan on giving them the Box, but not the one
they expect." Wilder said.

"First we'll have to track them down. When he e-mails you again, I'll be ready.
I've brought my own special software along," the Jew said with a smile.

"I'll leave that in your capable hands," said Wilder. "You're the expert."

"Where is the Box? I'll need to make a copy of it—warts and all," said the
Frenchman. "When I get finished, even Imhotep himself won't be able to tell
them apart. Once I'm finished with the copy, the Swede and the German can do
their thing."

"How big a bomb do you want?" asked the Swede.

"Big enough to take out the entire group—but don't overdo it. We don't want
to take out any more of the city than we have to," Wilder replied.

"Don't worry. It will have a small blast radius—but you had better alert the
local police to evacuate everyone within a block of the place—just in case," the
Swede said with a smile.

"Blast radius?" asked Hawatt.

"Uh-huh. I plan on giving them something they'll get a real bang out of," said Wilder. "Like I said, I don't deal with terrorists and kidnappers—except on *my* terms."

He stood up and leaned on the desk with both hands.

"Okay men. You know the situation and you all know exactly what to do. Once we locate the group, I want the Jap and the Spaniard to check the place out to make sure that Maria's still alive. Then we'll proceed from there," he said.

The Swede got up and opened his briefcase. He took out a piece of paper and handed it to Hawatt. Who looked at it with a good deal of puzzlement.

"Just a list of the things we'll need. Do you think you can get them?" he asked.

"I believe so," Hawatt replied.

"Gut. We'll need this stuff by tomorrow morning. Here's $100,000. You may have to bribe a few people to get some of the items," the Swede said as he handed Hawatt an envelope.

CHAPTER 15

▼

Anazhur looked over at the two guards standing in front of the one-way mirror outside the guest room. He walked over and smiled at them.

"What are you doing out here? Where is Mrs. Wilder?" he asked.

"She's inside. She asked us to leave so she could have a few minutes of privacy," said the first guard.

"Is she sleeping?" Anazhur asked.

"Not exactly," said the guard.

"Then what is she doing?" asked Anazhur.

"Come and see for yourself," the guard said.

What Anazhur saw made him smile. Maria was apparently unaware that they could watch her through the mirror in her room.

They watched as she unbuttoned her shorts. She let them fall a few inches to reveal the top of her panties as she lay down the bed. She then put her fingers to her lips and licked them until they were quite moist, then eased her hand down into her panties. At the same time, she closed her eyes and opened her legs.

"She's masturbating!" Anazhur whispered.

They watched as the material of her shorts moved seductively, barely masking Maria's hand movements. A few moments later, she undid her blouse then reached inside with her free hand to, play with her nipples.

She soon began to writhe on the bed. Her breathing grew heavy and they could see her legs tremble ever few seconds as she raked her swollen clit with her fingers.

Feeling restricted by her clothing, Maria stopped long enough to pull off her shorts and panties. She then lay back down and bent her knees as she reinserted her fingers into her swollen, wet cunt.

By now her watchers all had erections. They stood there in awe as the gorgeous Latina slowly brought herself to a thundering climax. When it was over, Maria laid still with her legs open wide. This gave her captors an excellent view of her beautiful brown muff.

"I'd like to fuck her," said one guard.

"Me, too," agreed the other. "Maybe we should go in and rape her."

"There will be no raping of Mrs. Wilder. I gave my word to her husband that she would be safe and unmolested. If any one of you touches her, I will personally shoot you. Make sure you tell the others," Anazhur ordered.

"I will," said the guard.

Just then, Maria stirred and got their attention again. She sat up and stretched. As she did, her knees parted again. She closed them, eased off the bed and retrieved her clothing.

"I don't know what came over me. I just *had* to do that," she thought.

Then she looked up at the mirror and wondered if they were watching her. As if to tease them further, she bent all the way over with her behind to mirror, then tugged her panties up halfway before turning and rubbing her cunt. Then she pulled her panties all the way up and donned her shorts.

The next evening Wilder, Hawatt and the rest of the crew returned to the dig site at the Sphinx. As Wilder was guiding his "A Team" through the site, a black and white car bearing the gold shield of the National Police Force drove up. The team stopped what they were doing and watched as Kallid Al-Rashid, the head of the NPF, emerged from the vehicle and approached the site.

Wilder exited the tomb and walked out to greet Rashid. The two men shook hands like they were old friends.

Hawatt and Kuyder soon joined them. Wilder introduced them to Rashid who also shook their hands.

"I have received a phone call from the President himself," explained Rashid. "He has instructed me to leave this matter entirely in your hands, Dr. Wilder. I am to give you any and all assistance you require but I am not, under any circumstances, to interfere with anything you do. You have complete control—and total immunity from any legal prosecution."

Wilder nodded.

Hawatt was stunned. The NPF chief was known as a demanding, take-charge, no-nonsense type of man who always insisted on having things his way. Yet here he was, willing to take orders from Wilder—but only because the President ordered him to do so.

"How does he do it? Who does he know?" Hawatt wondered as Wilder and Rashid conversed en route to the tomb.

Inside were the men Wilder referred to as his "A Team". They were seated on the floor when he entered with Rashid and Hawatt. They rose and shook hands with the NPF chief as Wilder made the introductions. Hawatt noticed that Rashid seemed to recognize a couple of the men, if not by name then by reputation.

This, too, surprised Hawatt.

"Just how did he know them? From where?" he wondered.

After the introductions, Rashid smiled at Wilder. It was a knowing smile.

"Well, Dr. Wilder. I see that you have this matter well in hand. I will pass any information we have on this group to you as soon as I return to headquarters. If you need the NPF for anything at all, please call me at my private number," he said.

Wilder escorted Rashid back to the vehicle. The chief climbed in then bade him farewell. As the vehicle vanished in a cloud of sand and dust, Wilder returned to the dig site.

"You never cease to amaze me, Art," said Hawatt. "Whenever you need to have something done, you just make a few phone calls. Just who do you know in such high places?"

"Lots of people. The type of people that can make things happen real fast," Wilder replied as they went back into the tomb.

Once again, Maria felt nervous and edgy. When she felt this way, she just *had* to relieve the tensions. By now, she figured out the guards must be watching her through the trick mirror, but she didn't care.

As if in a trance, she fell back on the bed with her legs parted and gently massaged the breasts. When her horniness reached an almost fevered peak, she undid her shorts, opened them, and eased her hand down into her panties.

"She's doing it again," said Habib. "She's playing with her pussy!"

"Let me see," said the other guard. "By Allah! That is so fucking sexy!"

They watched in silence as Maria, now oblivious to everything but what she was doing, fingered herself faster and faster.

By now, she was panting. She shoved her finger into her cunt all the way to the knuckle and moved it over her g-spot. That caused her hips to buck up and down a few times. As they did, her shorts and panties slid downward.

She threw her legs open wider, then realized that the clothing restricted her. She hurriedly removed her shorts and panties and tossed them onto the floor. Then she fell back and bent her knees. As she did, she parted her thighs as far as she could and once more eased two fingers into her swollen, wet cunt.

The two guards watched in admiration as Maria fingered herself to a good, hard orgasm. When she came, the humped her fingers wildly several times, then fell limply on the bed and took deep breaths until it subsided.

"I don't care what the boss said. I'm going to fuck her," said Habib.

"Wait for me! I want some American pussy, too," said his companion.

As Maria lay on the bed with her eyes closed, the two men entered the room. They stopped for a while to admire her nakedness, then decided to do the deed. As one of the guards attempted to grab her, Maria lashed out with her foot and kicked him in the groin as hard as she could. The startled man's eyes crossed. He emitted a high-pitched yelp and fell to his knees gasping for air. Maria stood over him and spat in his face.

"You pathetic hyena!" she snarled.

Her words caught the attention of the other three. They stared at her with open mouths as if uncertain of what she'd said. Maria saw the expressions on their faces and felt contemptuous of them.

"What the fuck are you staring at, dogs?" she demanded.

That's when everything went crazy.

Incredibly crazy.

All of sudden, Maria found herself standing in the middle of vast, ornately furnished, palatial room like the ones she'd seen in paintings and movies about ancient Egypt. The walls were decorated with colorful paintings and hieroglyphs adorned the lotus-topped columns that supported an atrium-like roof. Behind her stood a large golden throne and she realized she was dressed exactly like she saw herself in the shrine.

Her guards saw it, too. They were staring in awe as they looked around in bewilderment. That's when Maria realized they were dressed like Egyptian courtiers.

The men looked at her and immediate fell prostrate at her feet.

"What's wrong with you? What's happening?" she demanded.

Not one man dared raise his head or speak. She walked over and stood between them.

"Get up!" she ordered.

Immediately, the guards jumped to attention and looked straight ahead. She saw they were frightened—and then some.

"No," she said. "It isn't fear. It's awe. Why do you not look at me when I speak to you?"

"It is forbidden to look directly upon the face of our queen," one man blurted out.

"Queen?" she asked.

Then she realized something else. She wasn't conversing in Arabic or modern Egyptian. She was speaking an entirely different language—a language that had been dead nearly 2,000 years.

And she was speaking it as if she'd been using it her entire life. So were her guards. Somehow they'd been projected back in time. Back to ancient Memphis.

"You said I am your queen? Speak. I command you," Maria said to one of them.

"You are the queen of all Egypt and we are your loyal subjects," he said softly.

"Subjects? That means that you'll do whatever I order you to?" she asked.

"Yes my lady," said the guard.

That's when the scene shifted back to the present and they found themselves once more in the small back room of the concrete house.

That's when Maria also realized that she was still half naked. She hurriedly retrieved her clothes and slipped them back on. This done, she returned to her guards who were again prostrated before her.

But the vision had already passed. The men rose slowly from the floor and eventually forced themselves to raise their eyes to Maria. They stared at each other for some time as they shook their heads to clear them. There was no doubting that it had happened. There was also no doubting the reverential awe the guards now viewed Maria with. They no longer snarled or looked menacing.

Instead, they were polite and respectful. Whatever happened, they all shared it. They all felt it. They all lived it.

And from then on, Maria and her guards conversed in the ancient tongue of the pharaohs whenever no one else was around.

When they addressed her, it was always as "my Queen" or "my Lady". It was as if they were truly her subjects.

CHAPTER 16

▼

The Jew had made several modifications on the museum's computer. All were power upgrades so that it could handle the special spyware he'd loaded onto the hard drive. The spyware was designed to trace e-mails back to their point of origin and come up with a printout of the address.

The e-mail from Anazhur showed up at two p.m.. As soon as the spyware detected it, it went into its tracking mode. Just as Wilder expected, Anazhur used a false, generic numbering system as the return address.

The Jew pressed a few keys and sat back. Seconds later, a blue screen appeared with the words "SOURCE LOCATED".

The Jew downloaded it into a file and smiled.

"I have it," he said proudly as he opened the file to display the return address.

"How did you do that?" asked Hawatt as he looked over his shoulder.

"That's easy. I used the same tracking software that was designed for Interpol and the CIA. Only mine is much faster and more accurate," the Jew replied as he printed a hard copy of the e-mail and address.

He handed it to Wilder, who showed it to the Spaniard and the Jap. They nodded.

"Scout the place out. Make sure where the doors and windows are, how many men he has and which room Maria is in—just in case," Wilder said.

He read the e-mail.

"He wants to make the swap in three days. He said he'll e-mail the location to me then," Wilder said.

"Too bad he doesn't know we already have his address," said the Jew.

Wilder laughed. He looked at the Swede and the Frenchman who were standing nearby.

"Is that enough time for you to copy the Box?" he asked.

"More than enough. I'm almost finished with it now. I just have to include the special compartment for the explosives," the Frenchman replied.

"Before I make my explosives and the trigger device, I need to know the size of the house they are in and the layout of the area. I don't want to make something too strong or we'll level the whole neighborhood," said the Swede.

"You'll have all the information you need by morning," the Jap assured him as he and the Spaniard left the office.

The next afternoon, the Swede and the Frenchman emerged from the back office. Each of them was carrying a Box which they placed on the desk in front of Wilder and Hawatt.

"What do you think?" asked the Frenchman.

Both Wilder and Hawatt stared at the boxes for some time, then shrugged.

"I can't tell the difference," said Wilder. "Which one is it?"

"The one on the right is the copy," said the Swede as the rest of the team gathered around the desk.

"Incredible. Not even an expert could tell them apart," said the German. "How did you do it so quickly?"

"Trade secret," said the Frenchman smugly.

"What about the contents?" asked Wilder.

"There is ten pounds of high explosive hidden in a compartment that makes up half the box. It will go off ten minutes after you press the hieroglyph on the side of the box. That starts the timer," explained the Swede.

"What about accidents?" asked Wilder.

"It will not be activated until the glyph is pressed. Once it is activated, there is no way to turn it off," said the Swede.

"And the blast radius?" asked the Spaniard.

"About five hundred feet. That should take out most of the block," said the Swede.

"Most of the block? But there are other people living in those houses. *Innocent people*," Hawatt said.

"Don't worry, Nasi. I've already made arrangements with Rashid to have them quietly evacuated before I go to make the exchange. He's sent undercover officers to each house to tell the people to leave early in the morning, like they're heading to work or something. This way, the bad boys won't know what's going on,"

Wilder assured him. "By the time the bomb detonates, there won't be anyone else on the block but the kidnappers."

"It appears that you have thought of everything," Hawatt said.

"I tried to. It will all go to pot if they decide not hand Maria over to me once I give them the box," Wilder said.

"Then what?" asked Hawatt.

"That's where me and the Jap come in," said the Spaniard. "We'll be out back waiting. If Art doesn't come out of there within ten minutes, we'll go in and do it the hard way. With any luck, we'll be able to get Maria out before the fighting starts. Either way, there will be one less terrorist cell to worry about."

Hawatt looked at Wilder.

"You seem so calm. I wish I had your nerves," he said.

Wilder chuckled.

"I always try to put a good face on for such matters, Nasi. Inside, I'm a bundle of nerves," he said.

He looked over at the Jew.

"E-mail that bastard and make arrangements for the exchange. The sooner we get this done, the better for all of us," he said.

CHAPTER 17

▼

That night, Maria was awakened by the creaking of the door on her "cell". She looked up to see two shadowy figures. The nearest placed a finger on his lips.

"My Queen," he said. "It is I, Habib. Jahir is with me. We have come to rescue you."

Maria rose from the bed and grabbed her shoulder bag while Jahir listened at the door. He signaled that all was quiet, then slowly opened it and peered into the next room.

Maria looked at her rescuers. Apparently their trip back in time with her had convinced them that she really was an ancient queen returned to life and that they were her subjects and meant to serve her. And this meant freeing her from captivity. After all, no *real* Egyptian would willfully assist in the kidnapping of his queen. That would surely bring the wrath of the gods down upon him.

Jahir looked back at them and nodded. They quietly walked through the middle room to the next door. Finding it empty, they hurried to the front door of the house. Habib opened it and found himself staring at the angry faces of Anazhur, Hasmir and three men armed with rifles.

"Taking our prisoner for a walk, Habib?" Anazhur asked as he backhanded him across the face.

Habib recoiled, then swung back. As his fist connected with Anazhur's jaw, he swore to protect his queen with his life. Maria looked surprised. Habib's vow was in the old language and she understood it perfectly.

Before Habib could draw his pistol, the three riflemen fired into his face at point-blank range. As the air in the room filled with blood, bits of flesh and shattered bone, Habib hit the floor and rolled onto his face.

Jahir drew his pistol and fired. His shot hit the lead rifleman in the hip and spun him violently around before sending him to the floor. His second shot went wild. Then he, too, was brought down in a hail of bullets.

Maria glared at Anazhur and cursed him in the ancient tongue. Her words caused one of the riflemen to cast down his weapon and fall prostrate at her feet. Disgusted, Anazhur kicked him in the ribs—hard. The man remained in the same position and appeared to be praying.

"Get up, dog! Why do you bow before this infidel?" he demanded.

"She speaks the ancient words! She is our queen returned to lead us once more," the man replied without looking up.

Anazhur sneered.

"Fool! Of course she speaks the ancient tongue. She's a trained Egyptologist and skilled in the use of the language. She is just trying to trick you!" he said harshly.

Still the man refused to move. Anazhur turned to the others.

"Hasmir—take Mrs. Wilder back into our guest suite," he said. Then to the other rifleman, "Drag this fool outside and get his mind straight. Tell the others to come in and take these traitors to the city dump."

He then turned to Maria. The way she scowled at him rattled him somewhat. He recovered and sneered at her.

"We will have no more of your tricks, Mrs. Wilder. My men, as you have correctly guessed, are very superstitious. I don't want them subverted by you," he said.

Then Maria smiled. It was even more unnerving to Anazhur than her scowl had been. It made his blood run cold.

Maria replied in the ancient language.

"I do not play tricks, peasant trash," she snapped back. "Neither does my husband—as you will soon find out."

"Take her away," Anazhur said.

Hasmir led her into the bedroom and quietly advised her to leave the rest of the men alone. Then he lowered his voice so that only she could hear.

"You know the language of the ancient priests. How is this possible?" he asked.

"I don't know," Maria replied. "It just came naturally to me."

Hasmir nodded.

"I also know the language. It has been in my family for thousands of years. My ancestors served in the temples at Luxor for many generations. Yet, even I cannot speak it as easily as you," he said.

He stood back and looked at her. Then he felt it, too. Suddenly, there he was, standing before a beautiful queen seated atop the sacred throne of Egypt. The vision was very brief—and very vivid.

Hasmir began to sweat visibly.

"I think I understand now, my Lady," he said with a gentle bow of his head. "Either that or I am going mad."

He walked out and found Anazhur seated at his desk.

"What do you think?" Anazhur asked.

"She's good. Almost too good. Not even Dr. Hawatt can speak the old tongue as easily as she can," Hasmir said as he sat down.

"It's just a trick. Part of her training. They teach that in school," Anazhur said.

"Perhaps. But did you know that Mrs. Wilder has no formal training in Egyptology? She didn't start learning to read hieroglyphs until she arrived in Egypt," Hasmir pointed out. "Now, she speaks the old language as easily as if she was born to speak it. Like it is her *native tongue.*"

"It's a trick, I tell you," Anazhur repeated. He sounded like he was trying to convince himself of that.

Hasmir shrugged.

"Keep your eyes open. I expect our little gunplay to attract the attention of the police," Anazhur said. "I'm certain the shots have been reported by now."

And they had.

Yet surprisingly, not a single officer bothered to investigate. This made Anazhur even edgier and he began wondering just what was really going on.

Rashid phoned Wilder as soon as the shots were reported and assured him that Maria was still quite safe. In fact, his undercover men watching the house said they saw Anazhur's men carrying two of their own out the back door.

"They were quite dead," he said. "They simply stuffed them into the trunk of a car and drove away. I imagine they plan to dispose of them in the city dump."

Wilder laughed as he hung up the phone. The Spaniard who was seated nearby, asked him what was up. When Wilder told him, he laughed too.

"It seems like your wife has those fools fighting amongst themselves, amigo," he said. "There might not be any of them left to make the trade with."

Wilder chuckled.

"Maria's pretty resourceful under duress," he said. "Those idiots have no idea what they've gotten themselves into."

"They will know for sure after they receive the Swede's box," the Spaniard said.

Hawatt looked at him as he made an explosion sound with his mouth and moved his hands apart violently. Then he smiled at Hawatt.

"You're really sending him a bomb?" Hawatt asked.

"Let's just say that we'll be celebrating Independence Day a few months early this year," Wilder replied.

"What if they don't hand Maria over to you after you make the trade?" Hawatt asked.

"That's where me and the Jap come in. By the time we are through with them, they'll wish that they had taken the bomb," said the Spaniard.

"They're very thorough. I don't expect them to leave any survivors," Wilder added.

"I can't believe how *ruthless* you can be, Art," said Hawatt.

"Neither did the goons you sent to loot the temple in Guatemala. Remember what happened to *them?*" Wilder said.

He did indeed. In an attempt to discredit Wilder, Hawatt had hired a few soldiers of fortune. He sent them to the lost city that Wilder had discovered and told them to steal anything that might show a connection to Egypt.

These men were tough and experienced. They expected the job to be a cake walk. Instead, they wound up with their shrunken heads on poles outside the gates of the city.

They neglected to find out about Wilder's headhunter guards until it was too late. These headhunters were members of the tribe that had kidnapped Maria in order to sacrifice her. Wilder's explosive rescue of her left the tribe shaken to the core. Then the local policia arrived and rounded them up. They would have all gone to prison if not for Wilder's intervention. He talked the police into letting them go. In exchange, they vowed to protect the lost city from would-be looters.

And proud, fierce protectors they were. Hawatt's goons never knew what hit them.

As Hawatt thought back to the incident he had to laugh. Wilder smiled at him then used a quote from one of his favorite movies.

"They do not know who they are fucking with."

Hawatt nodded. He knew that the kidnappers were about to find out exactly that.

CHAPTER 18

▼

Maria lay on her back, twitching and mumbling as she dreamed of ancient temples and places and sailing gently down the Nile on a beautiful golden barge. Where ever she went, people prostrated themselves before her. Servants followed and provided for her every wish. Even priests treated with awe and respect.

In her dreams, she spoke the ancient language of the pharaohs. She spoke them out loud.

Her words unnerved her guards so much that they refused to stay close to her.

Hasmir paced the floor of the next room with a worried on look on his face. Anazhur sat and watched him for a while.

"What's wrong? Losing your nerve?" he asked.

"Damn right I am," Hasmir replied. "Don't you hear her? She even dreams in Egyptian. It's giving me the creeps."

"What have you learned about her would-be rescuers?" Anazhur asked.

"That's even creepier. They were about to rape her when she spoke to them. They both swore to the other men that they were suddenly transported to an ancient palace where Maria stood before them as a queen. It convinced them that she was divine and that it was their duty as Egyptians to protect her," Hasmir replied.

"That's insane!" snapped Anazhur.

"Is it? Those men were willing and ready to die for her. I am certain they would not have laid their lives down for you or this bullshit cause of yours," Hasmir shot back.

"What about Jusef? How is he?" Anazhur asked of the rifleman who fell at Maria's feet.

"I don't know," Hasmir replied.

"Explain," Anazhur demanded.

"He's gone! He took off last night. So did two other men. Apparently, they've decided not to have anything to do with this," Hasmir said. "They're afraid to bring the wrath of the gods down on themselves."

"Bah! There is only *one* god," Anazhur scoffed.

Hasmir leaned close.

"Are you *certain* of that? Allah is alien to this land. He is an interloper here. There are things here that are far older and wiser than Allah. Think about it, Mahomet. The men who guarded her were devout Muslims. After one night with Maria Wilder, they cast aside their beliefs and returned to the gods of our ancestors," he said.

"How many have we left?" Anazhur asked.

"Six—counting yourself," Hasmir replied. "She has two other men scared now. They may run off before too long."

"What about you, Hasmir? Why are you still part of my 'bullshit cause'? Why don't you leave, too?" Anazhur asked.

"Who says that I won't? Look, Mahomet. I advised you to steer clear of the Wilders. I warned you that they were too much for us to handle. Now do you see what I meant? Those people are bad news as the Americans say," Hasmir replied.

"You need rest. Check the guards, then get some sleep. It's been a strange day," Anazhur said.

Hasmir went over to the guards and assured them that it would all be over soon. He then stepped outside and lit a cigarette. As he looked up at the bright, full moon, he saw the face of it change into the unmistakable symbol of the Eye of Horus.

Horus was the hawk-headed god. He served Egypt as both protector and avenger.

To Hasmir, the omen was as clear as a bell. He tossed away the cigarette, put his hands in his pockets and walked away from the house.

He didn't get very far. In fact, he walked right into the arms of a half-dozen waiting policemen just three streets from the house. When they arrested him, Hasmir made no attempt to fight them off or escape.

"In fact, he almost seemed *relieved*," Rashid said to Wilder. "Just what in Hell is Maria doing to those men?"

"I have no idea. Looks like they're numbers have been cut in half," Wilder replied.

"Do you still plan to go ahead with this?" Rashid asked.

"Definitely," Wilder said.

"I suppose that you know what you're doing then," Rashid said.

"Definitely," Wilder assured him.

When Anazhur discovered that his right-hand man had deserted him, he went ballistic. He swept everything off his desk and swore loudly in Arabic while his men watched.

"I am surrounded by cowards and fools! I will personally shoot the next man who tries to leave. Tell the others. Make sure they understand!" he screamed.

Then he ordered his men not to speak with Maria unless it was absolutely necessary, lest they fall under her spell.

"But she speaks the tongue of the pharaohs! She is the reincarnation of our queen," one of guards insisted.

"She is an archaeologist. She knows the old tongue and can use it to her advantage. It was nothing more than a hoax on her part and you fools fell for it," Anazhur said in disgust. "I advise you not to fall for her tricks again or you'll end up like Habib."

The guards nodded in resignation. There was use telling their leader about the time warp or the fact that they, too, suddenly became fluent in the old language.

Maria was also perplexed. She'd never spoken the old language before and had only learned a few dozen hieroglyphs since her arrival in Egypt. Now she could speak, read and write Egyptian with ease.

That was her third time warp incident. Or were they ancestral memories? If so, why did they include other people? Why did they experience them with her?

The situation reminded her of her experiences in Guatemala. She began to wonder if they were somehow connected.

It was almost noon when three unmarked sedans pulled up to the curb across the street and around the corner from Mahomet Ali Anazhur's hideout. Wilder and Rashid got out of the lead car and leaned against it as they watched the Jap and the Spaniard climb out of the second car. Wilder nodded as they waved to him before running around the other side of the street.

"I'll give them five minutes to get into position. Then I'll go and make the swap," Wilder said.

The rest of the A Team members sat in the third car and waited. When the time was up, Wilder put the ersatz box under his left arm and headed for the hideout.

He walked up to the door and rapped three times. The door opened a few inches and a man wearing a checkered kerchief over the lower part of his face peered out. Once he recognized Wilder, he opened the door and motioned for him to come inside.

He led Wilder through a small front room where three similarly masked men sat sipping coffee and playing chess. One nodded as they walked by him and through beaded curtains into a larger second room. Wilder noted that the house was laid out shotgun style and figured that Maria must be in the last room.

But at that moment he was more concerned with the scarred man seated behind a desk and the two masked guards on either side that were pointing rifles at him.

"Mahomet Ali Anazhur?" Wilder asked.

"Ah, Dr. Wilder! You are very punctual. I see also that you have brought the Box," said his host.

"I said I would. You can tell your men to lower their weapons. I am unarmed," Wilder assured him.

Anazhur smiled and nodded. The guards lowered their weapons and tried to look tough. Wilder thought they looked pathetically comical and suppressed a laugh.

"Give me the Box," said Anazhur as he reached out.

Wilder held up his hand.

"Not so fast. First I want to be sure that you have Maria and she's unharmed," he insisted.

"Of course," said Anazhur. He turned to the man on his right. "Bring Mrs. Wilder out."

As the guard went into the last room, Anazhur looked at Wilder.

"Have you opened it yet?" he asked.

"No. We haven't been able to figure out its elaborate locking mechanism yet. We didn't want to force it open and risk destroying what might be inside," Wilder answered.

"You mean there is no key?" asked Anazhur.

"None that we could find," Wilder replied. "Tell me something—just what in Hell do you want with this box? What use is it to you? After all, it's not a weapon."

"That Dr. Wilder, can only be determined after we've opened the Box. If the legends are true, what's inside will make me a god, not unlike Thoth himself," said Anazhur.

The guard walked in then with Maria trailing behind. Wilder looked her over. She seemed fine.

"Are you okay?" he asked.

"I'm fine. They treated me well enough," Maria assured him.

"Okay then. We have a deal," Wilder said as he presented the Box to Anazhur. Just before he did, he made sure to press the hieroglyph on its side.

Anazhur seized the Box and smiled avariciously.

"It was a pleasure doing business with you, Dr. Wilder. Perhaps we will meet again one day under more pleasant circumstances?" he said with a smile.

"I doubt it," Wilder replied as he took Maria by the hand.

They walked through the beaded curtains and into the front room. As soon as the men saw Maria, they fell prostrate before her as if she were the queen of Egypt or some kind of goddess. Wilder squinted at them quizzically, then looked at Maria.

As they walked through the front door and into the street, he turned to her.

"What was *that* all about?" he asked.

"I'll explain later," Maria replied as they hurried across the street and around the corner where the three cars waited.

As soon as he saw them, Rashid got out of the car and held the door open. Maria slid into the back seat. Art got in next to her.

"I see that all went as planned?" asked Rashid as he climbed behind the wheel.

"As planned," said Wilder. "Where's the rest of the team?"

Rashid pointed to the two men racing around the corner. They watched as the Jap and the Spaniard got into the second car. Maria noticed that they looked a little rough—kind of like the men her husband had associated with in Central America.

"Your team?" she asked.

"I'll explain later," he replied. "Right now, we'd best get out of range."

"Hold tight," shouted Rashid as he stepped on the gas pedal.

"I can't believe that you actually gave the Box. It took you years to find it and now, because of me, you had to give it to those men," Maria lamented.

Wilder put his arm around her shoulders.

"I just gave them exactly what the deserved," he said with a wry smile.

Rashid drove down the side street. After three blocks, he stopped. So did the cars with the A-Team members. Maria looked at her husband quizzically as everyone got out of the cars.

"What's—?" she began.

Wilder held up his right hand and looked at his watch.

"Three…two…one…NOW!" he shouted.

That's when the ground literally shook with the vibrations from a very powerful explosion. As dust and debris rained down over several square blocks, Maria covered her head. That's when she noticed that the strange men that had come with her husband were happily giving each other the "high five" and slapping each other on the back. She looked at her husband. He was grinning from ear to ear.

"Like I said, I gave them *exactly* what they deserved," he said.

"That takes care of that bunch. Your plan worked so well I think we should send boxes to all the terrorist groups," said Rashid.

"Maybe we should," mused Wilder as they got back into the car. "But I'm an archaeologist. I'm not in the business of wiping out terrorist organizations. I don't mess with them if they don't bother me."

"Once word of this gets out, no terrorist groups will ever bother you again. After all, yours was an act of reprisal, not politics. They understand such things. In fact, they will probably respect you more for this," Rashid said. "You think and act as they do."

"When in Egypt…" said Maria.

They all laughed.

"What about the media?" asked Wilder.

"Don't worry about the media, Dr. Wilder. Leave them to me," Rashid assured him.

CHAPTER 19

▼

Art took Maria back to the hotel. She immediately threw her arms around his neck and gave him a long, deep kiss. The she stepped back and looked into his eyes.

"Looks like it's just you and me," Maria said with a smile.

She unbuttoned her shorts and let them fall to the floor. Art watched them slide down her pretty legs, then fixed his gaze on the prize between them. He was already rock hard as he slid to the floor and pressed his lips against her fleecy vagina. As his tongue entered, Maria sighed deeply. Usually, Art licked her pussy just long enough to get her ready for his cock. This time, he tongued her labia and clit until she came.

Maria groaned, then convulsed as her nectar gushed into Art's open mouth. He lapped up every drop, then stood up. Now, Maria knelt. She pulled down his jeans and stared as his throbbing cock. She gave it a few strokes with her hand then twirled her tongue around and over the knob. Art moaned.

Maria was good.

So very good.

She licked him to the balls then back several times before slipping the swollen head into her mouth. Moments later, Art grunted and Maria drank his first load of cum as it jetted down her throat.

"No one does that better than you, Maria. You're the best," Art said.

She smiled, then grabbed hold of his penis and led him upstairs to the bedroom. Seconds later, they were completely nude and locked in a hot embrace. Maria kept hold of his penis and pumped it until he was hard again. She spread her thighs, laid back and guided him into her open vagina.

He slid into her nice and slow. Her vagina felt tight, hot and comfortable as they began to love in their usual style. Both liked it slow, deep and easy.

Maria wrapped her arms and legs around his body and pressed her lips to his. As their tongues merged, the tempo of their union increased. Art used deeper thrusts now. Penetrating strokes that made Maria sigh with pleasure each time he moved inward.

She let her body take control and began driving her hips upward to meet him each and every time, taking his cock deeper and deeper into her hungry vagina. It was a hunger only Art could feed now.

Art moved his arms so Maria's legs draped over them. He leaned forward then, almost pressing her thighs to her chest, and driving his cock into her as hard as he could. Maria gasped and dug her nails into Art's shoulders. This was something new for her. Something exciting.

Art ground his cock into her and she shivered as magical sensations emanated from deep within her vagina and tentacled through her entire body. She was soon speeding uncontrollably toward orgasm.

Art shivered, too. Maria's vagina felt warm, tight and incredibly delicious as it clutched his penis. They humped good and hard now, sweat beading up on their naked bodies.

Maria came first. It was deep, hard come that rocked her to her very soul. She drove her hips up and down on Art's penis and cried out in Spanish as her pussy took complete control of her. She humped Art like she'd never humped before and begged him to come inside her. At the same time, she tightened her vagina muscles to increase the friction—as well as Art's pleasure—as much as she could.

That did it.

Art exploded—no erupted—and kept filling her vagina with what seemed like gallons of thick, hot cum.

Maria rolled him over and straddled his cock. He was still hard. She was still horny. And the day was young.

As she bounced up and down on his penis, Art played with her dark nipples. He was still coming, too, and his cum oozed out of Maria's vagina and covered his balls. Maria kept doing and doing. She seemed insatiable now. She lived only for the feel of Art's penis inside her vagina.

Art caught his second wind. He gripped her thighs and drove his penis upward into her vagina. This was, by far, the longest, most sensational love he ever had—that either of them ever had. They were as one now. Two halves of a whole who lived only to please each other. They humped until both ached from the strain. Just when Art thought he was about to collapse, Maria came.

She threw her head back, screamed with delight, shook violently on his penis, then fell on top of him. She lay in his arms, her eyes closed, emitting soft cooing sounds as she basked in the afterglow of their lovemaking.

After a short rest, Maria jerked Art off until he was fully erect once more, then gave his prick a few fucking licks. When she was finished, she got onto her elbows and knees and parted her thighs. Art smiled at her open cunt as he took his place behind her. He stopped to admire and run his hands over her shapely behind, and then eased his cock into her again.

This was Maria's favorite position. She was able to feel every move of Art's prick more intensely like this and each of his thrusts caused it to slide over her g-spot. When they made love like this, it sent shivers up and down her back and heightened her pleasure considerably.

Today was no exception. This love was slow, long and easy. After several minutes, Maria felt herself coming and began squeezing Art's prick with her pussy muscles. This made Art come, too. They came at the exact same instant and it felt spectacular to say the least.

Art pumped so much cum into Maria's cunt that it dribbled down the backs of her thighs. They kept going and going until exhaustion overcame them and fell asleep in each other's arms.

Heider stared at the Box on the table before him for a long time. The lid had a an intricately made bronze locking mechanism. He shrugged and passed it to the Frenchman.

"I think I can make an impression of the lock with some clay. Then we can use it to make a key that will open the Box," he suggested.

"That sounds good. Have you done this before?" asked Hawatt.

The Frenchman grinned.

"Many times," he said. "Shall I get started?"

"By all means," agreed Hawatt.

The Frenchman opened his briefcase and took out a small plastic bag. Inside was a wad of loose, gray clay. He took it out, kneaded it between his palms, then balled it up and pressed it against the lock. When he was sure it worked, he gently lifted it out of the mechanism and held it up to the light.

"Viola!" he declared.

"Now what?" asked Hawatt.

"Now, I will melt some wax and use it to make a mold of this key. When the wax hardens, I will remove the clay. Then I will pour molten metal into the wax mold. When that hardens, I will break away the wax, file the rough edges smooth, and try to open the Box," the Frenchman explained.

"I think we had better wait until Art returns. I think we should let him open the Box," Heider suggested.

The other men nodded in agreement.

Back at the suite, things had heated up again as the Wilders caught their second wind.

Maria lay on her back, her legs wide apart, enjoying the sensation of Art's prick moving in and out of her willing cunt. He fucked her slow, sliding in all the way to his balls on each thrust, then slowly easing upward and thrusting again.

On each downthrust, Maria sighed happily and drove her hips upward to take him all the way in. Each thrust brought her closer and closer to orgasm. Her body begged for more and more as she sailed into sexual Heaven.

But she wasn't there alone. Art was also lost in a sexual fog as he again enjoyed one of the best fucks of his life. The soft, moist flesh of Maria's cunt eagerly engulfed his cock, sucking it inside like a hungry mouth. She was tight and willing to please. Art delighted in the way she became as one with him.

He moved into her slowly until his glans touched the wall of her cunt.

Then he came out again, feeling her cunt gently gripping at his prick.

Repeat.

Again and again.

Maria groaned. Waves of pleasure raced through her and she dug her fingertips into Art's muscular shoulders and hugged him with her knees. Art increased his tempo. Maria fucked back, matching him thrust-for-delicious thrust as she started to come.

She used her cunt muscles to grip and release, then grip his prick on each downward thrust. Art moaned and smiled at her. Maria smiled back as she felt herself get ready to explode.

"I'm going to come," Art whispered.

"Me too. Fuck me harder, Art," Maria gasped as the first wave rippled through her. She trembled.

Art picked up the pace and really hammered her. Maria gasped, arched her back, and let herself go. Her orgasm was spectacular.

She cried out for more as she fucked Art with all of the might. Art grunted. His balls twitched and he emptied every bit of cum he had inside her lovely cunt.

"Yes! YES!!" Maria cried as she wrapped herself around him. She milked his prick harder as she came. They kissed as their orgasms peaked, then subsided, leaving both breathless and literally covered with sweat.

"Perfect!" Maria gasped.

Art couldn't agree with her more.

Art approached her, his prick now at full salute again. Maria looked at it, licked her lips and encouraged him to ram it home. They kissed once again. Maria gave Art's prick a few nice pulls, then spread her legs and sighed as he entered her.

As Art slid it home, Maria almost bit his tongue off. They waited a few moments to savor their union, then began a nice, steady fuck. Maria tightened her inner muscles to give Art more pleasure, then moved with him. She loved the way he felt inside her. He fucked her nice and deep, gently, lovingly.

And she did him the same way. Theirs was a controlled passion. It transcended mere sex and took it several level higher. They moved together perfectly, each deriving the utmost pleasure from the other.

Yes it was sex.

But it was so much more than that.

Whatever it was, neither wanted it to stop.

Not now.

Not ever.

Maria gasped and held on tight. Art's thrusts became harder and faster. So did hers.

"I'm coming, Maria," Art whispered between kisses.

"Me too. My God, this is good," she gasped.

"Very good. Perfect," he agreed.

"Give it to me, Art. Fill my pussy with your love," Maria gasped as she started trembling.

He did.

So did Maria.

Their movements grew erratic, shaky, as each strove to please the other. Art pumped away until his balls ached, then slowly withdrew his limp member.

Maria leaned back against the tree, her legs apart, Art's cum dripping down her left thigh. She smiled. It was a sweet, happy smile, too.

"Thank you," she said.

"You're very welcome," he answered as they kissed again.

CHAPTER 20

▼

The evening news was full of the disaster. Wilder, Hawatt and the rest of his "A Team" watched as television cameras filmed local firefighters and bomb squad detectives picking through the smoldering rubble of what was only hours earlier a row of neat cement block homes. As the reporter provided the information, hundreds of people stood nearby, watching the grim tableau.

Wilder chuckled.

"Of course the bomb squad will find nothing," said the Swede. "That explosive cannot be found unless one specifically looks for traces of it."

"Most likely, the police will declare that it was an accident, perhaps a gas leak," Hawatt suggested.

"There are no gas lines in that neighborhood, Nasi," said Wilder. "You know that."

"Then how *will* they explain this?" asked Maria as she handed Wilder a glass of beer and sat down next to him on the sofa.

Just then, the Chief of NPF appeared on the screen. The reporters placed microphones in front of him while he adjusted his fez.

"Have you any idea what caused this terrible explosion?" asked the reporter.

"We in the Security Police have been investigating the men in the middle house for some time now. They were suspected members of a small terrorist cell," the chief replied. "I believe the explosion was caused when one of the bombs the group was manufacturing accidentally went off."

Everyone around Wilder laughed.

"Good old Rashid. He covered our asses just like he said he would," said Wilder.

"He had to, of course. After all, he was under strict orders from the President's chief of security," Hawatt said.

He looked at Wilder now with a mixture of surprise and respect. Wilder's connections were far-reaching indeed. Just how he managed to pull this off without causing a major international incident was beyond Hawatt's imagination.

Wilder reached over and turned off the T.V. set.

"Now that this is over with, we can get on with our work," he said

The next day, Art, Maria and Hawatt said farewell to the members of the A Team at Cairo International Airport. Art shook hands with each of them and wished them well. Then he, Maria and Hawatt watched as they went through the gate to catch flights to places unknown.

"You have some interesting friends," Maria said as they walked back to the parking garage.

"Interesting is one way to describe them. I call them useful," Art replied.

"Where did you meet those men?" asked Hawatt.

"When you haunt places like I do, you get to know a lot of different people. I just happened to make friends with the right ones," Wilder replied.

Maria laughed.

She knew that her husband never "just happens" to do anything. He purposely sought out those men and recruited them as part of a special team. Like Art, they probably had friends in high places.

Very high places.

That's why the Egyptian police didn't interfere with the rescue mission or question them about the explosion.

Hawatt marveled at Wilder's ability to instantly reach out and pull the necessary strings to get things done. It made him glad that they were friends. He'd never fully realized just how dangerous an enemy Wilder could be.

They got into the limo and headed back into the city. The driver dropped the Wilders off at their hotel, then continued on to the museum with Hawatt.

Once back in their suite, Maria decided it was time to have some more fun. She took Art by the hand and led him over to the bed.

"What shall we do today?" she teased as she ran her fingers over the bulge in Art's jeans.

Instead of answering, Art untied her blouse, and then slowly undid the buttons to reveal her near perfect breasts and already erect nipples. He fondled them gently as he kissed her neck. Maria sighed.

She reached down and unzipped Art's jeans. Seconds later, she had his prick in her hand and was slowly jerking him off.

Art's mouth moved to her left nipple and stayed there to adore it while he unbuttoned her shorts and slipped his hand inside. Maria moaned softly as Art's fingers explored her soft pubic hair, then danced gingerly along her swollen labia and hard clit. She gasped with delight when two of those fingers slipped into her cunt and began to wiggle around inside her.

While Art was doing that, Maria's hand moved faster and faster along his erection. Soon, the knob was coated with sticky, clear pre-cum, which Maria then massaged into the rest of his prick.

She felt her shorts falling and allowed them to slip all the way to her ankles. Once there, she kicked free of them and spread her stance wider. This enabled Art to literally fuck her with his fingers, which now made slurping noises as they moved in and out of her hot, wet pussy.

Maria began muttering in Spanish. Her body was trembling now. Soon her head began reeling as waves of pleasure surged outward from her cunt and rippled through her entire body. As she came, she kept jerking Art off even faster. He tried to hold back, but the feel of Maria's soft, warm hand on his prick proved to be far too much for him.

He began spewing lines of thick, white cum all over Maria's belly, thighs and still-throbbing cunt. She didn't seem to notice though. She was still coming and her orgasm felt like a speeding, out of control, freight train.

She kept pumping Art's prick until it grew limp and slipped from her grasp, the stepped back and smiled at him. She looked down at her body. Art came a lot.

"That was nice," she said. "Let's get into bed now and fuck for real."

Art kissed Maria on the lips softly, then slowly undid her blouse and helped her off with it. Her nipples were still erect and he leaned over to tease them with his tongue.

"Ah, that's nice," sighed Maria.

Art sat up as Maria helped him out of his shirt, then she leaned forward and sucked each of his nipples until he felt his balls tingle. While she was doing that, she unzipped his jeans and pulled out his now fully erect prick. It felt even bigger now. Harder, too.

She gave it a few slow pulls. Art stood up and Maria undressed him altogether. She then leaned forward and played with his balls, then turned her attentions to his prick.

Art sighed happily as she jerked him off.

Maria took her time now. There was no need to hurry.

She stuck her tongue out and ran it all over his swollen knob a few times. Art moaned and put his hand on her shoulder. Maria kept licking for a moment, then pushed half of his cock into her mouth.

She never really liked to suck cock. But Art's was different. She loved the way he tasted. She loved to suck it. She especially loved it when he came in her mouth and the way his cum felt as it slid down her throat.

Art really loved what she was doing, too. What man wouldn't? Maria wasn't just sucking his prick. She was actually making love to him with her mouth.

And no one, he decided, could do that any better than her. Maria stopped and lay down on the bed with her legs dangling over the side.

Art knelt and undid her shorts, then slowly pulled them off. Naked, she looked gorgeous. He kissed and licked his way up her inner thighs to the soft, brown patch between them. She was already quivering with anticipation. Her labia and clit were wet and swollen and her sexual perfume permeated the room.

She smiled lovingly at Art.

"Eat me, darling," she whispered.

Then she sighed deeply as Art's tongue entered her more-than-willing cunt. He was marvelous with his tongue. He knew when and where to lick and how to fire all of her sexual triggers. Maria head been longing for this. She was so excited that she came within seconds. She threw her legs over Art's shoulders, gripped his hair and began humping his tongue with a wild abandon. Maria came again and again. So many times that. So many times that she could barely breathe or speak.

She didn't have to. Her body did all the talking for her and it was screaming for more. Art got the signal loud and clear and kept licking her quivering, dripping snatch until his tongue began to ache.

"Enough! That's enough," Maria gasped as she pushed his face away from her cunt. "Fuck me, Art. Please fuck me."

Her body was still trembling when Art took his place above her. He pressed his glans to her soft, moist labia then moved it up and down several times before easing into her. He went in slowly in order to get the feel of her tight, hot channel as it caressed his prick.

Maria spread her legs as far apart as she could, then bent her knees. She gripped Art's shoulders and drove her hips upward until she felt the head of his prick touch the opening to her womb.

"Oh yes!" she sighed as Art began to move his hips in a circular motion.

At the same time, he thrust in and out of her cunt nice and slow. He felt her inner flesh hug his shaft tightly as he pulled out, then part again as he slid back in. Each time, Maria moved with him in perfect unison.

Art had had many women in his life, but no one's cunt felt as exquisitely sexy as Maria's. She was warm, tight and silky smooth and she could really use her inner muscles. He felt as if her were making love with an angel. They were a perfect match.

That's why he was taking his time. This wasn't just sex. It was lovemaking at its best, with all of the emotional ties that went with the word.

They made love gently, slowly and with a lot of passion. They matched each other stroke for stroke, thrust for thrust. Their lips met again. Art reached beneath Maria and put her right leg over his shoulder, then drove into her a little bit harder and faster.

Maria emitted a loud moan and dug her nails into his back as his cock massaged her secret g-spot perfectly. She felt herself spinning out of control.

"Faster, Art! Do it faster," she begged. "Make me come!"

She closed her eyes and allowed the movements of Art's prick inside her cunt carry her away. She began crying out and gasping for air. She clawed at his back like a mad woman as an explosive series of orgasms raced through her body.

Maria felt his prick jerk a few times, and then relaxed as Art emptied his seed into her sucking pussy. Like earlier, he pumped a large amount of cum into Maria's love tunnel. Her body, which seemed to be suspended in time, eagerly accepted his seed, greedily making it one with her.

She let Art come inside her.

After a few more deep thrusts, Art eased his half hard member out of her and rolled onto his back. His prick glistened with their combined love juices. Maria rolled on top of him and they kissed once again. It was a long, deep kiss, too.

CHAPTER 21

▼

That evening, they joined Hawatt at the Royal Egyptian Bistro for dinner. As they ate, Maria described her weird time trip while being held captive. Hawatt listened intently as Art told him about Maria's similar experience in Guatemala when the natives believed her to be the reincarnation of an ancient goddess.

"I wonder which queen the guards thought you were?" he asked.

"And you say that you spoke ancient Egyptian with the guards?" asked Hawatt.

Maria nodded.

"I've also discovered that I can now read all of the ancient hieroglyphs with ease. Before this happened, I managed to learn less than a hundred of them," Maria said.

"Perhaps they thought you were the goddess Isis," mused Hawatt. "Many people here still worship her. In fact, she still has a worldwide cult. I understand that some of the cult members can speak the ancient tongue. Your guards must have belonged to the cult. But how did you come to speak ancient Egyptian?"

"I can't. Or at least I couldn't until it happened. It felt like someone else was inside my body and mind. A stronger personality that temporarily took control of me," Maria said.

"Sounds like channeling," said Wilder.

"Channeling? Is such a thing possible?" asked Hawatt.

"Oh yes. I've witnessed such things personally. The question now is who channeled through Maria and why was she chosen to be that channel," Wilder replied.

"Perhaps you are descended from an Egyptian priestess or queen?" suggested Hawatt. "Coming to Egypt may have triggered ancestral memories. That would explain why you have adapted so quickly to life here and why you have this deep and sincere love for our history."

"How much of what you spoke do you remember?" asked Art.

"All of it," said Maria. "Ancient Egyptian is no longer a foreign language for me."

"If that's true, then you have become the most valuable member of our team. Your newfound language skills can save us hours of translation time when we start going through the artifacts from Imhotep's tomb," said Hawatt.

"Speaking of which, how do you want to handle the opening of the Box? Should we do it in private or as part of an international broadcast?" Wilder asked.

"This is the single most important find in human history. What is inside the Box belongs not only to Egypt but to all of mankind. I think we should do it in front of the cameras," Hawatt replied.

"Good. When should we do it?" asked Wilder.

"It will take at least a week to gather the media together. How about next Tuesday in my office?" Hawatt suggested.

"Done. That will give us more time to go over the things we opened before," Wilder agreed. "There's still so much to do at the tomb."

"Let's have another round of beer and head out there. The sun has already set and it is cool enough to return to work."

CHAPTER 22

▼

Two days later, at eight in the morning, teams of reporters from several major TV networks were on hand in Hawatt's office to watch him and Wilder open the Box. Maria was on hand with her camera, too, to take snapshots of the contents for the museum catalog and Wilder's personal records.

They began the broadcast with the largest scroll that was found beneath the mummy. When Wilder removed it from its protective tube and gently unrolled it on the table, his eyes widened. He glanced at Hawatt.

Nasi walked over and peered over his shoulder. Then he turned to the cameras.

"This scroll, which appears to have been written by Imhotep himself, is a history of Egypt's Zaptepi or Golden Age," he began. "He has included a list of several pharaohs on one side. The other side details the important events that occurred during their reigns."

"I might point out that the Golden Age predated Dynasty Zero," said Wilder. "This list of kings goes back some 2,000 years before Dynasty Zero and proves once and for all that Egypt existed as a nation long before the first mud brick was fashioned in Sumer."

"This means that Egypt is at least seven to eight thousand years old. Yet there are references to an even *earlier* civilization in this scroll," Hawatt added as he examined the papyrus.

"If that's true, that would place Egypt's origins somewhere around the end of the Ice Age," Wilder said. "I knew it, Nasi! I said all along that Egypt was the true cradle of civilization. Egyptians had agriculture, art, architecture, the wheel and several other things that were erroneously attributed to other early cultures."

"Your theories are now scientific fact, Dr. Wilder. The proof is all here, in Imhotep's own hand. This scroll is the first actual written history known to mankind. You said his tomb was between the paws of the Sphinx. You were certain that we'd find evidence to prove your theories. And both were exactly where you said they would be," said Hawatt as they continued to study the scroll.

He then turned to Wilder and lowered his voice.

"How did you *know*?" he asked.

"I don't know, Nasi. I just *did*. Something inside me drove me to find this. Maybe it was the will of the Egyptian gods themselves. Maybe they wanted me to find this because they think we're ready to handle the truth," Wilder mused as he grew philosophical.

Hawatt scanned the document. He shook his head.

"Again there is no mention of who built the Sphinx., although Imhotep did describe the huge statue of a lion left behind by some mysterious civilization. One of the earlier kings had the face reworked into a hawk's head to honor the god Horus, but there is no mention of who actually built it or why," he translated.

"Like you said, perhaps there are some things we aren't meant to know. But at least this proves that the monument was indeed carved around 10,000 BCE. It also proves that some of the "crackpot" theories that the ruts in its body are the result of water erosion, not sand and wind as previously believed," Wilder added.

"Water? As in rain?" asked a reporter.

"Yes. The Sahara was once a lush rainforest with lots of water. It started turning into a desert about 6,000 BCE when the climate changed in this region," Wilder explained.

Wilder handed Hawatt the key the Frenchman had made and insisted he do the honors. Hawatt gently pushed the key into the locking mechanism, took a deep breath, and turned it to the left. When he heard the loud clicks, he smiled.

"Now we shall see what is actually inside the legendary Box of Knowledge, he declared to the camera.

Hawatt opened the box, looked inside, then sat back and scratched his head. Wilder looked over his shoulder and wrinkled his nose at the contents. Then, while the cameras rolled, he reached inside and removed a solid gold rod about 16" long with a set of grooves on one end.

The next object he took out was a pyramid shaped golden base with the top removed and hollowed out. Inside the hole were another set of grooves. Hieroglyphs virtually covered the underside of the pyramid.

The third object was a four inch tall painted gold head of Thoth. The neck was hollow.

Wilder displayed the object side-by-side on the table before him while the reporters moved in for close-ups.

"What are they for?" asked Maria.

"Beats the Hell outa me," said Art. "I've never seen anything like this before. They look as if they were made to fit together."

"What purpose would that serve?" asked a reporter.

"Whatever it's designed to do, it was deemed important enough to be buried with Imhotep. Important enough to be inside the Box of Thoth," Art replied.

"Maybe one of those scrolls that we found in the sarcophagus will give us a clue?" suggested Nasi as he reached for the second one and carefully removed the wooden cap.

When he removed the papyrus and unrolled it, his eyes went wide. There before him, in glorious detail, was a map of the stars.

"Incredible! I didn't know they had anything like this," he said. "It shows all the planets and major constellations in relation to—what? This looks off somehow. I see the belt of Orion but it is not where it should be."

"You're right. Let's take pictures of this and send it to NASA. They can run it against a computer and tell us when this map was made. I have a feeling it's a lot older than we think," Art suggested.

"Good idea. Of course, you have friends at NASA?" Nasi joked.

"Of course," Art said with a smile. "Let's open the third one."

This one was a real puzzle. It was neatly laid out in rows of small symbols in a pattern that appeared to repeat itself again and again and again. The symbols weren't of any known script that Nasi or Art had ever seen.

Mystified, Art rolled it up and put it back into the tube.

"We'll have to give this a good going over later," he said. "Let's check out the last scroll now."

This one really floored them. It showed Imhotep seated on the floor holding what looked like an assembled artifact. Next to it was a series of heiretic instructions on how to put the pieces together.

The next set of instructions also showed the Great Pyramid's inner chamber and the famed empty stone sarcophagus. It also showed a light streaming through the supposed air shaft either going from or to the object which sat atop the sarcophagus.

Below were more instructions that both Wilder and Hawatt poured over carefully.

Hawatt looked over to him.

"These are instructions on how to assemble the three artifacts in the box and where to place them once they are assembled. What is amazing is the fact the drawings show the Great Pyramid, which means that it was built *during or before* Imhotep's lifetime, not after as we believed," he said.

"But why should we place the artifact there? What exactly will happen if we do it? And when should we do it?" asked Maria.

"Perhaps we shall know all this after we have fully translated the scroll," Hawatt said. "Until then, we can only speculate—and I would rather not do that."

Art made a copy of the star map and sent it via overnight courier to his friend Ryan Brown at NASA's Astrological Research Center

Then he sat back and sipped his beer. A few moments later, Nasi, Maria and Heider walked in bearing the other two scrolls.

"What's up?" he asked.

"I've decided to burn the midnight oil as you say to translate this scroll," said Nasi as he tapped the bundle under his arm.

"What about the other scroll? The one with the weird symbols?" Art asked.

"We can't even begin to understand what that one's for. Maybe you can take a crack at it? Al said it has him pretty confused," said Heider as he placed a second bundle on the desk in front of Wilder.

Art nodded.

"But not tonight. I'm too tired to think right now. It's been a Helluva day," he said. "I think Maria and I will get some dinner at the hotel and call it a night."

"That's fine. If you need me, I'll be in my office for the next few hours," said Nasi as he headed for the door.

Wilder looked at Heider.

"Any idea what those symbols are? Any idea at all?" he asked.

"Not a clue, Art. The symbols are not any form of Egyptian that I have ever seen. You're more knowledgeable about early civilizations than me. Maybe you can make heads or tails out of it," Heider replied.

"I'll give it a shot tomorrow," Art said as he stood and stretched. "It's been hidden for almost 4,000 years. Another day or two won't make a difference."

Heider nodded as Art and Maria left the office and headed for the Land Rover.

"You're too tired to work. I hope you're not too tired for *other* things," Maria teased.

Art laughed.

"I'm *never* too tired for *that*," he said.

They walked hand-in-hand to the bed and sat down. Art stared into Maria's lovely eyes, then smiled. He reached up and removed her glasses and laid them on the nightstand. Then they kissed several times. Each kiss became hotter and more passionate. As they kissed, they undressed each other.

When Maria was naked, she grabbed Art's penis and gave it a few easy strokes until it was hard and long, then she laid back and opened her legs. Art studied her perfect vagina, and then he leaned over and flicked his tongue over her labia and swollen clit. Maria sighed happily and ran her fingers through his hair. No one, she decided, knew how to use their tongue as well as Art did.

Probably not anyone else on Earth could make her feel like Art made her feel at that moment.

Art swung around so that his erection was just inches from Maria's face. She smiled and stroked it until his knob glistened with pre-cum, then ran her tongue up and down the shaft, over his balls and finally around the head. Art groaned as she slid it into her mouth and sucked away.

Art came first. Maria felt his glans expand inside of her mouth, then he groaned and decorated her palette with gob after delicious gob of sweet, warm semen. Maria happily swallowed as much as she could. While she was doing this, Art sucked her clit. The sensation was unexpectedly intense. Maria cried out with pleasure, then rolled onto her back as she came.

Art watched her labia open and close rapidly as her orgasm washed over her. The sight was so erotic, he remained hard. Maria saw his erection and threw open her thighs.

"Now!" she gasped. "Take me now!"

Art did**.**

He slid his erection into her still-pulsing vulva and moved it around inside her. As his hard shaft massaged her love tunnel, Maria moaned softly and clung to his arms. They were doing what they were meant to do. What they wanted to do. There was no guilt. No one here to stop them as they made slow, passionate love.

Maria now matched Art thrust-for-thrust. Each time, he went in deeper. Each time, he moved his hips in a circle to massage her passageway. Each time, she saw stars and heard bells go off inside her head.

When they first began their affair years before, neither of them thought it would last. Now, here they were, nearly ten years later making love as if it was their very first time. It was as if time stood still when they were together. It was as if nothing else mattered but the intense pleasure they derived from each other whenever they were alone.

Maria felt herself coming again. She shoved her hips up at Art as hard as she could, then picked up the tempo of their lovemaking. Art knew what it meant and moved with her, determined to come with her. He felt her nails cutting into his skin as she arched her back. He saw her eyes close. Her mouth opened.

"Ahhh! Love me!" she gasped as she neared the edge.

Art now did her with short, sharp thrusts. The sudden change was just enough to push Maria over the line. She screamed with joy and humped him back furiously as she came. It was a good, hard orgasm that rocked her entire world. She came so hard, she barely noticed that Art came, too, and was merrily filling her vagina with an incredible amount of cum.

They held each other close for several minutes. Eventually, they settled back to Earth and began exchanging short, sweet kisses. After a few minutes went by, Maria took a deep breath. She looked down at Art's now-flaccid member, then at the cum oozing from her love box.

"Wonderful," she said.

CHAPTER 23

▼

Wilder sat and stared at the strange characters for what seemed like hours. They certainly weren't any form of the Egyptian language he'd ever seen. They also didn't fit in with any other early alphabets that he was aware of.

They were also arranged in odd groups, groups that repeated themselves over and over and over again.

Three triangles, four circles, three slashes, five large black dots, then seven more triangles with dots in them.

Then the whole thing was repeated several times.

But what did it all mean?

He scratched his head and sat back. Then he rubbed his eyes, looked up at the ceiling, then went back to the strange symbols.

That's when he had an epiphany.

"It's a code! It's all some sort of code!" he shouted.

But what kind of code? Who or what was it meant for?

He thought about many codes he had seen over the years. It was similar to Morse Code, but it was far too repetitious. It almost looked like a computer programming code.

"That's it!" he said.

It was so simple.

So basic.

So *mathematical.*

"That's it!"

He stood up and shouted for everyone to come into the office. Hawatt and Maria arrived first, followed by Kuyder and the others.

"I finally figured it out, Nasi," Wilder said. "It was so simple that we couldn't see it, even though it was right in front of us."

"And what did you figure out, Art?" Hawatt asked as he sat down.

"This isn't a language. It's a code. In fact, it's almost a *binary code,*" Art replied.

"Binary code?" asked Maria.

"A binary code consists of two numbers, one and zero, which are repeated in patterns that can be read by computers. It's a programming code. It tells a computer what to do and how to act," Art explained.

"And you think this is a code?" asked Hawatt.

"Yes. Look here—these symbols can be taken for numbers, much like the symbols used to program computers today. This code was created by Imhotep to be read by those who were in on the secret, probably priests," Wilder explained.

"A binary code? But isn't that meant to be read by a computer?" Kuyder asked.

"That's right," agreed Wilder.

"If that is the case, then where is the computer?" Kuyder asked.

Wilder pointed to his temple.

"Imhotep was a genius. His computer was his *mind.* He created the code, then probably passed it down to a select few. They, in turn, passed it down to other generations. Eventually, the code was forgotten—possibly right after Rome conquered Egypt," he theorized.

"Fascinating. But what was it used for? What secrets does it contain?" Hawatt asked.

"One way to find out—we send it off to our computer experts at NASA. Maybe they can figure that out for us," Wilder suggested.

Hawatt nodded.

"Good idea. Let's do that right now," he said. "I am most anxious to get to the bottom of this mystery."

He looked at Maria. She was obviously enraptured by the whole thing.

"Imagine! A binary code written thousands of years before computers. Is there no end to the surprises hidden beneath the sands?" he said.

Maria just stared at the papyrus blankly.

"It makes me proud to be an Egyptian," she said.

Her remark caused Wilder and Hawatt to raise eyebrows. Was Maria descended from the ancient Egyptians? She acted as if she was.

Hawatt also wondered if she was somehow reconnecting to her ancestral roots. If so, why? What was causing it?

The next morning, they gathered in Hawatt's office for a brainstorming session. On the tables and desks around them stood several of the artifacts they had recovered from the tomb.

Wilder looked them over carefully.

There were dozens of papyrus books inside wooden, leather-covered boxes, a large box containing Imhotep's surgical instruments, several books on how to diagnose, treat and do follow-ups on a variety of injuries and illnesses, a box containing his star-gazing implements (including a long, metal device with various lenses that could only be an early telescope!), maps and charts of the entire world, an early Book of the Dead, and the original papyrus with binary code. Then there was the mysterious black box of Thoth.

"This is an incredible collection," he said. "It's all we hoped for and much, much more. The ancient Egyptians were far more advanced than we ever suspected, medically, scientifically and spiritually. Perhaps they were far more advanced than *us*."

"There is an incredible wealth of knowledge here—and it would have remained hidden from us if not for you, Dr. Wilder," Hawatt said.

"I couldn't have done it without your help, Nasi, or the help of our great team. This is big, gentlemen. Really big. What we have here could turn modern civilization on its ear. It's like having a genie in a bottle," Wilder said.

"Then let us let the genie out. It has been locked up far too long," Hawatt said. "After the books are translated, we can make copies and send them off to the major medical universities for further study, along with anything else the staffs there might find important.

The originals will be kept here in the museum in our vault."

"I'll agree to that. We can make more copies and put them on display. In fact, you should set up an entire room just for Imhotep's artifacts. We can put everything we have in it, from canopic jars to the Box of Thoth," Wilder said.

"This will be the most popular attraction in the entire museum. It will be even bigger than Tut's exhibit," Hawatt beamed.

Wilder stood up and stretched as he walked to the window and stared out at the crowded streets.

"Maybe now we'll learn how they managed to accomplish such seemingly impossible things. Maybe now we'll learn how they really thought and if they were able to use their entire brain instead of the one third we now use," he said.

"Your friends at NASA should have the code this evening," Hawatt said.

"Good. I hope they'll be able to do something with it," Wilder said.

"Now what?" asked Kuyder.

"Now we return to the tomb and take more pictures and finish mapping it out. Who knows? We might find something else there," Wilder replied.

They founds several more chambers near the main vault. All were beautifully decorated with paintings or Imhotep and the Afterlife. In one, the paintings were more unconventional. They were very lifelike and highly detailed.

One scene showed Imhotep standing before the Sphinx. There was a beautiful woman dressed in white kneeling before him. In her upraised hands was the Box of Thoth.

Hawatt leaned back and studied the painting.

"Look at the woman. Does anything about her seem familiar to you?" he asked.

Art studied her face and laughed. Then he dragged Maria over and pointed.

"She looks just like you," he said. "And a lot like that painting we saw in the tomb in Guatemala. Here we go again."

"I hope not. I don't want to get sacrificed again," Maria said with a smile.

"Don't worry about that, Maria. Egyptians did not practice human sacrifice after Dynasty Zero," Hawatt assured her. "But the resemblance is *remarkable*. She could have been your ancestor, Maria. She's kneeling before Imhotep and pre-senting him with the Box of Thoth. It is as if he were some sort of god."

"I wonder who she was. She seems to have been very important to Imhotep. Maybe one of his wives?" Art suggested.

"From her dress, I'd say that she was a priestess of the Cult of Thoth. If so, then the cult itself gave the Box to Imhotep. That could only have been done by divine decree," said Hawatt.

"You mean Thoth told his priestess to give the Box to Imhotep?" asked Maria.

"Exactly. That is what this painting means. There can be no other explanation for it. And see here—it shows the Sphinx with the head of a hawk. This means it was originally a combination of Horus and a lion. Horus is the avenger of the god Amun Re The lion was a symbol of strength, especially kingly strength. Again it proves that the Sphinx existed during Imhotep's time and was not built by Khufu as previously thought," said Hawatt.

"The more we dig into this, the more incredible it gets," Wilder said. "I think I've seen enough for now. I'm going back to the museum to work on that mys-tery scroll some more."

"Good idea. I still have to finish my translation," agreed Hawatt.

The scroll was indeed a mystery. Wilder and his associates compared it with every known ancient language they could find in the data banks of the museum's computers. Sixteen hours of this produced "NO KNOWN MATCHES".

Frustrated, they ran comparisons to the Indus Valley script, the Vedic script and even Minoan. The results were the same.

Two days.

Nothing.

As Art sat back to clear his mind, the phone rang. He picked it up and heard a familiar voice on the other end.

"Hi, Art. It's Ryan over at NASA. That was one interesting map you sent me," he said.

"I bet it was. Whatcha got for me?" Art asked.

"Well, once I figured out that the main reference point was the belt of Orion, I fed it into our data bank to see what year that particular star pattern could actually be seen from the Giza Plateau. When it lined up, it put the three stars of the Belt *directly* over the Great Pyramids. And you won't believe the date we came up with," Ryan said.

"I'm all ears," Art said.

"The last time that pattern showed up was in 10,544 BCE. That means the map was drawn up around the end of the Ice Age," Ryan said.

"Good Gods! And since the pyramids were built to mirror the stars of the Belt, that makes them over 12,000 years old!" Art said.

"Bingo! That means that Khufu couldn't have built the Great Pyramid because they were there long before Egypt existed," Ryan added. "It looks like your theory of a much earlier civilization is right on the money, Art."

"I'm still flabbergasted, Ryan. Thanks a lot for your help. Can you fax me your findings?" Art asked.

"No problem. Anything else?" Ryan said.

"Yes. What about that scroll I sent you? Where's that at?" Art asked.

"Beats me. Aarons is working that angle and I think it has him stumped. Hey, thanks for giving me a chance to become part of this. It beats the Hell out of tracking asteroids all night," Ryan said.

"My pleasure. I'll call you later with our findings," Art promised.

"You won't have to, Art. Everything you guys do is all over CNN these days. It's a shame what happened to that terrorist bunch."

"Yes isn't it?" Art said smugly.

Both men laughed hard. Ryan was well aware of Art's penchant for taking care of loose ends and of the network of associates he had.

Art hung up the phone and waited for the fax. When it arrived, he took it down the hall to Nasi's office and laid it on the desk before him. Nasi perused it and smiled.

"You were right all along, Art. We are about to rewrite human history. What we discovered here blows all of our previous "truths" to atoms. Even the Bible has been proven wrong," Nasi said.

"To some extent. Remember, the Bible mentions no pharaoh by name nor does it date any of the events it purports to chronicle. Because of this, we don't know what time period it covers. For all we know, the events in the Bible predate Dynasty Zero and the sinking of Atlantis," Art said as he sat down across from Nasi and folded his hands over his chest.

"But you have always said that the Bible was mostly nonsense," Nasi reminded him.

"I still believe that. Yet the writers included several ancient cities that we have since uncovered and included enough historical characters to make their stories convincing. Yet I doubt that the Jews were the mighty warriors they claimed to be. Nor do I believe that they were God's chosen people. If they were, their God seemed to really enjoy fucking with them. He seems to have a real hard-on for the Jews," Art said.

Nasi laughed.

"If there was a chosen people, it had to be the Egyptians. Never before or since has any nation seemed so incredibly blessed by climate, harvests, knowledge and everything else. The ancient Egyptians had the best standard of living on Earth. Hell, we can't even match it!" Art continued.

"I also feel that the ancient ways are about to make a huge comeback, Nasi. Most people are disgusted with the modern way of life and long for a gentler, simpler lifestyle and a promise of a good Afterlife. What better model is there than Egypt?" he added.

"I think you really believe that, Art," Nasi said.

"I do, Nasi," Art said.

"You must have been Egyptian in a previous life. Maria, too," Nasi said with a smile.

Art smiled then looked over Nasi's translations of the one scroll.

"Holy cats! *That's* what it says on that scroll?" he asked.

"Yes. Just as we thought. These are precise instructions on how to put the artifact together, which is described as "The Scepter of Horus and Summoner of the Great Golden Hawk".

It also tells us exactly where to place the artifact," Nasi said.

"The only thing that's missing is a date and time—and that's probably in the part you haven't translated yet," Art said.

"I should have that done by tomorrow," Nasi promised.

CHAPTER 24

▼

Maria lay on her back with her smooth, sexy legs wide apart. Her eyes were misty and half shut as she enjoyed the slow, easy movement of Art's penis moving in and out of her hot, juicy vagina. Art did her slowly. On each downstroke, he slid into her until their pubic hairs meshed, wiggled his hips in a few tight circles, then eased out of her nearly all the way. On each of his deep, penetrating thrusts, Maria emitted a happy sigh and drove her body upward to take all of him inside of her.

She was actually savoring this love. Savoring every hard, delicious inch of the cock that was slowly and surely moving her toward orgasmic bliss.

She was in sexual Nirvana.

But she wasn't there alone. Art too, was savoring the way her vagina gently wrapped itself around his thrusting cock as if were some soft, warm glove. He loved it even more when she used her inner muscles to increase the friction and his pleasure as he pulled slowly out of her then eased back in. It seemed as if each love was better than the one they had before, as if their bodies—and their very souls—were blending into one.

She began humping Art harder and harder. Her hungry vagina all but devoured Art's erection with each sharp thrust of her hips. She soon looked up at Art and smiled. It was a soft, dreamy kind of smile.

"I'm coming," she whispered.

"I know," he said softly.

"Do it faster, Art. Faster!" she urged as she dug her nails into his arms.

Art stepped up the pace. Maria gasped and matched him, thrust for thrust. She began emitting moans and squeals of pleasure now.

As the first ripples of her orgasm erupted from deep within her vagina, she cried out and arched her back. The room exploded around her now and everything went white, then returned in a kaleidoscope of colors and light. Maria clawed at Art's arms now as she used her body to "beg" him to continue. She was all his now.

He owned her.

More, he possessed her.

And she obsessed him.

They moved faster and faster now. Waves of intense orgasmic tide washed over Maria's taut, sweaty body as Art continued to piston in and out of her now-quivering vagina.

Then Art came, too.

Like before, he pumped huge amounts of hot, sticky cum into her hungry body and kept at it until he stomach muscles ached and he could continue no longer.

He fell next to her, panting for air.

"Perfecto!" Maria gasped as she returned to her senses.

Art just couldn't agree with her more.

They rested for a few minutes, then Maria decided she wanted more. By then, Art was more than eager to comply.

He lay on his back with his hands behind his head, watching as Maria straddled his thighs. She grabbed his penis, gave it several easy pulls, then moved her hips so that the head of his cock pointed directly at her labia. Satisfied that he was hard enough, she guided his penis up into her slit. When she felt her pubic hairs mingle with his, she began to rock back and forth.

Art reached up and played with her erect nipples, sending delicious tingles all through Maria's taut, sweaty body. She gasped then began moving up and down on his penis as slow and a deep as she could. She kept at this until she realized Art was about to come. She stopped and waited a few seconds.

When she felt she was back in control, she continued. Four times, Art nearly came. Four times, Maria stopped until it passed, then loved him again. This was the longest love Art could remember. It was the longest time he'd ever been erect and it was the most his balls had ever ached.

By the time he was ready to blow again, he begged Maria to let him come. But she was already in the beginning throes of her own orgasm and didn't hear a word.

The room was spinning wildly for her now as her orgasm entered the explosive stage. She began shaking out of control as she raised her hips one last time then slammed herself down onto Art's cock as hard as she could.

They both came within seconds of each other. Art grabbed her behind and thrust his cock hard up into her vagina. Maria toppled backward onto her elbows, taking Art with her. He rolled so that he was on top and his penis was still inside her wonderful, quivering vagina.

He humped for a few more seconds as he continued to spew his cum deep inside her eager body. Maria clawed his back and used her pussy to milk him of every last drop.

"Love me, Art! Oh love me!" she cried as everything went white.

This was by far, the most intense, deep reaching sex she'd ever had and she didn't want to stop.

Not now.

Not ever!

To Art's surprise, his cock stayed hard. He could barely breathe and see now, but that didn't matter. All that mattered was the incredible sex he was having at that very moment and the beautiful woman on the other end of his penis.

He also realized that he was still coming like mad. Still pumping gob after gob of cum deep into her pussy. Then it hit him. One last, powerful eruption that left him shaking and weak all over. He moaned and fell onto Maria's heaving chest. She pressed her lips to his for a long, hot kiss as they waited to return to Earth.

"Ay caramba!" Maria gasped after a long while.

"That was magnificent, Maria. The best sex I ever had!" Art said.

"There's more where that came from, mi amor," Maria assured him.

Art laughed.

"But not until we've had dinner first," Art replied. "Where shall we go?"

"How about down the street?" Maria suggested.

"Sounds good to me. Let's get dressed. I'm starved," Art agreed.

"Me, too. Good sex gives me an appetite," Maria said.

As she pulled her clothes on, Maria smiled and thought about her situation.

It seemed as if she and Art were having sex constantly of late. This was fine with Maria. She loved Art and really loved the way her made love to her. Sex with Art was never boring.

She also trusted him like she had never trusted anyone before. She also knew that trust was mutual.

When Art and Maria got back to the museum the next morning, they were greeted by a tired-looking but grinning Nasi. Kuyder and Heider were also with him.

"I take it that you've finished the translation?" Art asked as they went into Nasi's office.

"Yes I did. Just as you guessed, the scroll contained an exact day and time to make the broadcast," Nasi said as they sat down around his desk.

He unrolled the papyrus and pointed to a series of heiretic glyphs.

"According to this, the broadcast must be made at precisely one minute past midnight of the Vernal Equinox. And it must continue for no more than one full hour," Nasi explained.

"Since the Egyptians had the same concept of time as we do now, can I assume that the instructions are completely accurate?" asked Heider.

"Yes, they are. There is no mistake," Nasi said. "I went over this many times to be certain of the date and time."

"Good. When is the Equinox?" Art asked.

"Ten days from now," Nasi said.

"But the air shaft used to point directly at the middle star in the Belt of Orion. That was over 10,000 years ago. The position of the Earth in relation to the stars has shifted by several degrees since then," Art pointed out.

"No problem. We'll compensate for the shift when we make the transmission. I've already made the calculations for that," Kuyder assured him.

"Then let's get it on. First, we'll inform the ladies and gentlemen of the press. They'll need some lead time for this. Then we'll get to work," Art said.

"I will make the necessary calls. Perhaps we should have the Egyptian military scan the area above Giza with radar to track anything unusual approaching the area?" Nasi suggested.

"Sounds good to me," Art agreed.

Nasi quickly informed the press and told them to put the information out to the general public. Naturally, they did just that—with unexpected results.

Almost immediately, planeloads of tourists began arriving in Cairo. Within days, every hotel was booked to capacity. So were youth hostels, YMCAs, YMMAs, motels and even spare rooms in private homes.

The tourists, mostly New Agers, came from every corner of the Earth for what many believed would be the greatest event in human history. It was their one and only chance to connect physically and spiritually with the elder gods.

The area around Giza soon took on a festive atmosphere. Enterprising Egyptians set up food, drink and souvenir booths. Tourists were more than happy to buy amulets, ushabtis, statues of Thoth and the other gods, books, candles—just about anything and everything that had some sort of mystical connotation.

Many of the tourists donned ancient Egyptian garb or wore wigs as if this would bring them closer to the long-sought-after "truth".

By the time the team was ready to start setting up the transmitter, there were close to two million people gathered at Giza with more arriving each and every hour.

Wilder found it all quite amusing. Kuyder and Heider found it distracting. Hawatt didn't know what to think of it all.

With film crews from several major networks on site, Kuyder and Heider began their work.

It took two full days for them to lug the sensitive electronic equipment through the narrow passages and up and down the wooden ladders to the King's Crypt of the Great Pyramid.

On the third day, Art, Nasi and Maria joined them in the crypt to watch them hook everything up. Maria took photos of the whole thing for Art's records while a National Geographic crew came in and filmed the final process of setting up the powerful transmitter in the exact center of the empty granite sarcophagus.

That evening, they team went out to dinner. Afterward, Art and Maria headed back to the hotel for another long night of wild, passionate sex. Tonight, though, Maria suggested something a little bit different.

"Are you sure that you want to do this?" Art asked.

Maria nodded.

"You really don't have to if you don't want to. You know I won't force you to do it," Art assured her.

"I'm sure," Maria replied. "Neither of us has ever done this before, so it will be exciting. Besides, I want to give you something special. Something that no one else ever had."

"It will probably hurt," Art warned.

"I know. I expect it to hurt. Let's try it anyway. I always wanted to do it that way," Maria said.

She got onto her hands and knees and took a deep breath. Art picked up the tube of K-Y and knelt behind her. He stopped to admire her sexy, shapely behind. It was perfect. One of the finest he'd ever seen or felt and now it was all his. He squeezed some K-Y into her crack and gently massaged it into her sphincter until she was good and slick.

The sensations caused by Art's fingers moving around and slightly into her asshole excited Maria more than she expected. She broke out in a cold sweat as ripples of pleasure washed through her quivering body.

"God!" she thought. "If this feels so good, what will it feel like when he enters me?"

Art pried her cheeks apart with his fingers with and teased Maria's sphincter with the head of his penis. When he felt she was ready, he began pushing it into her, slowly and cautiously so as not to hurt her.

Maria bit her lip to stifle a scream as Art's hard penis penetrated her virgin channel, tearing apart her soft, warm flesh as it moved slowly inward. The pain was tremendous. She wanted to scream. To tell Art to stop. But she didn't. She wanted him to have her this way, to finish what they started.

It seemed like an eternity before she felt his pubic hairs tickling her crack.

"He's in!" she thought. "He's really in!"

Art took a deep breath as he began loving Maria nice and easy. Tears rolled down her cheeks as the pain increased at first, then slowly subsided to be replaced by a rather pleasant sensation that seemed to move through her entire body. Maria moaned.

"Are you okay?" Art asked.

"Oh yes! I'm fine. This feels kind of nice," she replied dreamily as he continued to love her behind.

Art was in sexual heaven now. Maria's ass felt exquisitely tight and warm and he loved the way her sphincter muscles seemed to massage his penis on every in and out movement. After a few good strokes, Maria began to relax and enjoy it. She even began matching Art, stroke for stroke as if getting screwed in the ass was the most natural thing on Earth.

Maria realized that they were moving in perfect time with each other. And it was perfect, too. Just like everything else they did together.

Perfect.

So very perfect.

After a couple of minutes, Art felt his balls churn and realized that he couldn't hold off any longer. He began moving faster and faster then. Maria's teeth chattered as she tried to match his thrusts, taking his penis deeper and deeper into her asshole.

And it was on fire!

Art gripped her cheeks, leaned hard against them, and emptied his balls into her behind. Maria quivered when she felt his cum jet into her and consciously tried to squeeze him dry with her ass muscles.

Art had come.

But she had not. Nor was she close to orgasm.

She allowed him to keep riding her until he limp penis slid out of her channel, then rolled onto her back. She reached up, grabbed Art by his ears, and pulled his face down onto her open pussy.

"Eat me! I need to come!" she gasped.

Art happily obliged. Two minutes later, Maria was writhing in orgasmic bliss. Art kept tonguing her quivering clit until she literally begged him to stop.

"That's enough, darling! Please stop. I can't take any more," she begged as she pushed his head away from her crotch.

Art sat back on his heels and grinned down at her. Maria weakly returned his smile as she massaged her belly with both hands. Art recognized that as a sign that Maria had reached her sexual limits.

The next morning, Art received the long-awaited package from his friends at NASA. Naturally, a phone call came with it.

"Art, this is Ryan. It's just as you thought. Those symbols are indeed mathematical symbols. In fact, they're part of a code. From the looks of it, it was meant to be broken down into its numerical components, then transmitted somewhere—probably into deep space," Ryan said.

"Holy shit. Have you broken it down so that we can transmit it from here?" Art asked.

"We sure have. It's on the CD we enclosed with the paperwork. It should run about an hour. It should work. Our computers translated it exactly," Ryan answered.

"Thanks a million, Ryan. I owe you one—a big one—for this," Art said.

"No problemo, Art. We were thrilled to be part of this," Ryan said as he hung up.

Art hurried to the museum to explain everything to Nasi and the others. After he'd finished, he handed the CD to Kuyder.

"Can we do this, Al?" he asked.

"We'll give it one Hell of a try," Kuyder replied as he looked the CD over. "It's a good thing you have friends at NASA or we'd be at this for months. We would have missed the window."

"The code has to be broadcast through the artifact? How? And to where is it transmitted?" Nasi asked.

"My guess is that some outside power source, perhaps that ancient battery, was attached to the artifact. When it was fully charged, Imhotep used it to transmit his code into space," Art said.

"Can we transmit this code by modern means?" Nasi asked.

Heider nodded.

"We can hook a computerized transmitter to the artifact and broadcast the code via a series of electrical impulses," he suggested.

"How far?" asked Art.

"As far as you like," Kuyder said with a grin. "As to what is out there to receive the transmission, only Imhotep knows that."

"And he ain't talking," Art finished. "Or *is* he? The only way to find out what all this means is to give it a try. I just hope we don't start anything we can't control or cope with."

"I hate to tell you this, Art, but we already *have*. We've put things into motion that will change human history and science and our perception of the world we live in forever. Now, everyone on Earth is waiting for us to see this through. We have no choice," Nasi said.

"I suppose you're right. My friends at NASA have translated the code into electrical impulses for us. Now all we need is for Nasi to finish his translation of the second scroll so we know exactly when to make the transmission, Art said.

"I'll have that by this evening," Nasi assured him. "I want to double check a few things first to make certain I have it right."

"I wonder if there's anything still up there to receive the transmission after all these centuries?" Kuyder said as he looked out the window at the sky.

"We'll soon find out. I don't know about you gentlemen, but I am most anxious to see what will happen," Nasi said.

"Me, too. I think that Imhotep would want us to do this. I think that's why he had the scrolls buried with him. He *wanted* them to be found," Art mused aloud.

He looked at the clock.

"It's almost dinner time. I think I will head back to the hotel to eat and rest. We'll join you here again around eight this evening.," he said.

He smiled at Hawatt.

"You'd better get something to eat, too, Nasi. You look worn out. The translation can wait a few hours," he suggested.

"I think I will go home and get something to eat. I could use a shower, too. I'm starting to smell like Nile sludge," Nasi replied.

When Art arrived at the hotel, Maria greeted him at the door dressed in her very sheer robe. As soon as he walked in and shut the door behind him, Maria let the robe slide to the floor and stood before him completely naked. He gawked at her smooth, lovely body as his cock hardened.

Then Maria walked up to him and groped him. Within seconds, he, too was naked and Maria was kneeling before him stroking his cock. She had a hungry look in her eyes. Sort of like a cat ogling a canary.

Art led her to the dining room and had her lean forward on the table with her legs apart. Then he knelt behind her and lovingly licked her puckered anus for a few seconds before sliding his tongue up into her cunt.

Maria gasped as he explored her soft, flowery lips and nibbled at her clit. It was a very pleasant and exciting sensation that made her fidget. At the same time, Art reached up and massaged her nipples. That really made Maria squirm.

Now that she was good and wet, Art stood up and eased his cock into her channel. She sighed as his knob pushed past her labia and sunk deep into her pussy. It felt good to have a cock in there again.

So very good.

She felt him moving in and out. He did her slowly at first, trying to find his balance. When he did, he began laying her faster and faster. Maria sighed and trembled all over. Art grabbed her behind and humped her even faster. This caused her to shriek with delight as his knob raked across her g-spot several times.

Art fucked the way her cunt convulsed around his cock each time he thrust into her. She felt so good, too. So tight. So silky smooth.

In fact, this was one of the best fucks he'd had in weeks. And Maria had one of the best cunts.

Each time Art's cock moved inside her pussy, Maria sighed happily and trembled with lust. She felt herself growing wetter and hotter as they laid and she began thrusting her hips back at him to match his rhythm.

In and out.

In and out.

Each time, he pushed into her all the way to his balls. Each time, he thrust harder. And each thrust caused Maria to moan.

Maria felt herself coming. It was a good one, too. From deep inside her cunt. Art realized what she was going through and picked up the pace of his thrusting. Maria moaned and threw her head back.

"Oohh! That's it! Fuck me, Art! That feels so good! So laying good!" she moaned.

Art laid her even faster. He soon felt his balls spasm a few times and held onto her even tighter as he hammered away at her sopping cunt.

Maria shook wildly and sighed. Then she fell across the table and lay trembling while he continued to do her like a madman.

After several more deep thrusts, Art pushed his cock as deep into Maria's cunt as he could and released a flood of cum. The sensations caused by the hot cum slamming into her cunt walls triggered another orgasm in Maria and she began groaning loudly.

Spurt after spurt jetted into her. She felt each and every one of them, too.

And they felt delicious.

So wonderfully delicious.

Art kept humping away until his cock slid out of Maria's cunt. As it did, a shower of cum dripped from her open slit and splattered onto the carpet.

He fingered her slit while she slowly fell back to Earth. Maria turned and wrapped her fingers around his half-hard shaft. To her delight, it began to get hard again.

"Let's finish this in bed," she said.

Once in bed Art pushed Maria onto her back. She immediately opened her thighs so he could mount her. Since her cunt was still lined with cum, Art's long cock slid into her with ease and they began a slow, easy do.

After a few Seconds, Maria gripped his behind and began thrusting her pelvis upward with a wild abandon. Art stopped in mid-thrust and allowed her to do most of the work for a few seconds before he joined in with a vengeance.

"Aaaahhh!" Maria gasped.

They moved faster and faster now. Art felt her cunt convulse around his cock as she came and came hard. He laid her as fast as he could until, Seconds later, he emptied another large load of cum deep inside her pussy. But this time, he remained hard and he kept going at her with all of his energy.

Maria fell back with her arms and legs akimbo as he deep laid her until he fell across her chest. She felt his knob slam into her cervix. The impact was followed by yet another gusher of warm cum that blended with his earlier deposits.

They rested for a few minutes. Then Maria wrapped her fingers around Art's cock and jerked him off. He leaned over and licked her nipples as he fingered her slit.

When Art was fully erect once more, Maria straddled him and impaled herself on his cock. She rode him nice and slow this time as she savored the feeling of his meat moving in and out of her cunt. Art grabbed her behind and laid her back.

They soon got into a nice, steady rhythm. It took several minutes for them to come this time. Art did first. He drove his cock straight up Maria's snatch and drained his cum inside of her. He shot wad after wad into her. So much, in fact, that it leaked out of her cunt and coated his balls.

By then, she was riding him very hard. Her head was back and she emitted load, happy moans as she bounced up and down on his cock. When she came, she fell on top of him and sighed deeply.

But she wasn't satisfied.

Not yet.

She slid off him and grabbed his cum-coated cock. When it didn't respond after a few good pulls, she slipped the head into her mouth and sucked away until Art's balls ached and he had to beg her to stop.

She gave up and lay next to him.

"I guess we've reached your limit," she said. There was a definite tone of disappointment in her voice.

"I need to rest for a while. Then we can try it again if you like," Art offered.

"I like," she replied.

They did it one more time that day. This time, they did laying on their side, facing each other so that Art could suck on her nipples while they laid. This time, they did it until they could barely move and Art had added yet another shot of heavy cream to the lake of cum inside of Maria's cunt.

When it was over, they lay next to each other gasping for air. Neither one could move for several hours. When they did, they staggered into the shower.

CHAPTER 25

▼

When Wilder and the others returned to the museum, they noticed that the light in Hawatt's office was still on. Wilder stuck his head inside and saw Hawatt leaning over the scroll.

"Checking the translation again?" he asked as he walked in and sat down in a the leather chair across from him.

"As a matter of fact, yes," Hawatt replied with a smile. "According to this, the artifact must be assembled and placed in the exact center of the sarcophagus in the King's Chamber of the Great Pyramid at precisely eleven p.m. of the Vernal Equinox."

"That's only six days from now, but we already know all of that. Anything else in there we need to know about? Like what the Hell it's supposed to contact?" Art asked.

"No—and yes. It is very cryptic in that it describes the Golden Hawk Horus that will come and transport the true believers to the Sacred Place. But what the Golden Hawk is or where the Sacred Place is remains obscure," Nasi said.

"Well, placing the equipment in the chamber was the easy part. But getting that stuff down into it was a little tricky," said Kuyder. "It was tough getting up and down those ladders. Running the power cables from the generator into the crypt will be just as tricky."

"The scroll said that the code must be transmitted through the head of Thoth and sent through that air shaft directly in front of and above the sarcophagus," Nasi added.

"Well, we can easily simulate that part of it to make it seem like the transmission is coming from the head," Heider said. "How much of a window do we have on this?"

"The scroll seems adamant on that," Nasi replied. "If we are off by so much as a minute, it won't work."

"That's provided that this works at all," Kuyder said. "That scroll was written nearly 5,000 years ago. Whatever was up there then might not be there now. It's a longshot that anything *will* happen."

"I know," said Wilder.

"But it is worth a try, is it not? If something is out there, I want to know what it is. Don't you?" asked Nasi.

"I sure as Hell do," said Art. "We have been handed a rare opportunity to connect with something from our distant past. We can't it slip through our fingers."

"How will you send the transmission?" Nasi asked.

"Radio wave impulses that are the mathematical equivalent of the symbols of the code. If the boys at NASA get it right, we should be able to connect with whatever is up there," Heider explained.

"And if nothing happens, then there's no harm done or there's nothing left to connect with," Kuyder added.

"Then let's do it, gentlemen," Hawatt said enthusiastically.

"Damn straight!" agreed Art.

The others simply nodded.

When Art arrived at the hotel fifteen minutes later, all Maria had on was a T-shirt and panties that barely covered her pubic patch. Art got an immediate erection when he saw her—a fact that did not go by Maria unnoticed.

She knelt before him and undid his jeans. Art stripped to his birthday suit and sighed happily as Maria first jerked him off, then applied her tongue to the undersurface of his penis. By the time she reached his knob and began sucking on it, Art was moaning with pleasure.

"You're getting real good at that," he said.

"It's easy to get good at something you enjoy doing," she replied between licks.

She stood up and threw her arms around his neck.

"Where do you want to do me? My pussy or my asshole?" she asked.

"Your asshole again," Art replied.

Maria nodded and moved toward the dresser. Art followed close behind her, his cock bobbing with anticipation at entering her tight hole.

Maria leaned forward onto the dresser and spread her feet apart as Art slowly peeled down her panties. He dropped to his knees behind her and eased his tongue into her tight asshole. At the same time, he slipped his middle finger into her vagina. Maria gasped at the double action.

When she was good and wet, Art worked his finger up into her behind and gently stretched her inner muscles. Maria shivered, then groaned. Caught between pain and pleasure, she bit her lip as he worked her still virtually untapped nether entrance. It still felt weird to have something inside her like that.

She spotted a bottle of Vaseline Intensive Care lotion on the dresser and handed it back to Art. He squirted a large amount onto his fingers, and then worked it into her asshole until it was nice and slick. He stood up and removed his briefs.

Maria reached back and grabbed his erection. Art sighed as she jerked him off a while. Then she let him go and dropped to her elbows. Art spread her cheeks apart with his thumbs, then slowly eased his penis into her hot, tight ass until he was in her up to his balls.

"Yes!" she sighed. "God, yes!"

Art did her nice and easy. On each thrust, he went in all the way then withdrew several inches and entered her again. At the same time, he played with her nipples. Maria moaned. The sensations were intense and oh-so delicious. Her entire body tingled with excitement now.

She decided that she actually liked being loved this way. Even more than she ever expected. She also decided that Art could do her this way any time he liked.

Art reached around front and massaged her clit. His thrusts were becoming erratic and Maria knew he was about to come. She thrust her ass back at him now, trying to take every wonderful inch of his cock as deep into her ass as it would go.

Then she felt it.

Art's cock stiffened and jerked inside her. She felt his balls jump against her cheeks as he did her faster and faster. She felt his cum jet into her several times, then everything suddenly went white.

Maria had come, too.

And it was a huge one.

They kissed for a while, then Art slid his limp penis out of her asshole. Maria laughed as she teased it.

"You have a fabulous ass," Art said.

"Is it as good as my pussy?" Maria asked.

"Nothing's that good," Art assured her.

It took several hours of climbing and back tracking to hook the power cables into the transmitter from the large generator they had placed outside of the Great Pyramid. Several times, Kuyder and Heider had to stop to untangle to cables after they had knotted or wrapped themselves around protrusions inside the narrow tunnels.

By the time they emerged from the structure, they were bathed in sweat and looking pretty grimy and work out. Art handed them bottles of cold water and watched as the gulped them down.

"It's done," Kuyder said as he wiped his lips. "We are ready to test the connection now."

They walked over to the generator and flicked the switch. There was a low hum as it powered up. They studied the display on the screen and watched as the indicators rose to full power.

Kuyder held his thumb up and grinned. Art slapped him on the back.

"Good work, Al. Now all we have to do is wait for the right time," he said.

"How many more days have we?" Heider asked.

"Four," Art said.

"I can hardly wait," said Heider. Then he sniffed his armpit and winced. "I think I'll go to the hotel and shower. From there, I'm going to the bar."

"I'll meet you at the bar," said Kuyder.

"I guess I'll head back to the hotel, too," Art said.

When Art opened the door to the suite, there was Maria in nothing but an unbuttoned white shirt, proudly displaying her gorgeous young body.

"I need to fuck you, Art," she said with her usual sexy smile. "I want to feel your hard cock in every hole of my body. I want to love you until neither of us can move."

"Pretty lady, you have got yourself a date!" Art said as he grabbed her hand and led her into the bedroom.

It proved to be a wild ride for them both.

They started off with lots of playful feels, kisses and nibbles on various parts of their bodies. When Maria began squirming, Art made love to her missionary style until she had her first orgasm. He then flipped her onto her belly, pulled her to her knees, and screwed her from behind.

Maria yelled as she came a second time. This time, Art also shot his first load deep into her tight little vagina.

They rested for a few minutes, then Maria used her hands and mouth to bring Art back to full salute. She straddled his cock and impaled herself on it with one fast motion, then proceeded to love the Hell out of him. This time, they both orgasmed at the exact same instant and Art pumped what seemed like a gallon of cum up into her pussy. It soon ran down her thighs.

They stooped for few seconds. To Maria's delight, Art was still hard. She moved up and down on his cock again. This time, they did it nice and slow. Again, they both came at the same time. It was a long, breath-taking come that left them trembling on the bed.

Both were covered with perspiration. Maria kept teasing and sucking on Art's cock for a long time before he was able to get it up again.

"Love my ass, Art," she said as she got onto her hands and knees and faced away from him.

Her ass looked so damned good, Art simply couldn't say "no." He then discovered that Maria was no stranger to anal sex. His penis slid in easily and she didn't even gasp with pain. She then used her ass muscles to work his penis until he was dizzy with lust.

Art grabbed Maria's thighs and started fucking her nice and slow. She just knelt there and smiled. They kept at this for what seemed like a long, long time before Art rammed his cock into her as deep as he could and emptied his balls into her deliciously tight ass.

Maria came, too. She shook violently, then collapsed onto the bed. Art fell on top of her, his penis still buried between her smooth cheeks.

"Caramba! Mucho caliente!" Maria gasped dreamily.

Art and Maria sat down in front of Nasi's desk. The older man looked at Maria and smiled.

"I have been thinking about your—er—flashbacks for want of a better term, Maria. You never had any of them before you visited Egypt. Is this correct?" he asked.

"Never. It's really strange, Nasi. Because when I have them, the people that are close to me have them, too. Now, I can even speak ancient Egyptian and understand the symbols," Maria answered.

"Well, I have contacted some of the best psychics we have in Cairo. They all say these episodes indicate that you have lived here many centuries ago. In other words, you are experiencing past life regressions," Nasi said.

"That could explain many things," Art said. "But we need some sort of definite proof."

"If you will indulge me, I would like to try an experiment. It may prove nothing. It may also prove a theory of mine," Nasi suggested.

"What do you have in mind?" Art asked.

"We still have the DNA test results from Imhotep. I would like to take a sample of DNA from Maria and run a comparison," Nasi said.

"And what would that prove?" Maria asked.

"It may show that you have some ancient DNA code that could pinpoint your ancestry here in Egypt. Many of us have DNA that are very similar to that we have taken from mummies in the past. This shows that we are, indeed, Egyptian. I want to see if that is the case with you. Are you game?" Nasi explained.

"What do you need?" she asked.

"Some strands of your hair will do nicely," Nasi said.

Maria nodded. Nasi took scissors from his desk drawer and handed them to her. Maria then clipped some hair from near the top of her scalp. Nasi took them, placed them in a vial and buzzed for his secretary.

When the woman entered, Nasi handed her the vial.

"Take these to the lab and get a DNA test run," he said.

The secretary took the vial and hurried out of the office. Nasi turned to Maria.

"That should take about three hours or so. Want to join me for lunch?" he asked.

When they returned to the museum that afternoon, the envelope from the lab was on Nasi's desk. He opened it and took it over to a light table. Then he took the film strip from the envelope and placed it on the table beneath a strip that was already on the screen. Nasi turned on the light and peered at the strips.

"This is fantastic! I can hardly believe it!" he gasped.

"What is it, Nasi?" Maria asked.

"Come here and see for yourselves," he said as he stepped to the side of the table.

Art and Maria stepped closer and studied the DNA strips.

"The top one is the DNA we took from Imhotep. The bottom strip is Maria's DNA. Look at them and tell me if you see what I see," he said.

Art's eyes grew larger as he realized what Nasi was getting at.

"The two strips are *identical*," he said.

"Exactly identical. It is as if they both came from the same person," Nasi said.

"You mean that I'm *descended* from Imhotep?" Maria asked. "But I'm from Puerto Rico! My family has lived there for many generations. I'm not Egyptian."

"But the evidence shows that you were at one time. How your family got from here to Puerto Rico is a mystery, but there is no doubting the evidence. The

DNA unmistakably shows that you are a direct descendant of Imhotep himself," Nasi explained.

He turned off the light table and they returned to his desk and sat down. Nasi looked at Maria. She looked so much like the woman in the paintings in Imhotep's tomb. Even their hair color was the same. Their likeness to each other was almost chilling.

"Do you still have the visions?" he asked.

"Yes. They're becoming more frequent. I dream the same dreams each night, too," Maria replied.

"That explains why you feel so at home here in Egypt and how you learned the language so easily—like you were born to use it," Art said.

He was quite familiar with past life regressions from all of his travels. He had no doubt that such things were real. He touched her hand. She entwined her fingers in his.

"When conditions are right, you are able to reach back through the ages with your subconscious mind and relive parts of your previous life. Many people can do this under hypnosis or through feelings of déjà vu. But you're the only one I've ever seen who can take others back in time with you," he said.

"Being a descendant of Imhotep, perhaps you have inherited some of his legendary magical powers?" Nasi suggested.

"You don't really believe in magic, do you, Nasi?" Maria asked.

"My dear, when it comes to someone like Imhotep, I believe in everything," Nasi replied.

"But what does this all mean?" asked Maria.

Nasi shrugged.

"I may mean nothing. I would not worry about it," he said.

"Worry? Hell, I'm *proud* to come from such an ancient and noble family. What's our next step?" Maria said.

"Tomorrow, Kuyder, Heider and I will begin setting up the transmitter inside the Great Pyramid according to the diagram we found inside the Box. That leaves you the entire day to yourself," Art said.

"That's fine. I won't be bored," she said with a wink.

While Art was overseeing the installation of the transmitter in the Great Pyramid, Maria decided to pay another visit to her friend at the local sex shop. As she walked down the street, she had a weird feeling that this would be the last time they saw each other. The feeling would not go away.

"Maria! I'm glad you came. Please come in," she said.

That's when Maria realized that The Woman was wearing a knee length T-shirt that clearly highlighted her erect nipples. Maria caught herself staring at them.

"It's funny. I've seen you without a bra before but this is the first time I noticed how big your nipples are," she said as she followed The Woman upstairs and into the bedroom.

"I just finished showering," The Woman explained as she pulled back the covers on the bed.

"I've been thinking of you all night, about what we did the last time," Maria said as she unbuttoned her blouse.

The Woman stared at her nice, firm breasts and pert, brown nipples. She smiled.

"Me too. That was very nice," The Woman said as she helped Maria out of her jeans.

Her eyes went straight to the soft, brown triangle between Maria's thighs. That's when Maria realized The Woman had no panties on. The Woman pulled off her T-shirt.

Naked, they fell into each other's arms and kissed passionately as they virtually melted into the bed. Hesitant at first, Maria cast away all doubts and threw herself into the affair with wild abandon.

It soon became a wonderful, wild ride. Lips met lips, then graced necks, chests, nipples and navels. As their tongues played across their bodies, excited fingers explored their moist, warm folds and danced deliciously within eager slits.

This being new for Maria, she let The Woman do as she pleased with her at first, then followed her lead until both women were burning with lust.

Incredible lust.

Neither woman could recall being so horny before. They were both very wet and their sexual perfume hung heavy in the humid afternoon air of the bedroom.

Maria's muff fascinated The Woman. Her labia were like tender flower petals. Soft and pliant, they quivered noticeably when The Woman caressed them. Her slit was long, moist and deep pink in color. It glimmered in the sunlight and her wonderfully swollen clit peeked at her invitingly from beneath its fleshy cover. This marvelous cunt was covered with a rich, brown carpet of silken pubic hair.

"You're so beautiful," The Woman said.

Maria shivered, still amazed that her friend was touching her most intimate place. She was having sex with a beautiful woman for the first time in her life.

As The Woman gently caressed her now-trembling cunt, Maria wondered just how far The Woman would to go.

Would she go beyond touching?

Probably.

If so, was Maria ready for that?

Most certainly.

Despite her earlier inner conflicts, Maria soon gave herself willingly to The Woman. She simply closed her eyes and allowed her more experienced lover to take her wherever she wanted.

The Woman inserted two fingers into Maria's cunt and moved them in and out. Maria groaned with passion as The Woman kissed her navel and licked her way slowly downward.

"Do it, The Woman! Eat me!" Maria whispered. Her words surprised her. She never once imagined that she'd be begging another woman to go down on her.

When The Woman's soft, warm tongue touched her swollen clit, Maria nearly jumped off the bed. She grabbed The Woman's head and opened her legs wide as that wonderful, knowing tongue played and danced between her thighs.

"Aiee! Aiee—yes!" Maria yelled.

No one had ever eaten her like this. No one, that is, except Art.

The Woman used her fingers to pull Maria's labia open so she could suck on her clit. This caused Maria to cry out with pleasure. She felt her orgasm mounting from deep within her cunt and clawed at the mattress.

The Woman understood what was happening. She responded by dipping her tongue deep into Maria's cunt. Then she slowly moved one of her fingers into her and teased her g-spot.

That did it.

Maria came like she'd never come before.

It was an explosive, deep-from-inside come that rocked her sweat-covered body from head to toe. Maria grabbed The Woman hair and pulled her face hard against her vulva. She humped The Woman's face wildly now as orgasm after orgasm surged through her body. At the same time, The Woman slid another finger deep inside Maria's cunt and massaged her g-spot even harder.

This increased the intensity of Maria's orgasm and she shook all over as the stars exploded in front of her eyes.

She let go of The Woman's hair and fell, arms akimbo, back onto the bed. The Woman moved upward so her cunt was merely inches from Maria's lips. The delightful aroma of The Woman's open pussy enticed Maria. She reached up, gripped The Woman's behind and pulled her down onto her tongue.

Then Maria ate her.

The Woman tasted sweet.

Inviting.

Intoxicating.

Maria felt wicked. She was eating her best friend's pussy—her first and only pussy—and she fucked it. She fucked the smell, the feel and especially the flavor. She explored The Woman from cunt to asshole several times, then settled down and concentrated on her pretty little clit. She was so enraptured by what she was doing that she barely noticed that The Woman was eating her again.

The Woman came.

She actually made The Woman come.

Maria felt her bittersweet juices jet into her mouth and hungrily lapped them up. The taste was sensationally erotic. It blew Maria's mind so much, she came again and they both held on to ride the waves that surged through them.

"Th-that was unbelievable!" Maria gasped. "My head is spinning like crazy!"

"Mine, too. You are a good lover, Maria. You eat me almost as good as Art does," The Woman replied as she came down from the clouds.

Maria smiled at her lovely sex partner, then reached out and ran her fingers over her soft, black pubic hair. It felt so natural to be with The Woman like this. Maria told her this, too.

The Woman smiled.

"If you want me, Maria, you can have me anytime you like," she said. "I am all yours."

She was feeling Maria's pussy now. As she inserted two fingers into it, Maria moaned and glanced at the clock. It was only 11:00. The day had just begun…

Maria was surprised how easily she gave herself to The Woman. She never had any real lesbian inclinations before, even though she often fantasized trying it just once to see what it was like.

As she lay naked on the bed, she looked down at the pretty woman licking her cunt and smiled. It seemed and felt so natural now.

And so very, very good.

She closed her eyes and enjoyed the ride. Soon, she would sink her tongue into The Woman's delicious cunt. She sighed as The Woman nibbled her clit.

God, she was good at this.

"The best," Maria thought.

A sudden surge of pleasure roared through her. She arched her back to take The Woman's tongue deeper into her cunt, then came seconds later. As she did, she humped The Woman's tongue and cried out in Spanish.

Sex with The Woman was intense.

Very intense.

Maria groaned and fell back to the mattress. The Woman stopped licking and sat back to watch Maria's petal-like labia throb visibly as her orgasm subsided.

"You're very beautiful, Maria," she said.

"You are, too. Let's fuck," Maria replied.

Wordlessly, The Woman got on top of her and began rubbing her cunt against Maria's nice and easy. Maria's eyes went wide. The Woman was actually screwing her! It was the most incredible thing she ever felt. She moaned softly and dug her fingers into the bed as her body took control and fucked her back.

"Yes!" The Woman gasped. "Yes! YES!!!"

Maria didn't hear her cry out. She was completely lost in the sex they were having. All she cared about was the way her cunt felt as it ground into The Woman's and the fact that she was coming…and coming…and coming…

She couldn't recall ever coming so much, so many times. Sweat covered her—and The Woman—from head to foot as they continued to make love all through the warm afternoon. The bedroom was filled with their sexual aromas now. The scent only served to heighten their lovemaking.

They soon switched positions. Now, Maria was on top and the two women fucked away in the scissors position until their bodies literally ached. They were tired, sweaty and almost unconscious by the time they'd each come for the umpteenth time that afternoon.

As Maria lay next to The Woman, she smiled. She felt good all over now. The Woman looked content, too.

I got a new toy," Maria said.

She walked to the dresser, opened her purse and produced a large double-headed latex cock. It was at least two feet long with a double set of "balls" in the center.

The Woman watched with anticipation as Maria slid one end up into her hot juicy cunt and climbed onto the bed. The Woman spread her long, sexy legs, then grabbed a pillow and stuck it under her behind to elevate her pelvis.

"This lets me take it deeper," she explained.

The Woman closed her eyes and moaned as Maria slid the dildo into her cunt. It was a nice, easy screw. A long, slow, deep one that had The Woman begging for more and more. Maria had never really fucked another woman until she came to the sex shop. Until then, she never knew women actually laid other women. It seemed weird then. Now, it seemed like the most natural thing on Earth.

Maria savored every stroke. Each inward thrust also drove her into her cunt deeper so that it was really a mutual fuck She was living out one of her fantasies and she wanted to make it a memorable time for both her and The Woman.

The Woman suddenly spasmed and stretched her legs out to the sides. She dug her nails into Maria hips and began laying her back as hard as she could. By some miracle of timing, they both orgasmed at the exact same moment.

And it was a long, powerful and wonderful orgasm.

"Now, it is *my* turn," The Woman said as she picked up the dildo.

She slid one end of the huge dildo up into her cunt, then got between Maria's thighs. Excited beyond imagination, Maria threw her legs open wide and closed her eyes. If the sex she was about to get was anywhere near as good as what The Woman did to her with her tongue, Maria knew this was going to be something special.

The Woman bent over and licked Maria's cunt to moisten it, then slowly eased the dildo into her until their pubic hairs touched.

"Aiee!" Maria gasped.

The Woman smiled, then began to do Maria nice and slow. She used deep, easy strokes that stoked Maria's inner fires until she was white hot. It took a little while for Maria to grow accustomed to this huge, latex prick working her gash, but she soon learned to enjoy it.

Really enjoy it!

She was being laid by another woman. An older, sexier woman who really knew how to use a "prick". Maria began fucking her back, matching The Woman thrust for thrust as she dug her fingers into the woman's soft back. Now, Maria's legs were wide open and her knees were bent. She was getting the ride of her life, one of the best ever. And it was from a woman!

"Oh, God! That feels so damned good!"

"You're very beautiful, Maria. You have the most gorgeous cunt I've ever seen. I could do this with you forever," whispered The Woman as she increased the tempo of her thrusts.

Maria took a deep breath, and matched her. She knew she was about to blow and gripped The Woman's ass tightly.

"Fuck me harder. Ohh, yes!" Maria cried.

The Woman complied. It was just enough to push Maria over the edge and she erupted into an orgasmic bliss. She trembled all over and cried out in Spanish. The Woman did her even faster, sending more waves of pleasure surging through Maria's taut, sweaty body. Then The Woman came, too. She shook all over, then fell next to Maria. Both women were breathing very hard.

"Enough. I cannot do it anymore," The Woman said after a while. "You are almost insatiable today. It is like this will be our last sex together."

"That was incredible. I've never felt so totally satisfied and worn out. I can hardly move," Maria said.

"Then don't. Rest here with me," The Woman suggested.

Maria laughed.

"I can't. If I do, we'll be at each other again and I'm not sure my pussy can take anymore today," Maria said. "It's sore."

"My pussy is also sore, but a nice kind of sore," The Woman said.

"You taught me a lot about making love with a woman. I want to thank you for bringing this out in me. I think it has made me a better lover for my husband, too," Maria said.

"To be the perfect wife and lover, you must know the secrets of great sex, with both a man and a woman. By knowing how to satisfy a woman, you can better guide your husband in new ways to please you—and him as well," The Woman said knowingly. "My ancestors knew these secrets and practiced them. I think that is why Egyptian society lasted as long as it did. Of course, we have never forgotten those secrets."

"Where did you learn to be such a good lover?" asked Maria.

"My mother taught me," The Woman replied.

An hour later, Maria left the shop. She went back to the hotel and showered, then ordered room service.

When Art returned from the Great Pyramid two hours later, he found Maria asleep in the large chair in front of the TV set. He smiled, then picked her up and carried her over to the bed. Once he was sure she was comfortable, he went into the bathroom and took a nice, long shower.

Maria was awake when he came out. She handed him a cold beer and they walked out to the balcony and watched the sun set.

"It's beautiful here," Maria said.

"Yes," Art agreed as he sipped the beer. "How did you spend your day today?"

Maria told him what she did. Art listened and chuckled in a few places. Then she looked at him as he pulled her close.

"How did it go today?" she asked.

"The computer and transmitter are already in place in the King's Chamber. Heider and Kuyder are still running the power lines to the generator. The whole things should be ready on time," Art said. "We get the package from NASA?"

"Not yet. I checked when I got back this afternoon. Maybe you should call Ryan?" Maria replied.

"I'll give him one more day. If it's not here by tomorrow night, I'll call him and see what's up," Art said.

"What happens then?" Maria asked.

"Heider converts it to a series of electric impulses that can be transmitted through the artifact via computer. Then we go in on the equinox and set up the final stages," Art answered.

"Do you really think this will work, Art? Do you really think that something's out there?" asked Maria.

Art shrugged.

"Who knows? But we won't find out if we don't give this a try," he said.

He looked at her barely covered body and touched her thigh.

"You have anything left for me?" he asked.

Maria smiled and led him back into the bedroom...

CHAPTER 26

▼

Maria lay on her back, her legs wide open. She reached down and pulled her labia apart, enticing Art with the dark, pink moistness of her cunt.

Art climbed on top of her and slid his hard prick all the way inside. Maria sighed happily and opened her legs wider as he began that slow, soft, delicious fuck she loved so much.

Maria let herself go with the flow, allowing her body's natural rhythms match Art's every thrust. She savored every moment of their lovemaking—for that's what it was to her.

Lovemaking.

It went well beyond just great sex.

Each time Art thrust his cock into her steaming snatch, it felt better. More natural. More excitingly delicious than anything she ever felt before. His prick felt perfect inside her and she hungrily accepted every thrust.

Art was in Heaven, too. He didn't care that he was fucking his sister-in-law or that his wife had set this up for them. All he cared about was that sexy brown body writhing beneath him and the incredibly silky-soft cunt that was devouring his prick.

Maria felt herself coming. She arched her back. Art felt it, too and began screwing her faster. Their timing was perfect.

Unable to hold back any longer, Art exploded deep inside Maria's cunt. The force of his last hard thrust caused Maria to come, too. They laid erratically for a few more moments and Maria groaned with each thrust.

She pulled him to her and stuck her tongue into his mouth. At the same time, she laid him as fast and as hard as she could. He was still very hard and Maria refused to let go of him until she had drained him of every last drop of cum.

That was fine with Art.

Maria's body was small and lean and her cunt was tight. In fact, it was the tightest one he had ever sunk his cock into and this little lady really knew how to use it.

They kept at it for several minutes more. By then, sweat covered them both and Maria began to feel a little sore between her legs. This was the longest do she'd ever had—and the best.

When Art came for the last time, she exploded, too. It took a long time to get back to Earth. When she did, Maria smiled happily at Art.

"Again!" she said.

Her body was still trembling when Art took his place above her. He pressed his glans to her soft, moist labia then moved it up and down several times before easing into her. He went in slowly in order to get the feel of her tight, hot channel as it caressed his prick.

Maria spread her legs as far apart as she could, then bent her knees. She gripped Art's shoulders and drove her hips upward until she felt the head of his prick touch the opening to her womb.

"Oh yes!" she sighed as Art began to move his hips in a circular motion.

At the same time, he thrust in and out of her cunt nice and slow. He felt her inner flesh hug his shaft tightly as he pulled out, then part again as he slid back in. Each time, Maria moved with him in perfect unison.

Art had had many women in his life, but no one's cunt felt as exquisitely sexy as Maria's. She was warm, tight and silky smooth and she could really use her inner muscles. He often felt as if her were making love with an angel. They were a perfect match.

That's why he was taking his time. This wasn't just sex. It was lovemaking at its best, with all of the emotional ties that went with the word.

They made love gently, slowly and with a lot of passion. They matched each other stroke for stroke, thrust for thrust. Their lips met again. Art reached beneath Maria and put her right leg over his shoulder, then drove into her a little bit harder and faster.

Maria emitted a loud moan and dug her nails into his back as his cock massaged her secret g-spot perfectly. She felt herself spinning out of control.

"Faster, Art! Do it faster," she begged. "Make me come!"

She closed her eyes and allowed the movements of Art's prick inside her cunt carry her away. She began crying out and gasping for air. She clawed at his back like a mad woman as an explosive series of orgasms raced through her body.

Maria felt his prick jerk a few times, and then relaxed as Art emptied his seed into her sucking pussy. Like earlier, he pumped a large amount of cum into Maria's love tunnel. Her body, which seemed to be suspended in time, eagerly accepted his seed, greedily making it one with her.

She always let Art come inside her. She always would.

After a few more deep thrusts, Art eased his half hard cock out of her and rolled onto his back. His prick glistened with their combined love juices. Maria rolled on top of him and they kissed once again. It was a long, deep kiss that spoke volumes of their feelings for each other.

"I love you," Maria whispered.

"I love you," Art said.

At long last, the day for the transmission arrived. The festive atmosphere that had permeated the plateau for the past several days was now more subdued. Wilder thought the atmosphere had taken on a more religious tone, as if the people gathered there was expecting the arrival of their savior or the return of the ancient gods.

But no one knew exactly what to expect. All anyone knew was that a transmission would be made at 12:01 a.m.. No one knew exactly where it was going or what would respond to it.

Nasi noticed that the plateau seemed strangely devoid of politicians. Instead of flocking to the place for a rare photo op, world leaders avoided Giza. It was if some higher power had contacted them and warned them away. Perhaps they thought that their presence would somehow abase this incredible event.

Wilder said they were probably afraid.

"Most politicians are cowardly, backstabbing liars and would never go anywhere where they might be at risk. Besides, I don't think the gods would appreciate their presence here right now," he said.

With his typical bravado, he dared the members of the press to quote him.

"Make sure you get it right, boys. I meant every word!" he said.

"It is almost time to begin the transmission," Heider shouted.

"Let's make it happen!" Wilder said. "Let's get this show on the road!"

Kuyder looked at the timer as he counted down.

"Three…two…one…NOW!" he shouted as he pointed to Heider who hit the switch. There was a short humming sound.

"We're transmitting. All systems are up and running. Now all we have to do is wait," he said.

"Yes. But for what?" Nasi asked.

"Whatever's up there. *If* it's still up there," Art said.

"I wonder what type of signal we're transmitting? I can't tell from the electronic pulses," Kuyder asked.

Art looked up at the stars.

"My guess is that it's some sort of homing signal designed specifically to summon this Golden Hawk thing on this particular night, provided, of course, that my friends at NASA got it right," he said.

As the signal beamed onto space, the millions of onlookers at Giza sat down in the sand and looked skyward. Many of them started to chant. It was as if someone had cast a powerful magic spell over the area.

Maria felt it, too.

She walked away from Art and began climbing the face of the Great Pyramid. Art and the others stood and watched as she made her way slowly upward until she reached the halfway point. There, she stopped and turned. As she did, she cast her arms skyward and started to chant.

Hawatt stared up at her.

"What is she doing?" he asked.

Art studied her for a few moments before answering.

"It looks like she's praying. She might be caught up in another flashback. I'm starting to feel it, too. It's like I'm being pulled toward the pyramid by some invisible force," he said.

The chanting of the crowd increased steadily in volume. Before long, every person gathered on the plateau joined in.

"Nasi! The Egyptian Air Force called. They've picked up something on their radar screens. Something big and it's headed right for the plateau!" shouted Heider.

Everyone looked up and stared into the clear night sky. After a few minutes, a speck of bright light appeared. The speck grew brighter and brighter as it slowly fell toward the plateau. As it got closer and closer, the chanting of the crowd grew louder and louder.

The light emanating from the object was almost as bright as the sun and bathed the entire area in its golden rays. Many people shielded their eyes from it as it slowly filled the sky. Then the light began to dim. As it did, the chanting abated.

It stopped altogether when the object slowly touched down right in front of the Great Pyramid and scattered the crowd by kicking up clouds of sand and dust.

Wilder and the others shielded their eyes and watched as the glow faded and they were finally able to see what their signal had summoned.

"I don't fucking believe it! It's amazing!" gasped Wilder as he took a few steps toward the object.

"Incredible! Simply incredible!" echoed Hawatt.

The crowd was now completely silent. All anyone could do was stand and gawk at the huge, bird-winged craft that stood before them.

And what a craft!

It was over one hundred feet long. It's fuselage was shaped like a bird and its outstretched wings spanned nearly fifty feet. Its landing gear looked like the talons of a huge hawk, and its head was an exact likeness of the ancient Egyptian god, Horus. And the entire ship looked as if were covered in the purest gold.

By now, Maria had descended from the pyramid. She walked over to her husband and smiled up at him. She looked serene, too. More serene than Art had ever known her to be.

"It has come, my beloved," she said.

Nasi and Art stared. Maria was speaking the ancient tongue again.

"Incredible! That ship has been waiting up there for nearly five millennia," said Heider as he looked the craft over.

"But where is it from? Who built it? What was it waiting for?" Kuyder fired. "We must know the answers!"

"I agree," said Art. "But the only way to get them is to go aboard that craft. Right now, I don't see any sign of a door or window on that ship."

"We're looking at ancient technology that blows away anything we have today. Imagine it, Art! They built an interstellar craft that was still able to respond to a pre-programmed signal 5,000 years after it was built! Think of the science behind it!" Heider said.

"The ancient Egyptians had starships. They actually had the capability of traveling to and from distant planets! Art! We *have* to get aboard that ship! Think of what we could learn from it!" Kuyder added.

"This poses many more questions than it answers," said Nasi. "Like what did they use this ship for? Where did they go?"

"Actually, a more important question is just where did they come *from*? What if human beings didn't originate on Earth? What if we're all from someplace else?" Art asked.

"Something is happening! Look!" shouted Heider.

They watched as an opening appeared in the side of the craft just below the left wing. The opening grew to the size of a large doorway, then a long metal ramp slowly emerged from the it and touched the ground.

Everyone stood and waited for something to happen, for someone to emerge from the doorway and descend the ramp. But nothing happened. The craft stood silent.

Foreboding.

Inviting.

Wilder took a deep breath. He looked back at Maria and held out his hand. She took it and they began walking toward the ship. Hawatt watched, then finally worked up the nerve to follow them.

"Are you sure you want to do this?" he asked.

"I *must* do this, Nasi. You *know* this. This could provide us with the answers to all of our questions. The very questions that Man has been asking since the beginning of time," Wilder replied. "This is one chance I dare not miss."

He looked back at his wife. Maria was staring up at the ship as they walked toward the ramp. She seemed to be a million miles away.

"I'm going with you, Art," she said. "I have to. The ship is calling to me. I can hear it inside my head."

They soon reached the bottom of the ramp. Wilder turned to Hawatt and offered his right hand. Hawatt shook it warmly as he fought down an urge to go into the ship with them.

"We must go now," Maria said as she hugged Nasi. "We must go where the ship takes us."

Hawatt stepped back and watched them walk up the ramp. Before they went inside, he shouted.

"But where is it taking you?"

Maria turned and smiled softly at him.

"Home," she answered. "It's taking us home."

Hawatt stepped back to the crowd. Everyone stood and watched in silence as the ramp slid back into the ship and the hatch closed behind it. There was a faint humming noise next. Then the great golden ship rose slowly off the ground and hovered above the plateau for a few seconds before rising quickly into the air.

Everyone stood and gawked until it vanished from sight. Hawatt walked back to his Jeep. Before he got in, he looked up at the sky. It was empty now and the crowd was dispersing slowly. Only the New Agers stayed behind to pray.

Kuyder and Heider stared at the sky for some time. When they were certain the ship was gone, they headed back to the Jeep. Nasi was already behind the wheel when they climbed aboard.

"Damn it! Now we'll never know anything about that ship," lamented Kuyder. "That was our one and only chance to learn about the ancient technology behind it."

"Then you don't believe they will come back?" asked Heider.

Kuyder shook his head.

Nasi sighed and started the Jeep. The engine sputtered a few times, then finally kicked in.

As he drove back to the museum, he wondered what Maria had meant.

Where was "home"?

Where did the ship come from?

The Wilders were going home—wherever that was—and he was sure that they were never coming back. He stopped the Jeep on a hilltop and looked up the stars. For one brief moment, Hawatt wished that he had gone with them…

0-595-33515-2

Printed in the United States
22835LVS00004B/286-288

9 780595 335152